"The last few years," Fu told [...] [...]ce with Earth has become increasingly frag[...]. A complete break is not far off. A new generation of leaders is gaining power, the economic and environmental situations grow more desperate—"

"They have only themselves to blame," Derek said.

"And they certainly aren't going to do that, so who does that leave? It has to be us, and the answer has to be another war."

"Another war?" There had been none in Derek's lifetime. Life could be hard and dangerous enough in the Belt without people deliberately trying to kill each other. There were hazards in plenty: the slightest mistake was usually rewarded with instant death. Systems failures and particle collisions took a tragic toll, and every year dozens of vessels and their crews simply disappeared. Prosperous colonies were occasionally discovered with all personnel dead. Sometimes, mysteriously, they were found abandoned.

War was something else. "Do you think it will be soon?" Derek asked.

"Much may depend on the nature of your artifact. It may be the answer to the problems that have defeated us since the last war."

ERIC KOTANI AND
JOHN MADDOX ROBERTS

BETWEEN THE STARS

BAEN
BOOKS

BETWEEN THE STARS

A Baen Books Original

Baen Publishing Enterprises
260 Fifth Avenue
New York, N.Y. 10001

First printing, March 1988

ISBN: 0-671-65392-X

Cover art by Alan Gutierrez

Printed in the United States of America

Distributed by
SIMON & SCHUSTER
1230 Avenue of the Americas
New York, N.Y. 10020

For Alayne, Angela, Beatrice,
Cynthia and Valari

ONE

Rhea is an insignificant chunk of lunar material orbiting Saturn at a distance of about 327,000 miles. It is not as negligible as glorified asteroids like Atlas or Telesto, mere fugitives of the solar system captured by Saturn's immense gravity. Still, Rhea has nothing like the glory of spectacular Titan, the next moon out.

All this was on Derek Kuroda's mind as he exited his solo explorer craft, *Cyrano*. He was nineteen years old, one year out of the Ciano Academy, and he felt he deserved something better. He had applied for Titan. He had applied for Ganymede and Callisto, where serious terraforming projects were in the works. He had not applied for Rhea. Rhea he got, nonetheless.

"Ethelred," he said, stepping onto the Rhean surface, "I want it on record that this mission is a waste of the time and talents of Derek Kuroda, who is destined for better things."

"Recorded," said Ethelred, his ship's computer, who had heard many such complaints.

Like the other Saturnian satellites, Rhea had one sterling quality: its view. The sight of Saturn at close range was a spectacle that stole the breath from hardened spacers. The impact of the thousandth viewing was no less powerful than the first as the eye was drawn

1

into futile analysis of the dazzling bands of color, their interfaces twisted into patterns of infinite complexity. Settlers of the Jovian moons claimed that the swirling colors of Jupiter were even more beautiful, but no other body in the system had anything to compare with the majesty of Saturn's rings. *If the big move comes in my lifetime*, Derek thought, *this is the only thing I'll regret leaving behind*.

"You need the experience," the man back at Crater Station on Mimas had told him. "You're a kid just out of school. Nobody gets the big, demanding jobs first time out. Pull a few of these routine surveys, survive and don't screw up too bad, and we'll see about giving you something more important." Straight out of the academy, Derek had signed on with McNaughton Enterprises, in the exploration department. When he found out what he was expected to do, he would have chucked the job and looked elsewhere, but he needed the money to keep up payments on *Cyrano*.

With such thoughts, it was more pleasant to look up at Saturn than down at where he was stepping. Thus it was that, when he made the greatest discovery in the history of man in space, he stubbed his toe on it. Had Rhea had any gravity worthy of the name, he might have literally tripped over it. When he looked down to see what had made him stumble, he froze. It was not a natural object.

It was egg-shaped. Derek had seen pictures of eggs and he knew that degenerate Earthies actually ate the horrid stuff inside them. He lowered himself for a closer look. It was perhaps ten inches on its longer axis and half that in diameter. The material appeared to be glassy, a transparent green shading to opacity at its center.

Who had made it and why had it been left here? Was it man-made or might it be some freakish but natural object? Glass produced by a meteor impact, flung upward and cooled into this oddly regular shape? He had never heard of such a thing, but crazy things were always turning up in remote corners of the solar system. It hadn't moved when his toe had struck it, so it had to be fastened to the ground in some fashion. He grasped its narrow ends and tugged at it. It came up, but reluctantly. It was not fastened to the ground, but he had to exert himself to lift it.

Sweat sprang out on his scalp when he realized how much this thing had to weigh. Rhea's gravity was infinitesimal, and this thing was barely a double handful, yet he had to strain to lift it. He ran his hands over it to get a reading from his palm-sensors. The instruments in his transparent helmet took a quick visual scan.

"Ethelred," he said, his voice a little shaky, "what do we have here?"

"An object of tremendous density," the computer said. "In Earth gravity it would weigh a few tons."

He looked up at Saturn, hoping for inspiration and finding none. "Only matter at the center of collapsars has that kind of density!"

"So it has always been thought."

"You can't just pick up a hunk of collapsar and hold it in your hands, Ethelred."

"It is not possible at our current stage of technology," the computer agreed.

"Ohmigod!" Derek closed his eyes and swallowed hard. "You know what we have here, don't you? What we have here is an alien artifact."

"Not proven, but that seems to be the most likely hypothesis."

"For around two hundred years people have been looking for alien artifacts. Nobody's found any. Until now." Since it wasn't a question, Ethelred didn't bother to answer. Derek set the thing down and made a quick scan of the area. A few yards away, he found a second egg. It took two arduous walks to carry them back to his ship. He gave their readings to a robot probe and sent it in a widening spiral, searching for more.

Derek stripped off his EVA suit and went straight to the ship's tiny food synthesizer. He punched in a double tequila and it delivered the icy bulb in two seconds. With its straw clamped in his teeth like a cigar, he stared at the two objects on his deck. The moonlet barely had gravity sufficient to give him up-and-down orientation, but the two eggs sat there as if they were welded to the substructure. On Earth, they might have sunk through the crust.

"X-ray analysis?" he asked.

"The centers are opaque to X-ray," Ethelred said.

"Give them the full battery: spectrographic, chemical, everything." Carefully, he lowered one of the ovoids into an analyzer. Within one minute, the instruments had adjusted themselves to the size and shape of the specimen and began busily testing it. For the next several minutes, while the tests were being run, he stood in deep thought. The moon's gravity was too low to bother with unfolding the little ship's only chair.

Derek would have been tall if spacers had bothered much about comparative height. In the mostly zero-gee environment of the Island Worlds, such considerations were irrelevant. His bronze-colored hair was tied in a neat samurai topknot, which was both fashionable and convenient for wear in an EV helmet. Despite the hairdo and his family name, there was little Asiatic about his looks. Only a very slight epicanthic fold in the inner corners of his green eyes revealed his Japanese ancestry. His body was beautifully proportioned—lean, but with far more muscle mass than most spacers had. Since childhood he had taken special treatments and performed special exercises so that he could function in planetary gravity up to Earth normal.

Idly, he tugged loose his hair-ribbon and his implanted static charge fanned his hair into a leonine mane, a style popular with his age group in recent years. On Derek it looked better than on most. His strong face, with its broad brow and wide cheekbones, was equally leonine. He tossed the white ribbon away, and it was attacked before it could settle to the deck. A furious furball shot through the air, squalling hatred of anything small, white and moving. The shipcat was nearly spherical, with a flat, wide tail that paddled the air for added velocity. It caught the ribbon with its forepaws and tore at it with needlelike fangs. The cat twisted in air and cushioned its impact against a wall with its hind paws.

"Good move, Carruthers," Derek said. The shipcat ignored him and batted the wadded ribbon across the chamber, giving it a tiny head start before setting out in pursuit. In the early days of Lunar settlement, white lab rats had escaped and infested first Luna, then all other settlements and ships. They were a mutated stock, unnaturally intelligent, and all attempts to eradicate them had failed. Cats, mankind's oldest ally in the war with rodents, became the third spacegoing species to spread from Earth. Much research had been devoted to developing a suitable cat box.

"Ethelred," Derek said, "you are to forget that I found two of these things. You will report that I found only one."

"As you instruct." The computer's tone was mildly reproving, but it would follow orders. "As soon as the probe returns, start plotting a course for the Academy. I need to pay a visit to Aunt Sieglinde."

Hours later the probe returned, having found nothing. It was possible that there were other artifacts somewhere on Rhea, but if so, they were beyond the probe's range. Derek spent part of the time arranging Ethelred's figures so that it would look as if *Cyrano* had been accelerating only the mass of one of the eggs. The automated tests turned up absolutely nothing. He had expected as much. Whatever these things were, they were totally outside all human experience. Turning them over to his instruments was like handing a computer to a medieval alchemist and asking him for an analysis.

Under his contract, anything he found on his explorations became the property of McNaughton. For an event of this magnitude, he was willing to bend the rules. Come to think of it, did the rules apply in this case?

"Ethelred, what are my contract obligations vis-á-vis alien artifacts?"

"The United Nations pact of 1997 stipulates that any alien artifact found by anyone automatically becomes the property of the U.N. Confederacy law likewise makes any and all such finds government property."

"Hmm, this could be tricky. Well, Aunt Sieglinde's sort of an institution. That's close enough." Actually, she was not his aunt. But, as a member of the extended Ciano-Kuroda-Taggart clan, Derek had access to the legendary Sieglinde, and the right to address her as his aunt. It had been her genius that had pulled the Confederacy's chestnuts out of the fire in the space war three decades before.

"Ethelred, what are chestnuts and why do they need to be pulled out of fires?"

The computer made an electronic sigh. Derek often asked such questions. "It is an archaic and largely meaningless metaphor indicating—"

"Never mind. Do we have the power to accelerate and brake one of those eggs all the way from here to the Academy?"

"Fuel level is insufficient, but the ship can make it within distress call range of Avalon."

"Not good enough," Derek said. "They'd send out a tug to take us in tow and they'd detect all the extra mass. Will my credit cover a fuel delivery and transfer?" He studied Saturn again. Through the curved square of his main viewport, it looked like a holographic projection.

"No. In fact, the emergency service will probably impound this vessel until you pay the towing bill."

"Probably. Sometimes I think we carry this free enterprise stuff too far." Immediate credit was the rule in the Belt, and the entrepreneurs of Avalon were more demanding than most others. Derek tossed the drink bulb into the recycler and punched in another. As he sipped the drink he told himself that, at this rate, he would be an old drunk before his time. The thought of old drunks gave him the much-needed inspiration.

"Ethelred, how about the Ciano Museum? Will our fuel get us that far?" This might work out better, if he could pull it off.

"If we leave within twenty-four hours."

"Then let's button up and head for the base vessel."
He strapped himself into his acceleration couch while
all loose objects were automatically secured. His head
was swimming with thoughts, plans, schemes, counter-
schemes and just plain fear. A few hours before, he had
been despairing over his boring, dead-end job. Now,
he was in the middle of the biggest drama he could
have imagined. Life in the Belt, he reflected, never
stayed dull for long.

The base vessel, "mamaship" to its dependents, was
a cluttered complex of modules and engines, constantly
changing in configuration. Ships usually had names, but
larger ones could be broken down into a number of
smaller vessels, limited only by the number of engines
available. Only the smallest vessels, like Derek's *Cyrano*, retained their identity throughout the vessel's
lifetime.

Derek's mamaship was the *Jardine*, named for an
illustrious nineteenth-century opium smuggler to whom
the McNaughtons claimed kinship. *Jardine* orbited Titan, occasionally firing canisters of gene-engineered bacteria into the giant moon's murky atmosphere. The
bacteria were transforming the atmosphere and surface
of Titan into something inhabitable by humans. Real
colonization was slated to begin within the next generation. Already, it was possible to see the surface from
orbit. When Derek was born, the atmosphere had still
been opaque, resembling thin tomato soup.

After a tricky braking maneuver, Derek left one of
his finds in Tital orbit with a locator, to be picked up
later. With the other, he proceeded to *Jardine*. When
he was still a few minutes out, the face of his first-line
supervisor appeared in the holo tank.

"Kuroda, why are you back so soon? Are you having
mechanical difficulties? I remind you that the company
accepts only limited responsibility for the repair of vessels personally owned by employees."

"Oh, blow it out your—" He took a deep breath and
started over. "Solo explorer craft *Cyrano*, Derek Kuroda

commanding, returning to base vessel *Jardine* with alien artifact aboard."

The supervisor didn't seem to hear him. "State your reason for returning early, Kuroda."

There was no talking to a company man. "I said I have an alien artifact aboard, goddamn it! Get me the base director right now!"

"You have a what?" Obviously, the supervisor wasn't equipped to handle anything unexpected. Abruptly, a new face appeared in the holo tank, this one broad and black.

"Base Director Helen Jackson here. What's this about an alien artifact?" He knew her by reputation. Jackson had been a Marine in the Earth forces during the war. Taken as a POW, she had opted to stay in the Confederacy after cessation of hostilities. She was probably somebody he could deal with.

"Just what I said. I picked it up on Rhea. All the tests I could make say it's not of human origin. It's a bit massive, so I have to brake easy."

"Can you make it into the Emergency Dock?" She was all business, as if she had handled this sort of thing before.

"Sure. No difficulty there."

"I'll have it cleared. When you're secured, stay right where you are and I'll meet you with a research team. Does this thing look in any way dangerous?"

"It seems to be inert." He sent her a holo of the ovoid in its actual size. "Look at the rough readings."

Her brow became a mass of wrinkles as she read the figures. "Never seen anything like that. *Nothin's* that dense!"

An hour later, she came aboard with her team. The group crowded *Cyrano's* tiny interior space. Two wore some sort of protective clothing and carried between them a container that looked like a baby bank vault. They all looked at the egg with awe. In zero-gee it floated like everything else, but their instruments proclaimed its utter alienness.

"I want this kept secret," said a man who wore blue

collar tabs. The Confederacy made little use of uniforms or insignia, but Derek figured he was some kind of official.

"Whaffor?" Jackson said. "The Confederacy has no Official Secrets Act that I ever heard of."

"There must be an exception for this," the man insisted stuffily. "This is an event of the first magnitude and it may be of vital strategic significance to the Confederacy."

"Are we at war?" Derek asked. "I hadn't heard."

"Of course we aren't at war!" snapped blue-tabs. "But scientific data constitute vital intelligence which may be crucial in any future conflict."

"That true, Ethelred?" Derek asked.

"Truth of the statement is immaterial," the computer answered. "Free exchange of scientific information is one of the bedrocks of Confederate policy and any infringement of it is quite illegal."

"The law was never intended to extend to such events as this!" blue-tabs insisted. "To noise this about would be totally irresponsible. It will draw every Earthie agent in the solar system!"

"Nonetheless, that's how policy stands," Jackson said. "I just looked up state policy for this kind of discovery. It says any such objects are to be transferred to Aeaea for analysis." She turned to a subordinate. "Cut loose the *Carnegie*, sober up her skipper, and send her to Aeaea with this thing immediately."

"I shall protest," said blue-tabs.

"Knock yourself out," said Jackson, affably. When the others were gone she turned to Derek. "Just in the thirty-odd years I been out here, we got bureaucrats, fuctionaries, all that stuff. The business kind are bad enough. The government kind are worse."

"I don't know what the procedure is," Derek said, "but I'm quitting. I'm heading back toward Avalon as soon as I get clearance."

She cocked an eyebrow at him. It was an Earthie gesture that the spaceborn didn't have. "Wanna get there ahead of the artifact? Figure you can snag all the

glory, have all the holorecorders on you when it gets
unveiled?"

He bristled but restrained himself. "Sure, why not?
How many people get a chance like this? I'd be a fool to
pass it up."

She shrugged, another piece of Earthie body language. "Nothin' to me. Seein's you didn't make it to
your first payday, I don't have to worry about paying
you. Law says any man wants to quit his job he's free to
do it." She began to leave, then turned at the hatch.
"You figure on dropping in on old Sieglinde?"

He hadn't expected that. "Why do you mention her?"

"Because I know how tight your clan is. And I think
you're holding something back. Now, was we back on
Earth, you might be under arrest right now, answering
some hard questions. As it is, you're free to go. When
you see her, tell her Helen Jackson says hello."

"You know Sieglinde?" he asked, realizing as he said
it how stupid the question sounded.

"Sure, I known Linde since I first come out here. She
got me my first job with McNaughton, after I got out of
the POW pen. You take care now." She drifted out
through the hatch, a bulky, gray-haired woman who
would never look like anything but an Earthie.

Within the hour he was on his way to artifact number
two.

The Ciano Museum was a featureless hunk of rock
drifting in a solar orbit not far from Avalon, as distances
were calculated in the Belt. Fortunately for Derek, it
was, at this time, somewhat closer to the termination
of his route from Rhea than was Avalon. He knew his
luck was holding when he saw that there were no ships
parked near the museum. It was a popular site for
school outings. He hit the museum frequency.

"Roseberry? Are you there?" He waited a few minutes, then an incredibly ancient face appeared in his
holo tank. It was extravagantly wrinkled and surrounded
by wispy white hair and whiskers. Roseberry, who had
only one name, was believed to be the oldest human in

existence. He was nearly two centuries old and living proof that longevity and hard drinking were not mutually exclusive.

"Well, if it ain't young Dmitri! How you doing, boy?"

"Dmitri was my uncle, Roseberry," Derek said. "He's been dead for twenty years."

"Wait a minute, I'll get it in a minute! Derek! That's it, ain't it? Ivan and Mitsuko's boy?"

He grinned. "That's right. How's it going, Roseberry?"

"Dull, just like always. Since the war, it's all been dull. Hardly anybody ever comes by. Even the kids. They don't bother to teach young folks about the past anymore." He sighed heavily.

Derek knew better than to contradict him. The old man had probably conducted about a thousand schoolchildren through the museum in the last ten days, but to mention it was to invite an hour-long harangue on the neglect of the younger generation.

"What brings you by, Derek? I know you seen this place plenty of times."

"Well, I thought we'd have a drink," he saw how the old man's eyes lit up, "and I wanted to talk to you about something exciting. It's the most exciting news since the war. I knew there was only one man to come to with this."

The old man began to cackle. "Well, you come to the right place, all right! Dock your ship and come aboard and tell old Roseberry all about it."

Twenty minutes later, Derek exited *Cyrano*. The museum had a spin sufficient to create a faint artificial gravity. With the gliding, low-grav walk of the spacer he passed the holographic image of Ugo Ciano and threw the tiny man a respectful salute. Ciano looked like a miniature King Lear, with his swirling white hair and beard and his perpetual furious glare. Ugo Ciano had been the Newton of the space age, and never shy about admitting the fact.

"Come on in, Derek," Roseberry called. "I got the sake all heated up."

Derek went to the old man's quarters, just off the

dock. Even seeing the old derelict so close, Derek still felt a sense of awe. Roseberry had lived through the entire span of man's expansion into space. He had known all the giants: Sam Taggart and Ugo Ciano, Martin Shaw, Thor Taggart and Sieglinde Kornfeld. It was even rumored that, as an infant, he had sat on the lap of Wernher von Braun. Even Derek didn't believe he was *that* old. They sipped sake for a few minutes before Roseberry, unable to contain his curiosity, broke the silence.

"Come on, what you got for me?"

This was touchy, but Derek knew that Thor and Sieglinde had put the museum, once Ugo's personal lab, under Roseberry's care because they considered the old drunk to be absolutely trustworthy.

"Rosesberry, I've found it. What everybody's been searching for. Out there in my ship I have an alien artifact."

In the blink of an eye, the old man sobered. "You wait right here. I got a couple of things I gotta do."

"I need to talk to Sieglinde," Derek said, "secretly."

"That's one of the things I gotta do," Roseberry said. "I have to set up a meet between you and her. Other thing is, you gotta talk to Ugo."

Derek groaned. Ugo had been dead for almost a century. He had left behind numerous holographs of himself, dispensing advice and orders. All of his descendants had to endure them.

"This is one nobody ever seen before," Roseberry insisted, "not even me. It's for when one of you finds the alien artifact. He always knew it'd be someone of his blood."

"That's because he was crazy!" Derek protested. "It was pure chance I stumbled across this."

"Ugo had him some theories about chance," Roseberry said. "He always held there was rules to chance that most of us didn't understand. Must've been something to it. Man played a mean crap game. Couldn't play poker worth a damn, not like old Sam could. Too much skill and what Sam called human interaction to that, but

Ugo could always ace 'em at craps and blackjack, because it was all chance, you see. He—"

"Okay," Derek said. "Go warm up Ugo's holo. It'll be something to see a new one." He thought for a moment. "And tell Sieglinde I'm out of fuel."

"You know what old Ugo used to say about his kids when they called up from all over out of fuel and credit?"

"I can imagine."

"Well, lemme go make my calls. I'll send Ugo in. Then I want to see that artifact. It got any writing on it? Anything like that?"

"Nothing like that, but it's plenty weird."

"Hot Damn!" Chuckling, Roseberry hurried off on his errands.

Without preamble, Ugo Ciano was in the room with him. The tiny man was, as always, ebullient and manic, positively erupting with energy. "So you done it! Congratulation! Jesus, I envy you, kid!" How did he know the discoverer would be young? Derek wondered. "Now, lissen up. You just found out we ain't alone. Philosophically, that's the greatest discovery ever made. See, all the big discoveries are the ones that change how we see the universe. Mostly, they're made by big geniuses like Newton and Darwin and me, but sometimes an ordinary jerk will find something that changes everything. That's what happened to you." The grating Brooklynese dialect still sounded awful after a hundred years.

"We useta live in a cozy little world," Ugo lectured on. "It only stretched as far as the horizon and we was right in the middle of it, with the sun going around us. Copernicus theorized, and Kepler and Galileo further demonstrated, that we wasn't the center of anything, that the universe didn't revolve around us. Other astronomers showed that we was just riding on a dirtball way the bleedin' *hell* out on the edge of a second-rate galaxy." He punctuated his speech with explosive, extravagant gestures that set him spinning in zero-gee.

"Darwin came along and showed that the universe wasn't created for us, that we just evolved right along with everything else. That was some blow to the collective ego right there. Then along came Freud, and he hypothesized that there was whole big chunks of our own minds we had no knowledge of, that we just had an imperfect understanding of the conscious part." He stopped spinning and held up a cautionary finger. "Now, what you gotta remember is, all these people got their butts kicked for demonstrating these unwelcome facts. You just found out that we ain't alone in the universe, that God or nature or whatever don't consider humanity to be the ultimate product. So prepare to get your butt kicked.

"Now, don't get too alarmed," he said, conspiriatorially. "After the initial butt-kick period, you can make a pretty good deal outa this. Freud did. And look at me!" He threw his arms wide, as if inviting inspection. "All my dumb but highly placed colleagues said I was crazy. But I'm richer than all of 'em put together and I've already outlived all but a few!" He went into convulsions of chortling, then shut it off abruptly and went dead serious.

"The next part's for if you was alone when you found whatever it was. Keep it to yourself for as long as you can until you got some real understanding of what it is. It's gonna be a real power for human motivation, even if it's just a piece of rock with alien writing or something. If it's real evidence of a technology superior to ours, it can be truly explosive. But, above all," he waggled the admonitory finger again, "publish it all over hell and die doing it before you let it become a government or corporate secret. That kind of thing can be a death sentence for all humanity."

"Be careful who you trust. If you trust nobody, you might as well be dead, but there's no sense overdoing it. Trust your close family, except for the ones you can't stand. In-laws don't count. You can trust Roseberry, if he's still alive. If you go public right away, it goes to everybody: Earth, the planets, the orbiting colonies. I don't care what your political situation is. One last thing." He glared into empty space as if trying to project his will into the far future. Which, in a sense, he was doing.

"If you're already in other solar systems and you found your alien artifact there, no sweat. But, if you found it somewhere in ours, remember this: They can come back someday." The image winked out. Derek let out a long-pent breath. Listening to a Ciano lecture was as strenuous as a bout of zero-gee wrestling.

TWO

Anthony Carstairs relaxed, as much as he ever could be said to relax, in his office overlooking a park in Greenwich. It had been for the park that he had chosen Greenwich instead of nearby London. The park had been landscaped by Louis XIV's gardener. It amused him that the Sun King's gardener designed his view. Visitors never understood his choice of locale, and that amused him as well. My own little Versailles, he thought, only without all the courtiers and parasites.

Carstairs was Coordinating Director for United Nations Services and Activities. The title was deliberately meaningless. What he was in reality was all but absolute ruler of Earth, and had been for the better part of four decades. During that time, he had wielded power behind a series of figurehead Secretaries General. Every few years he changed his title to something else equally obfuscatory. He was little known to the great masses of Earth's people, but that suited his personal style. Everyone who counted knew him for what he was. Far more important than his U.N. title was his Party title. Anthony Carstairs was General Secretary of the Earth First Party. For a generation, the Earth had been ruled by a one-party government and Earth First was that party. They made a pretense of parliamentary

17

democracy, but it was a sham and everyone knew it. Fortunately, the planet's population had grown so passive that there was little serious protest.

He was a squat, bullet-headed fireplug of a man who looked like the dockworker he had been in his youth, following his father and grandfather. He had gone from gang boss to union chief to Party secretary to virtual dictator by a combination of intelligence, brute force, astute political maneuvering and ruthlessness.

He opened a desk drawer and took out a bottle of Newcastle Brown Ale, twisting off the old-fashioned cap with fingers still powerful despite his years, which were nearing the century mark. Advances in medicine kept his appearance and health those of a man in his mid-fifties. As he emptied the bottle, he thought of the long road that had brought him to this desk on this day.

The early years had been brutal: the street-fighting it had taken to establish Earth First, the years of conniving with loathsome pseudo-capitalists who only wanted monopolies and protection from competition. There had been the opportunistic politicians who had scented a powerful new bandwagon, and corrupt military officers eager to trade favors for future promotion. Carstairs had used them all, and most of them he had, eventually, imprisoned or executed. He had never persecuted anyone for personal reasons, nor from spite. All had been done in accordance with his personal vision for the salvation of the planet. He was absolutely certain that, had it not been for him, the planet would have lapsed into utter barbarism decades before.

It was a lonely job being dictator. Even as the thought came to him, he smiled thinly at the silliness of the platitude. A man who wanted to have friends had no business seeking power. It was an irony of his life that most of the few people he had liked had been enemies— Thor Taggart, Sieglinde Kornfeld, even old Martin Shaw, whose name still gave him the shudders after all these years. They had been people of character and force, not like the sheep he led or the hyenas who wielded power for him.

He nursed the brown ale along, putting off his next appointment. It was uncharacteristic of him to put anything off. Ordinarily he tackled each problem immediately and got it behind him. He knew that procrastination was the greatest sin of the statesman. The man in the outer office was Mehmet Shevket, Deputy Chief of Staff of the U.N. Armed Forces.

Face it, Tony, Carstairs thought, he scares you. In all these years, he's the first human being since Martin Shaw to throw a real scare into you. And why? He's a bloody savage, but you've dealt with them before, used them and discarded them. This one is different, though, he told himself. He's brilliant, he's just like me, only he has no morals or scruples whatsoever. I want to save a planet and he just wants to rule it. Kill him, then. But he's the only military man I have who's worth two hairs on a rat's arse. I may need him soon. And, admit it, he has a private power base. Killing him could be your own death warrant.

And I'm getting old. Twenty years ago, I'd have squashed him like the Turkish bug he is. Now, I'm not so sure. Yes, Tony, old age is a terrible thing. Now quit feeling sorry for yourself and see what he wants.

Carstairs addressed the empty air above his desk. "Send him in."

Mehmet Shevket had been born in the sprawling slums of Istanbul, the child of parents he had never known. Growing up in the streets, with minimal state schooling, he had become a ruthless, prominent gang leader by the age of fifteen. A local politician who had made use of his services took him on as protégé and sponsored young Mehmet for admission into a U.N. military school.

From the first, the young man's military career had been remarkable, both for his brilliance and for his stunning capacity for violence. He had been commissioned into the World Peace Force, a much-hated body dedicated to putting down insurrections worldwide. His successes were noted and he was marked for better things. From one post to another, he was renowned for his capability and brutality. After holding the position of Chief of Military Intelligence, he had stepped into the Earth's number-two military slot. Effectively, he was generalissimo, because the number-one slot was largely ceremonial.

Anyone who, from his name and history, expected to see a classical Turkish bandit would have been surprised to see the man who walked confidently into Carstairs' office. Mehmet Shevket was a tall, powerful man with the physique of a competition bodybuilder. He was as handsome as a holostar, with wavy blond hair and ice-blue eyes. At forty-five, he looked ten years younger, not much changed from the Olympic boxer and gymnast he had been during his military academy days. A slight beefiness of neck and jaw were the only signs of age and dissipation visible. If half the stories about him were true, Carstairs thought, the man had the best degeneracy-hiding system since Dorian Gray.

Shevket saluted smartly. "Mr. Secretary, good of you to see me on such short notice."

"Have a chair, General. What's on your mind?" *As if I didn't know*, he thought.

Shevket sat and crossed his elegantly booted legs. Since modern warfare was largely vehicular or spaceborne, the drab camouflage uniforms of the twentieth century had given way to handsome garb designed by the best couturiers. Shevket's was his own design—severe black pseudo-leather with white facings. He wore no insignia of rank and the only trace of color was the hilt of the *jambiya* dagger at his belt. It was carved from a single piece of blood-red coral. It was the only weapon he bore, unless one counted the three-strand horsewhip of knotted leather that dangled from his black-gloved wrist.

"I won't waste your time, Mr. Secretary. Military Intelligence has picked up a report from the Confederacy." He said the word as if it were a unique blasphemy. "It seems that an alien artifact has at last been found."

"Been hearing that one all my life," Carstairs said. "It's never panned out so far." His own spy network had reported the finding the day before, and he suspected that Shevket's personal sources had kept him informed likewise.

"This one seems to be authentic. We have no word as to the exact nature of the find, but it seems that it is no mere passive evidence, writing or the like, but something of a new principle and possibly of vast importance, both militarily and politically."

"Bloody hell," Carstairs said. Neither man gave the slightest thought to the philosophical implications of the find. "We have to get our hands on it, then, or at least learn everything about it that *they* do." The Island Worlders were the bane of Carstairs' existence. They had been siphoning off Earth's most adventurous spirits and best scientific brainpower for three generations.

"The find was made by one Derek Kuroda," Shevket said, "apparently quite by accident."

"Kuroda!" Carstairs spat. "Every time there's trouble from those buggers, it's a Kuroda, a Ciano, a da Sousa or a bloody Taggart! All their talk of freedom and democracy and they're just a pack of primitive clans."

"I agree," Shevket said. "And it is time we did something about them."

"It's not time for another war, General," Carstairs said.

"There are those who disagree," said the Turk. Idly he flicked his horsewhip, snapping the lashes against the side of his chair. "Some think it is high time we had a war against somebody other than petty rebels. This time, we must not settle for a humiliating peace."

"Oh?" The comment was dangerously bland. "As I recall it, the Confederates submitted to a demonstration of overwhelming force." The face-saving charade had fooled few people, but it was unwise to point that out to Carstairs.

"So it may be. The fact is, the new generation has not tasted war, and that means they have never known defeat. Now is the time, before they grow jaded and defeatist."

"Bloody convenient, isn't it?" Carstairs said. "Every

twenty years or so, a bunch of dumb kids grow to military age thirsting for blood. By the time they find out what it's really like, it's too late. No, General, we wait. The Confederacy's never been anything more than a loose-knit coalition facing a common enemy. Now their commercial interests are pulling them apart. Another few years and they'll be ripe for picking."

"You have been saying that for a good many years now," said Shevket. "Yet we are no closer to resuming hostilities. I have forged our armed forces into a superb instrument of conquest, but the finest weapon grows dull with disuse. Bismarck said, 'The problem with a bayonet is that you can do anything with one except sit on it.' You can't sit on our armed forces for much longer, Mr. Secretary."

"They'll stab me arse if I do, eh?" Carstairs grinned mirthlessly. "Well, we'd better make no move until we know what this alien whatsit is. Might be the ultimate weapon, and then we'd look pretty silly, wouldn't we?"

"Therefore, we must have it," Shevket said. "With your permission, sir, I shall send a team to locate it."

You already have, you deceitful bugger, he thought. "By all means, General. Report to me the moment you find anything of value."

"I shall take my leave, then." Shevket rose, saluted and left. Carstairs watched the broad, leather-clad back pass through the door.

"Bloody butcher," he muttered. Then, to the air above his desk, "Get me Valentina Ambartsumian."

Valentina was on the Moon when she got the summons. She lay amid the elegant luxury of the Mondberg development. To build it an entire mountain had been hollowed, its interior devoted to services, its exterior to housing for the very rich. All the dwellings had exterior windows facing onto the Lunar landscape. Status was differentiated by altitude and the quality of view of the Earth.

The bed where she lay was in a penthouse apartment on the very peak of the berg, with windows facing both east and west. All its appointments and services were so modern that to someone living just twenty years previously, they would have seemed like magic. Even in this age, even on Luna, even in the Mondberg, there were few who could afford such luxuries.

The man who lay in the bed next to her was such a person. He was the head of six major corporations. On the Moon, that was not meaningless, as it had become on Earth. He was also suspected of backing several national separation movements on the motherworld. It was Valentina's task to stay close to him. Orders to terminate might come at any time.

She winced when her implanted summoner went off, a hand going involuntarily to her ear.

"What is it, my dear" said the man who dozed next to her.

"I pulled a neck muscle playing mercuryball this morning," she said. "Nothing to concern yourself about. I think I'd better pay a visit to the pharmacy, though."

He waved a hand toward an alcove curtained with a sheet of shimmering red light. "Be my guest. I'm sure I have something to soothe your pains."

She glided from the bed and made her way gracefully to the alcove. She had a lean, muscular, athletic build, because that was the fashion on Luna at this time. Plasticity of physique was one of her specialties. Any native Lunaire would have thought her a native as well, so perfect was her mimicry.

Safely inside the light barrier, she muttered, "What is it?" Her voice was almost inaudible.

"Return to head office immediately." There was no identification or priority, nor was any needed. Valentina had only one superior, and only one transmitter could reach her summoner. All orders from that source were absolute.

"Present subject," she said, "terminate?"

"Negative. Contact may prove valuable in future. Neutral status meantime. Out." Neutral status meant left alive. Suspended death sentence.

Early the next morning she made hasty excuses to

her wealthy lover/victim and arranged for a descent to Heathrow Complex. His personal conveyance (moon-buggy was entirely too prosaic a word) deposited her at the VIP lounge of the Armstrong space facility. In the lounge she sipped an Irish coffee as a cat crawled into her lap to be petted. The lunar breed were long and ferret-like, with short legs to negotiate the narrow passages and tunnels that riddled the Lunar settlements.

She felt no disappointment that her months of preparation, of arranging introductions and working herself into the magnate's trust and finally his bed, had ended inconclusively. She knew that some of her colleagues thirsted for the kill, but not Valentina. If a termination had been ordered, she would have executed it. As it was, she had done her job and done it well. Now she would see what new task Carstairs had for her.

She had been chosen for her work at the age of ten, after a complex series of physical and psychological tests. Her scores had lifted her from the squalor in which nearly ninety-nine percent of Earth's population wallowed and propelled her into higher State schooling. Her schooling was quite different from that of ordinary children or of the children of high Party members. Besides an intensive course of conventional eduction, with emphasis on languages, she took years of ballet, acting, computers and security systems, armed and unarmed combat, codes, extraterrestrial anthropology, sabotage and a score of other subjects even more arcane.

When her schooling was finished, she was picked for Carstairs' personal security team. She had seldom met any of the others. Most of his people preferred to work solo. The fewer people on a given assignment, the less opportunity for betrayal. Also, it made for less difficulty should it become necessary to assign one of the team to terminate another.

She was beautiful today, as she usually was. She was black-haired and green-eyed because that was what her lover/victim liked. Her skin was perfectly white, because that was true of most Caucasian Lunaires. She could look like anything she wanted, even a man. But she had found that beauty seldom hindered an operation and usually got her more cooperation than ugliness.

As she waited, she reflexively fended off the polite advances of male travelers. It was not difficult in the VIP lounge. The very rich are seldom crude. Simultaneously, she kept her acute hearing occupied eavesdropping on nearby conversations. Important people usually talked about money, business and politics. She caught, from three different places in the large, luxurious chamber, a new subject: alien artifact. It was out of place here. She had been hearing it all her life. From the dawn of the space era, the popular media had been full of unsubstantiated reports of alien visitation and artifacts. None had ever panned out. Anyplace else, she would have tuned out all such talk. Not here.

When she reached Heathrow she took a tube car to Greenwich. After a long stay on Luna, she always found London depressing, and this way she avoided it. The city had changed little since Victoria's day, except to grow shabbier and more dilapidated. The hideous council housing of the previous century still stood, each unit now holding five or six times as many inhabitants as originally intended. With unemployment nearing seventy percent, most people spent most of their time on the streets. For the average citizen, participation in government was practically nil. Holovision, gang fighting and soccer riots provided the major pastimes.

The truly sad part, Valentina thought as the tube car sped toward Greenwich, was that London was one of the most prosperous cities on Earth. The wretchedness of what had once been called the Third World was simply beyond human comprehension. For generations, the resources of the planet had been squandered to provide for the growing, unproductive surplus population. The long-promised development of the Third World with its attendant employment opportunities never occurred.

Catastrophe might have been averted had population been controlled. It had been assumed that education and growing sophistication would take care of the problem. In the late twentieth century, a sudden, unforeseen resurgence of primitive religion had changed everything. The priests, mullahs, imams, evengelists and whatnot condemned birth control as unnatural. Alarmed at the booming population of Third World countries and afraid of being swamped, First World nations encouraged larger families, while decrying everybody else's lack of restraint.

After several nightmare decades during which even a modest, conventional war could kill hundreds of millions without putting a significant dent in the birth rate, the iron-fisted rule of Earth First had descended, slowing the deterioration without stopping it. There had been a sort of recovery during the Space War years, but the war had ended inconclusively. It was significant that those slightly less miserable years were being looked back on with nostalgic longing.

Carstairs glanced up as she entered his Greenwich office. As usual, he wasted no time. "Evening, Val. Special assignment this time—maybe the most important you've ever had."

"Alien artifact?"

His eyes widened slightly. In all of known space, she was one of the few people who could still surprise him. "Christ, you haven't been idling, have you now?"

"I heard some talk about it before I left Armstrong. Serious talk from people who don't fall for con games. You don't have many agents who can work in the Belt."

"Right you are, love. Have a seat." He took a bottle of Glenfiddich from his desk and poured two gills. "Official word reached here two days ago. The U.N. Academy was informed that something strange as all hell was found on Rhea. It's being studied. They promise to share all data with us. The trick is, they have the bloody thing and we don't, so do we trust them to tell us everything they find?"

"Have we any choice?" She let the smoky taste of the Scotch roll over her tongue.

"That's where you come in. I'm sending you out there. I want you to get close to whoever's analyzing the thing and report back to me. It's more complicated than it sounds, but we'll get to that in a minute."

Her stomach tightened. An assignment in the Belt! She had smuggled herself out to the Confederate asteroids on two occasions, but only to train and learn how to pass as a native. She had never had an assignment there.

"Our esteemed Secretary General made a brief statement to the media this morning," Carstairs went on. "Made a bloody fool of himself by calling Rhea one of Jupiter's moons, but who notices these days? Now Secretary Larsen's in the act. This came across about an hour ago." He waved a hand and a wall of the room ran a holo display. From his office in the Geneva Complex, Secretary for Planetary Security Aage Larsen was addressing a flock of unseen reporters. Like Shevket, the Dane was the opposite in appearance from what one would guess. He was a small, dapper man with shiny black hair and a dark-complected face dominated by enormous brown eyes. His small mouth made a prim line below a pencil-thin mustache.

Valentina heard Carstairs chuckle. "Bastard's had those basset-hound eyes surgically enlarged. Thinks it makes him look more compassionate and humanitarian." Valentina said nothing. Surgical alteration to fit a role made perfect sense to her.

"Today," Larsen began, "we received notification from the Confederacy of Island Worlds that an artifact of extraterrestrial origin has been discovered. There seems no reason to doubt the truth of the find. The scanty data we have been provided thus far, if accurate, indicate that the Confederates are in possession of a secret of cosmic significance. If Object X, as it is being called, is not surrendered to us, it could endanger all of us here on Earth. This afternoon, I intend to place a motion before the U.N. demanding that Object X be brought to Earth for study. A refusal to comply from the Confederates must be considered an act of hostility." Before the questions could begin, Carstairs cut off the holo.

Valentina was puzzled. "He's making war talk. Is the situation so serious?"

He shook his head. "No, but Security and Military have been in bed together lately. Larsen and Shevket want to start a war. In wartime you can do all sorts of things and get away with them, like shunt aside the Party old guard in favor of ambitious younger men. Good time to get rid of the political enemies, too. Lots of treason charges and summary executions with nobody looking into them too closely. Shevket would handle the butchery while Larsen spouted his humanitarian poppycock for the public."

"They'd start a war to do that?" She was interested, not shocked.

"Too right. Takes people's minds off their problems for a while as well. A big war is always a tempting short-range fix for your problems. I should know." His wry grimace vanished as a yellow globe of light flashed above his desk.

"Well, I've finally gotten through. Sit where you are and say nothing, Valentina. This will be the Confed Ambassador. I've been trying to reach him for hours. You should see this anyway." He arranged his transmitter so that she would be invisible.

The man who appeared from nowhere by holographic exchange was sprawled on a couch. The massive discomfort of the spaceborn when subjected to Earth gravity was evident in his features. The strain added years to his apparent mid-forties. He looked vaguely Hawaiian.

"Mr. Ambassador," Carstairs said, "good of you to spare me some time from the reporters."

The ambassador mopped his forehead with a damp towel. "God, anything but more reporters! Keep me as long as you want. I notice that this is a secure line, though. I have orders from my government not to engage in any secret talks while I'm here."

"Show this to anyone at your own discretion," Carstairs said. "I just don't want anyone eavesdropping right now."

"Fire away."

"To begin with, just what *is* this buggering thing?"

The ambassador made a hand gesture that was equivalent to a shrug. "I'll send you exactly what I was sent."

A near-translucent, glassy ellipsoid appeared above Carstairs' desk. A complicated readout appeared below it. "Not very damned impressive, is it?" he mused. "Looks like a paperweight."

"It's on Aeaea now. This thing is so odd they're having trouble just figuring out how to test it."

"You've heard Mr. Larsen's comments by now," Carstairs said. "How do you propose to respond?"

"We are not trying to keep it to ourselves," the ambassador insisted. "Send out all the scientists you want; they'll be welcome to study it firsthand."

Carstairs snorted. "Except that our scientists are not allowed to leave trans-lunar orbit."

"It was Earth First's law," said the ambassador. "You wrote it yourself, I believe."

"I'll have to see what I can do about that," Carstairs said. "So why don't you bring it here?"

"Aeaea has the most advanced scientific research facilities in the solar system. Besides, as you know well, Aeaea is the only really neutral territory between us."

Taking Carstairs' silence as consent, the ambassador continued. "Look at the readout, Mr. Secretary."

Carstairs shrugged. "Means nothing to me. I never passed my O levels."

"The figure refers to mass, not size. Object X masses better than a ton per cubic centimeter at the opaque core. It may not be as large as a football, but it's as massive as an elephant."

"Bloody hell," Carstairs said, impressed. "Physics isn't my field, but a thing like that could be useful, couldn't it?"

"The technology could open up the stars to us. Now think of the race that could develop such technology."

"Right." Carstairs thought for a moment. "Is Sieglinde Taggart studying it?"

"Who knows where that woman is? She's been notified, but she hadn't showed at the time of my last communication. Nobody controls her movements, but she must be far away to miss something like this."

Carstairs knew her habits better than most. Once, when his intelligence service had her located in Jovian orbit, she had walked into his maximum-security office in Geneva. "Thank you for your time, Mr. Ambassador. Please keep me informed of future developments."

"I'll keep the whole world informed, Mr. Carstairs. This could be the beginning of a new age for humanity." The hologram faded.

He shook his head. "Bastards still talk like that. Rough as it is out there, I don't know why they haven't had the optimism kicked out of them yet."

Valentina shrugged and finished her Scotch. "Pioneer spirit, I would imagine. You want me to find out what they really know about Object X?"

"Exactly. It won't be easy, because you'll not only have Confed security to contend with, but another U.N. team or two on the same mission. Also, Larsen and Shevket will send someone as well. That's where the real danger will be. Whatever this thing means, I don't want it in the hands of those two."

THREE

Sieglinde wasn't alone when she arrived. Derek broke off a chess game with Roseberry to meet her at the airlock. She smiled at him as she came in. Her appearance had changed little in the previous three decades. She was a small, compact woman with short, blonde hair. As she hugged him, he saw the man behind her. He was Chinese, wearing the utterly incongruous robes of a Confucian scholar. He knew this had to be Chih'-Chin Fu, another of the legendary figures of what were, to Derek, the "early days" of the independent Island Worlds.

"It's so good to see you, Derek! You know Chih'-Chin Fu, don't you? You don't? Well, surely you've heard of him."

"Who hasn't?" Derek said. He took Fu's hand. Spacers never actually shook hands, an operation that could be dangerous in zero-gee. Fu had been the media wizard of the war. While the Confederate forces and the outlaw Defiance Party had fought the military end of the war, Sieglinde had dominated the scientific end and her husband, Thor, had been the leader in Confederate Diplomacy. Throughout, Fu had handled the propaganda war, for years bombarding Earth with a relentlessly accurate picture of exactly what was happening.

Everyone agreed that it had been Fu's propaganda campaign, enabled by Sieglinde's inventions, that had finally brought Earth to the peace talks.

"Honored, sir," Derek said. As he looked more closely, he saw that the frail old man before him was actually in his vigorous middle years. The elderly effect was the result of makeup, for what reason he couldn't imagine. People like Sieglinde and Fu were renowned for their eccentricities.

"So you are the young man destined for the history books?" said Fu. "I envy you."

"Maybe on Rhea they'll build a monument to my sore toe," he said. As he led the pair to the lab where the egg was stored, he told them his story. At the lab, Sieglinde stared at the thing in rapt silence for a full twenty minutes, then she turned to Derek.

"Finding it may have been blind luck," she said, "but getting this one here undetected was sheer genius. From now on, you can write your ticket with the family."

"Actually," Derek said, "what I really need is some fuel. See, I—"

"I brought it. This is an unbelievable opportunity. Now I can conduct my own investigation without bother from those idiots on Aeaea, or the Institute for Arts and Sciences." It seemed odd to hear the most formidable institute for applied technology and the most distinguished body of abstract scientists in human history thus referred to, but Derek said nothing.

"I think," Roseberry said hesitantly, "old Ugo has a message for you, Linde."

"I know he has. He has them for everybody and every occasion. I'll be damned if I'll listen to another one. I still think it was that last one that got poor Thor killed." She looked at the others as if they were strangers. "Excuse me, but I want to be alone with this—this thing. I have some ideas about it. I work better alone."

"Perhaps," Fu said, "we might avail ourselves of Mr. Roseberry's excellent refreshment facilities."

"You talking about the bar?" said Roseberry. "Sure,

sure, come on. Linde, don't you starve in here. I seen you like this before."

"Certainly," she said, distracted. "Just send in meals. I promise to eat. Now go."

Discreetly, they made their way out. Had their been any real gravity, they would have tiptoed. Sieglinde never took her eyes from the green egg. In the bar, they drew drinks all around. It was a spherical room detached from the main body of the museum and consisted mainly of windows open to the starry vastness of the Belt.

"Now, young Derek," said Fu, "it is time we got to know one another. Since your clan is as numerous as my own, you must forgive me for not having made your acquaintance before this." The Fus were not prominent in the Belt, but there were incredible numbers of them on Luna, on Mars and in the orbital colonies. Chih'-Chin was one of the elders and by far the most famous of them. "Do you know Sieglinde well?"

"I've seen her maybe a dozen times in my life," he admitted. "Mostly at family functions—weddings and funerals and so forth. She's not what you'd call one of the family favorites." He hastened to avoid a misunderstanding. "I mean, it's not like anyone's hostile, it's just," he groped for words, "I guess we're all in awe of her."

Fu smiled. "She is not the most approachable of women. I must tell you her story some time. The real one, not the one everybody learns in school. My old friend Thor was probably the only human being to penetrate beneath the armoring she constructed around herself. She is not always as forbidding as when hot on the trail of some new scientific principle."

"Fine woman," Roseberry said. "Crazier'n hell, but a fine woman." He nodded in vigorous agreement with himself.

"One way or another," Fu said, "your discovery shall be of tremendous significance. It could not have come at a better time for us. Sieglinde believes that it may turn the balance in our favor for the coming conflict."

What conflict? Derek thought. "Does she know what it is?"

"She has a theory, based on the data released so far by Aeaea. On the way here she was devising tests to prove or disprove this theory. She did not tell me much."

"You mentioned a conflict. I've been sort of out of touch in the Saturn orbit. Has something been going on?"

"Ah, the young," Fu said with a heavy sigh. "They have so little grasp of public affairs. Of course, their elders have little more, but that is no excuse."

Derek dialed himself a beer. He was in no hurry.

"The last few years," Fu continued, "our peace with Earth has become increasingly fragile. A complete break is not far off. A new generation of leaders is gaining power, the economic and environmental situations are growing more desperate—"

"They have only themselves to blame," Derek said.

"And they certainly aren't going to do that, so who does that leave for them to blame? It has to be us, and the answer has to be another war."

"Another war?" There had been no wars in his lifetime, and it wasn't something the Confederates glorified. Life could be hard and dangerous enough without people deliberately trying to kill one another. Once piracy, hijacking and raiding had been a constant hazard in the Belt, but no longer. After the Space War, the Confederacy had made use of the extensive intelligence and security networks built during the conflict to obliterate the outlaw gangs. Under the leadership of the redoubtable Hjalmar Taggart, the campaign had been brief and brutal. Since then, criminal activity had been rare. The Belt was no longer used as a dumping ground for Earth's undesirables, and the rougher element among the immigrants had settled into steady, if hard-bitten, citizens.

That was the elimination of one hazard. There were others in plenty. Space was the most unforgiving of environments, with the possible exception of ocean depths. The slightest mistake was usually rewarded with instant death. Even using the greatest care, disaster could come from sheer bad luck. Systems failures and particle collisions took a tragic toll, and every year dozens of vessels and their crews simply disappeared. Prosperous colonies were occasionally discovered with all personnel dead, and sometimes, mysteriously, found abandoned.

As a result of the uncertainty of space life, the Belt dwellers had become cheerfully fatalistic. You did your best, and if you got killed anyway, that was tough luck. There were definite advantages to the life for those with the guts to live it. Low- to zero gravity eliminated many physical infirmities and bestowed a greater life span. Second and more important, spacers were the freest human beings that had ever lived. At least, they believed themselves to be, which was the same thing.

War was something else. Derek had seen violent death in plenty, amid the dangers of asteroid life, but the organized butchery of warfare was something different. If anybody would know about it, it would have to be Chih'-Chin Fu.

"Do you think it'll happen soon?" he asked.

"Much may depend upon the nature of your artifact. It may be the answer to the problems that have defeated Sieglinde since the last war."

Derek knew something of what Fu was talking about. In the years after the war, Sieglinde had labored over the obstacles to superluminal travel, and had reached a dead end every time. She had hoped to have large-scale emigration to the stars under way within twenty years, but her development of Ciano's pioneering work had never reached fruition, due to the inadequacy of the technology. Despite her many successes, these failures had cost her. Lesser, envious scientists used them to accuse her of being a mere crackpot.

"How is this thing going to affect a war?" he asked.

"We shall have to wait for her to tell us," Fu said. "But I have had many years to learn respect for her judgment. She has never disappointed me and has invariably confounded her adversaries. That is a good record."

"Looks like we're headed into excitin' times," Roseberry said. "I was hoping I was through with that kind of thing."

"Come, Mr. Roseberry," Fu said, "surely you are not intimidated by another time of danger?"

"Naw, I was just hoping to be on my way out of the solar system by now anyhows."

"We might still make it in our lifetime, Mr. Roseberry," Fu said. "Sieglinde has only dropped hints, but I believe she thinks the Rhea Objects are tied to some sort of propulsive device, and that she might be able to duplicate them."

"She's come up with that already?"

"I have no idea," Fu said, "but I have learned never to discount her hunches."

By the time Derek reached Avalon, the initial flurry of interest in the Rhea Object was waning. There had been no immediate revelations from it, and there were always plenty of other things to occupy people's attention. Avalon was the capital of the Confederacy of Island Worlds and it always swarmed with activity. Government functions were minimal, but business was roaring along at a great clip.

Cyrano safely docked, fees paid and reprovisioning operations arranged, Derek happily made his way toward the Hall of the Mountain King, social center of Avalonian life. He had expected some kind of hero's welcome as the discoverer of the alien artifact, but nobody paid him any special attention. This seemed to be a clear case of injustice, but he was prepared to live with it as long as nobody found out that he had secreted away a second egg.

HMK had been expanded greatly over the years and was by then the largest non-planetary open area in existence. Avalon's spin gave it artificial gravity, roughly Earth normal at the equator near the outer skin of the asteroid, dwindling to zero-gee at the axis. Within the huge, wheel-shaped chamber were stacked tiers of business facilities, provisioning yards, restaurants, hotels, entertainment centers, media facilities and other attractions, in vast profusion. Everything seemed to be thronged. He had come through an access tunnel onto a tier devoted mainly to entertainment. There were roughly equal numbers of tiers above him and below.

"Derek!" He turned. Recognition at last. Then he saw who it was. "You owe me, boy! You and your friends busted up my place and I intend to be paid. You want the debt police after you?" The debt police were mythical. The phrase meant that Derek stood in danger of being posted as a deadbeat or welsher. In Belt society, that was several degrees lower than being dead.

It had been a graduation party months ago that had grown a bit raucous toward the end. Derek muttered as he handed over his credit crystal. "There were twenty of us at that party. Why didn't you get one of the others?"

"You were the first one to show his face." The barkeeper fed the crystal into his belt counter, then handed it back. "Besides, you're the one who discovered that thing, so I knew you'd be able to pay up."

"Nice to know my fame is good for something." He broke off when he saw the man who was coming toward him with an intent, bouncy stride. "Oh, no." It was François Kuroda, possibly his least favorite living relative. There were, however, many others in competition for that position.

"I heard you got fired," François said without preamble.

"I quit," Derek insisted. "It's different. What kind of welcome is this, anyway? I made the most important discovery in the history of humanity and I get treated like an Earthie."

"The way I heard it," François said, "you practically tripped over the damned thing. Nobody's found a use for it anyway. What kind of discovery is that? I also happen to know you left your job broke and low on fuel, and here you are after a mysterious absence getting your ship reprovisioned and your fuel topped off. I just saw you repay Fischetti for busting up his place. Where did this sudden wealth come from?"

"I put the touch on a soft-hearted relative," Derek said with his best fake sincerity.

"Crap. You don't have any soft-hearted relatives. Just us."

"Who appointed you my watchdog?"

"Ulric," François said, grinning.

Derek winced. This sounded bad. Ulric Kuroda was the head of clan security. One of his duties was the disciplining of members who strayed too far from clan standards of propriety. He lacked a reputation for tolerance. "I suppose he wants to talk to me."

"Immediately," François confirmed. "Come on."

They walked to a tube station for the short ride to the old Sidon mining site, where the Kurodas had their stronghold. All the way, Derek kept hoping for a reporter to stop him for an interview about his exotic find. Nobody seemed to be interested.

The Sidon district was a large, mined-out hollow surrounded by residential tiers. More than half of them were claimed by the Kurodas and collateral families of the extended clan. The warren was protected by the latest vault doors and all units were interconnected by a maze of tunnels, in which certain family members were rumored to be still wandering around lost after a massive party at the Ciano place twenty years previously.

The largest door was marked with the Kuroda plumblossom *mon*. It slid open at their approach and a battery of security devices trained on them just in case the door's system had been faulty. The place seemed to be deserted, which was nothing unusual. The family's mining and freighting operations kept most members on their ships or at their sites most of the time.

"After you," François said, gesturing toward a door bearing Ulric's personal wolf-head crest.

Derek took a deep breath. The spin-induced gravity at Sidon was Mars-normal, about one-third of Earth's. He tried to use the gravity to achieve a confident stride as he walked into the wolf's den.

Ulric sat cross-legged on the polished stone floor, glaring up at him from beneath bushy white eyebrows. His silver hair flowed almost to his shoulders and a walrus mustache overhung his piranha mouth. His black coverall was embroidered with a wolf-mask in silver thread.

"Greetings, Elder Uncle," Derek began formally.

"Hand it over, nephew," Ulric barked, holding out a platter-sized palm.

"Hand over what?" Uh-oh, he thought.

"Don't insult my intelligence! I mean the other artifact! You found more than one, didn't you?"

Derek assumed a look of wounded innocence. "Who, me?"

Ulric's ice-blue eyes went into liquid-nitrogen mode. "Don't talk like an idiot, you product of a sperm bank for the hopelessly defective! Do you believe your elders have lost their capacity to think logically? Your recent actions are so transparent I am ashamed to call you my kinsman. I could have come up with a more convincing subterfuge while sleeping off a three-day drunk!"

Derek kept silence. This was going to be even worse than he had feared. It never occurred to him to turn and walk away, as was his perfect legal right. Clan obligations went far deeper than mere constitutional technicalities.

Ulric continued his tirade. "You're a glory-hungry young whelp, with an over-inflated idea of your own importance—a common failing of the young. Yet, after finding the now-famous green egg, you did not accompany it back! You passed up your chance to be holographed throughout human-occupied space. You'd have been famous for whole days!

"Instead, you terminated your employment and ran off as if you were publicity-shy; a laughable concept if ever there was one. There is only one possible answer: There was another alien artifact and you made off with it. Now hand it over."

"I have no such thing," Derek said, being truthful after a fashion.

"Then where did you hide it? Don't be cagey with me, Derek. Are you planning to sell it? No, you may be dumb, but you're probably not a crook." Ulric sat back and folded his arms, glaring ferociously. Derek tried not to quake. "Damn!" Ulric muttered at last. "You've given it to that woman, haven't you?" Before Derek could frame an answer, Ulric silenced him with an abrupt wave. "No, don't try lying to me, you just aren't good at it. Everybody wondered why the green egg didn't bring Sieglinde powering into Aeaea on her mythical super-luminal drive."

"She might've been on Earth," Derek said, helpfully. "Or Luna. Or even farther away. It takes a long time—"

"Silence." Somehow, Derek thought, Ulric sounded even deadlier speaking quietly than when raging. "She was here in the stronghold not thirty days ago. Now she's hiding out somewhere with that artifact you gave her, you unthinking young wretch."

Derek decided to drop all pretense. "You're acting like I gave it to some Earthie, or an outsider. Sieglinde's part of the clan; she's a Taggart."

"By marriage," Ulric grumbled. "She's crazier than the Cianos, and they're all lunatics."

"She's the greatest theoretical *and* experimental physicist alive," Derek said, loyally.

"So she tells everybody. Her faster-than-light schemes have never panned out, but they've cost a bundle."

Derek relaxed a little. The worst seemed to be past. "It's all been her own money."

Ulric twisted the end of his mustache and signaled to Derek to sit. With great relief, the younger man did so. A squat, domed robot with a flat bottom came gliding from a wall on a cushion of air. A pair of low-grav beakers rose through a door in its top. Bubbles rose lazily through amber liquid and raised a slow-motion spray on the surface. Derek took one and sipped it. After all these years, he still couldn't believe that Ulric's favorite drink was champagne.

"It could be worse," Ulric said at last. "My main worry is that that madwoman will destroy the thing trying to take it apart. It was another of the eggs, wasn't it?"

"Yes, identical to the one sent to the Aeaeans, as far as I could see."

"As soon as the *Althing* hears of this, and believe me they will hear of it, people will be calling for your head. Still, maybe it's not such a bad thing that two are being analyzed independently. But why did you do it?"

Derek finished his beaker and tossed it to the robot for a refill. "First of all, because I knew the McNaughtons would try to claim ownership of it, which seems absurd even if it's legal."

"I'll grant you that. And second?"

"Sieglinde's working on the Drive. Whatever these aliens are or were, they had some kind of interstellar drive to reach Rhea. If there's a chance the thing could help her to break the puzzle, I wanted her to have it."

Ulric seemed almost to smile, but it was hard to tell beneath the overhanging mustache. "So that's it. Still anxious to make the big move, are you?"

"What do you think?" He took a drink from his second beaker. At least it was *good* champagne. "What's left for us here in this solar system? The resources may be virtually inexhaustible, but the Earthies' patience certainly isn't. It's only a matter of time before there's another war. Anyway, I want to go and see what's out there."

"Only you don't want to spend your entire life covering the first tenth of the journey, is that it?"

"Naturally. Subluminal travel is a dead end at interstellar distances. I want to actually *see* what other star systems are like. Why else have I been training for planetary activity all my life? I certainly don't plan to go to Earth!" Another thought occurred to him. "When it gets out what I did, the McNaughtons will be after my blood." His former employer seemed far more dangerous than the rather nebulous *Althing*, as the Confederate congress was termed.

"Let us worry about the McNaughtons," Ulric said. The families had at various times been friends or fierce rivals. They were connected by marriage ties, but the McNaughtons were not members of the clan. "Still, you're out of a job and you need something to keep you occupied and out of trouble. How would you like to work in security?"

This was unexpected. There had to be a catch somewhere. A man like Ulric just didn't turn off the hostility so easily. "What kind of work?" he asked, cautiously.

"Bait. The Earthies must have agents heading here by now, if they aren't here already. Most will try to break into Aeaea's infonet, but somebody will decide you're worth interrogating. That might be convenient."

At least Ulric hadn't gone soft. "It's good to know the family still finds me valuable. This sounds like dangerous work. What's the pay?"

"Pay?" Ulric looked mortally stricken. "Where's your family loyalty?"

"Where it always is. On the other hand, it wouldn't do to let people think I work cheap."

"Who would know?" Ulric said. "Besides, they'd be after you anyway, even if you weren't working security for me."

"I was thinking of going to a body shop for a new face. I already have several alternate identities worked up. They'd never find me." He watched with satisfaction as Ulric's face went through several color changes. Then he wondered whether he had pushed his luck too far.

"All right," Ulric said when his breathing returned to normal. "Third-level pay with full seniority rights."

"And you'll pick up the payments on *Cyrano?*" Derek asked.

Ulric stared at him in utter astonishment. "Your insolence surpasses belief. You talk like a Ciano."

"Hell, I'm related to them by about fifteen bloodlines, just like you."

"Out!" Ulric pointed toward the door with a rage-trembling finger. "Get out of here, and don't come back unless you have something worthwhile to report!"

"But what am I supposed to do?" He backed hastily toward the portal.

"Circulate. Go out carousing with your worthless friends. Be prominent and make a target of yourself. What do I care so long as you show results? Rig yourself with recording gear so if you get killed we know who did it."

Derek backed out and the door slid shut, almost catching his nose. He found Francois still waiting outside with his grin unchanged. "How did it go?" he asked.

"Not bad," Derek said. "I've been hired on with security at third-level pay with full seniority. And he's picking up *Cyrano*'s payment schedule." The look on his cousin's face was worth all the trepidation.

FOUR

Shevket leaned over the green baize and carefully plotted his shot. His right hand swung in a brief, precise arc. The stick slid between the gloved fingers of his right hand, and the leather tip struck the cueball on its outer surface in a perfect line with its center of mass. The white ball rebounded from two cushions and struck another white ball, this one with two black spots. The spotted ball caromed off another rail and clicked elegantly into a red ball. He stood back and lightly stroked the leather tip of the stick with a cube of blue chalk while he planned his next shot.

Larsen stood patiently, awaiting his turn. He had no interest in the game and did not play it well. Shevket was a man of action and preferred to speak while moving about and performing some function, preferably competitive. Larsen was willing to put up with it, if in the meantime the Turk would speak his mind.

"Carstairs," Shevket said, sighting along the cue stick. "He has to go. The man has stayed around too long. He is in our way."

"Carstairs did not reach his present eminence by being soft," Larsen said. "He has not stayed there by being foolish. He has dealt with attempted coups in the past, always successfully." He flicked imaginary lint

45

from his impeccably tailored Saville Row sleeve. He detested Shevket, who was an uncultured beast from a part of the world not distinguished for its devotion to humanitarian behavior. However, the Turk was invaluable as an enforcer.

"Carstairs now is not the man he once was. In any case, he came to power in an easier world, when people still believed in a better future. He is accustomed to gaining his ends through political maneuvering, and that's a thing of the past. Only force counts now." He made another perfect three-cushion shot. "He was never a military man. He never understood the needs of the military."

"Yet he used the military quite efficiently," Larsen pointed out. "He had no difficulty in bending the generals to his will."

Shevket's next shot was a bit too forceful and he missed the red ball by a fraction of an inch. "The military system of four decades ago was weak and corrupt." He placed his stick on a rack, apparently no longer interested in the game. "In those days, the upper ranks were held by political officers—old cronies of whatever Secretary General was in power. That was why he could manipulate them. It is also why they were so easily defeated in the First Space War."

"The First?" Larsen's dark eyebrows arched. "Since it was the only space war, why this numerical distinction?"

"Don't be obtuse," Shevket said. From a shelf in the billiard room he took his riding whip and slipped his hand through its wrist thong. With infinite care, he placed his hat at exactly the proper angle. His gloved fingers left no mark on its gleaming obsidian bill. "It was Space War One because there will be another, and soon. I've completely reformed the military. My officers are superbly trained. They hate the offworlders with intense passion. They are also perfectly loyal and willing to undertake any mission of conquest upon which I order them."

"In other words, they are fanatics?"

"Exactly. But they cannot be kept waiting forever. I

have forged an army of conquest, and such an army will disintegrate from sheer boredom without worlds to conquer. Come, our luncheon guests await."

As they left the billiard room, their bodyguards fell in behind them at a discreet distance. Shevket's wore the black uniform of his elite guard. Larsen's were anonymous men and women in civilian clothing.

The Great Palace of the United Nations overlooked Lake Geneva. It was a grandiose structure, architectural propaganda designed to impress the citizenry with the majesty and power of the state. Every wall, pillar and decoration was outsized, scaled to inflict the viewer with a sense of awe and of the insignificance of the individual.

Larsen considered it to be garish and horrid, but he had to admit that it served its intended purpose well. The corridor they now occupied was floored with a single Bokhara carpet more than one hundred meters long and ten meters wide. The walls were of sea-green marble, covered with famous paintings. Many of the world's great masterpieces had been removed to the Palace for "safekeeping."

Larsen paused before one of his favorites, a Picasso from the artist's Blue Period, depicting an old man playing a guitar. "So, is policy to be formulated for the happiness and well being of the military?"

"Naturally," Shevket said, ignoring the painting. "At this moment, there are only two power structures of any consequence: the Party and the military. Over the years, all other organizations claiming rival power have been demolished. On this planet, the only power that can destroy the Party is the military. The Party cannot threaten the military at all. Therefore, the military wields the whip. Logical, is it not?"

Shevket strolled across the corridor and stood before a gigantic painting of lurid color and furious action. "That is my favorite," he said. "The French of the First Empire had spirit, unlike your bloodless Picasso and his whining post-World War One generation."

The painting was Delacroix's *Death of Sardanapalus*.

From atop his funeral pyre, the monarch whose city was about to be overwhelmed calmly surveyed the spectacle below him. On the slopes of the gigantic pyre, his wives, concubines, horses, dogs, slaves and treasure were being slaughtered or placed for immolation. It would be impossible, Larsen thought, to find a painting that more accurately expressed the personality of Mehmet Shevket.

Shevket pointed with the handle of his whip at the most prominent group in the foreground. A savage-looking warrior held a beautiful, naked odalisque by her pinioned wrists. The painting froze him in the action of plunging a serpentine dagger into her breast as she struggled futilely for her life. "This is a wonderful detail. Do you notice how the curve of the soldier's yataghan precisely echoes the curvature of the woman's body? A nice touch, the yataghan: It's a Turkish blade."

The idea of Shevket as an art critic was mind-numbing. "Your plans of military supremacy are a bit premature, aren't they? Carstairs is still there, and neither of us truly knows the extent of his power."

"His power is a myth," Shevket insisted, slapping the knotted thongs of his whip against the side of his boot. "Now is the time to prove it!"

"No," Larsen said coolly. "Now is the time to find out what the Rhea Objesct represents. A few weeks ago, I might have agreed that this was a good time for a test of power. Now, I do not. The heads of the Academy tell me that this could be one of those rare discoveries that changes everything. To act, one must have the greatest possible certainty of the situation. A situation of such fluidity, with so many unknown factors—" He shrugged his narrow shoulders. "It is not a good time to take irrevocable action."

"You think too much, Aage. If you think too much, you never take quick, decisive action. But then, that is probably why we make a good team, you and I. Rest assured, though; when I know that the time is ripe for action, I will act without consulting your overcautious advice." He whirled on a chrome-spurred heel and strode down the corridor. Larsen hurried to catch up, cursing this sudden loss of initiative.

"I agree, though," the Turk went on, "that this alien artifact business is of great importance. It could be a powerful new weapon. I've assigned some of our best teams to the task."

"I know," Larsen said. "I've gone over the reports from Intelligence. Who is your personal operative on this?"

"I've given it to Daniko Vladyka. The other teams may fail, but not Vladyka. I've also given him orders to kill the Kornfeld woman. She was our most dangerous adversary in the last war. I do not want her on the other side in the next."

Larsen stopped and faced Shevket. "You didn't consult with me about that."

"It isn't your department," said the Turk. "You are forbidden by law to order an assassination unless you have assumed your wartime powers, and that must be voted upon by the Security Council, remember? It's an old custom among military men to save their superiors embarrassment by acting unilaterally. Deniability is a wonderful thing."

Larsen was still fuming as they entered the dining room. It was not one of the State dining rooms, where the scale was as lavish as the decor, but one of the more intimate chambers, with small tables and few distractions, as befitted a room where serious discussions and decisions took place.

Still, this was a facility for the Party elite, so a complete absence of luxury was unthinkable. The waiters were human rather than the cheaper robots, and these were all Caucasian North Europeans. This was flattering to people from the former Third World and earned the Party cheap points for respecting the sensitivity of the poorer brethren. Even in a world with an enormous and idle surplus population, human domestics were hard to find. The Party solved the servant problem by the simple expedient of using military recruits.

Four men already sat at the table, waiting for Larsen

and Shevket. As two of the most highly placed Party members, it was their privilege to be late. Three of the others were also important Party members: Hua, a deputy welfare minister; Chalmers, Chairman of the Council for Military Affairs; and Ghose, secretary to the Minister for Finance. The fourth man was a nonentity— the President of Tanzania, one of the beggar nations that made up the majority of the U.N. Such persons were included at luncheons where no significant business was to be discussed in order to stifle complaints that the leaders of small nations were denied access to the inner sanctums of the mighty.

Larsen greeted the others with professional warmth, Shevket with barely concealed contempt. The waiters began bringing drinks and hors d'oeuvres and the men talked of inconsequentialities. Larsen was relaxed and charming in the familiar milieu. Shevket was bored and restless, and he drank heavily.

The Tanzanian fidgeted and sweated for the better part of an hour, then worked up his courage to break into a conversation about the upcoming Party convention.

"Sirs," said the African, "I have come here to Geneva to discuss matters of great importance, but I can find no one who will listen!"

The others were startled at this rudeness, but Hua smiled broadly. "Mr. President, you are among friends here. Speak freely. How may we be of assistance?"

"Sirs, my people are starving! I do not exaggerate here. There is real starvation in the cities and the countryside. This year, the rice harvest in China has been exceptionally abundant. The wheat harvest in North America has also been excellent. Why has there been no distribution of this grain to my nation?"

"Ah, Mr. President," Hua said, spreading his hands in an appeal to reason, "there are many needy people among whom this largesse must be divided. Some are suffering far more hardship than your people."

"Dead is dead," the president insisted. "You cannot suffer more. If you will not aid us, then you must let me open the Serengeti to farming and grazing."

"That is out of the question, Mr. President," Ghose said. "The Serengeti is an irreplaceable natural resource. It belongs to all humanity." In truth, environmentalism was a dead issue. The Serengeti was a game park available only to party VIPs and their favored guests.

"My people must have food or I shall not be able to control them!"

"Then perhaps," said Shevket, leaning over the table, "it is time your people felt the whip! Do not be so sure they have reached the limit of their capacity to suffer. I can teach them what those limits are."

He sat back and drained a wine glass, holding it out to a waiter to refill. The others stared at him in stunned silence. Such talk was simply not heard within the Palace. Hesitantly, conversation picked up and Larsen exerted his best skills to smooth over the breach. Shevket said no more for the rest of the meal.

After the luncheon broke up, Chalmers and Hua walked with Larsen on the terrace with its spectacular view of the lake.

"Bit of a shock, wasn't it?" said Chalmers, a thin man with perfect military bearing and an Oxford accent. "Shevket speaking out like that, I mean."

Inwardly, Larsen cursed the Turk's premature assertion of power. "I think the general had a bit too much to drink this afternoon. I am sure he would not—"

"Oh, not at all," Chalmers interrupted. "I think it's high time such talk was heard."

"Exactly my thought," Hua said. "It is time we curbed these petty potentates of worthless nations. We are all tired of this quagmire of sub-Saharan Africa. General Shevket is just the man to settle them."

"Oh, I don't think military action is really called for, old boy," Chalmers said. "Just cut them loose and let them starve."

"I agree," Hua said, as Larsen's mind worked furiously. "There are more important enemies to consider than the African primitives. Australia, for instance." The Australians had stubbornly resisted U.N. confiscation of their resources. The population was hard-working, independent and notoriously reluctant to part with their hard-earned wealth.

"Am I to assume, then, " said Larsen, "that you two would support the general, should he advocate, shall we say, a harder line with the member nations? Not just the rebel movements, but with the nations themselves?"

"You may," said Chalmers. "And we are not alone in this. Quite a few of us would like to see a bit of discipline thrashed into the surplus population of this planet. They've come to take too seriously all the rhetoric about freedom and equality."

"Yes," said Hua. "We have grown decadent. We need to return to the original principles of the Party. It is time for a long-needed purge as well. You may tell the general that."

Later, back in his office, Larsen thought over what he had heard. Chalmers and Hua must have been looking for an opportunity to speak as they had. Shevket's outburst had provided the excuse. They would never have spoken so, had there not been many others in the Party elite who were like-minded. Shevket was right. The time was growing ripe for a coup. If only it were not for the great unknown factor: the Rhea Object. Just what did it represent? He pounded a fist on his desk top in sheer frustration. Just what was the damned thing?

Vladyka decoded the microburst message in his ship, *Ivo the Black*. It had been months since he had been given an assignment, and his smile widened as he read this one. It was more than he could have hoped. And the implications were enormous. It meant, for one thing, that Shevket was ready to take power, and that his most valuable followers would rise with him.

It would be difficult, and by far the most deadly and dangerous operation he had ever undertaken. But, he thought with satisfaction, that was why he had been chosen for the job: Daniko Vladyka was the best. He would have to crack Aeaea's legendary security, and he would have to get close to the equally legendary Sieglinde

Kornfeld-Taggart. His mind whirled with ideas. He would have to contact his various agents and team members, scattered as they were throughout the Belt. Fortunately, most of them were concentrated in the vicinity of Avalon.

He would set up a careful operation. The message had given him no time frame, so he was free to set his own schedule. From all reports, the Aeaeans were no closer to solving the puzzle of the Rhea Object than they had been when they had first seen the thing. As for the Kornfeld woman, she would not be far from the alien artifact. Come to think of it, it seemed strange that she wasn't on the thing the minute it showed up. It probably meant that she was secretly on Aeaea, studying the problem. Everyone knew about her fetish for secrecy.

Vladyka was a burly man in his mid-thirties. He told people his muscle mass was due to treatment and training for planetary environments. A generation before, few except the Earthborn carried so much redundant muscularity. The prospect of convenient interstellar flight caused a demand for treatment to ready the pioneers for exploration of planets with real gravity.

Once he had been dark, with dense, coarse black hair and a drooping mustache. For life in space, his head had been depilated and his skin lightened. He especially missed his mustache. In his homeland it was all but synonymous with manhood. Well, when he pulled off this feat, he could return to Earth and look as a man should look once more. Surely, Shevket would reward him with a high positon, perhaps even Chief of Intelligence.

After allowing himself a few moments to revel in the prospect, Vladyka dismissed all such fantasies from his mind. From now on, he would allow only the job at hand to concern him. In sequence, he brought up the faces of his team. As each appeared before his mind's eye, he weighed their merits and faults for the plan that was already beginning to take shape within his mind. Which should he contact first?

When he had his plan roughed out, he ordered *Ivo's* computer to take him to Avalon.

Valentina watched through a small port as the transport docked at Avalon's North Polar terminal. The trip out had been tedious, but she had used the opportunity to study recent Confederate history. From London she had travelled to Luna, and there she had arranged for a clandestine outbound passage to the Belt. It was not difficult, using her contacts. Once among the Island Worlds, her mobility was all but unrestricted because the Confederacy did not use internal passports.

Personal suspicion was another matter, and she had carefully built up a believable personality, and the physiognomy to go with it. Her hair was now dark, parted in the middle and drawn back tightly. Her skin was pale and she appeared to be wearing no cosmetics whatever. Her beautiful features were unchanged, but she managed to radiate plainness by her expression and bearing.

"We have arrived at North Pole Dock on Avalon," said the captain's voice over the intercom. "Docking is complete. Passengers may now disembark."

Valentina unclipped her landing harness and floated toward the exit hatch. Around her, twenty or so other travellers did the same. Experienced spacers, they managed to make the transit without jostling or kicking each other's faces. Very few people who were not spaceborn could manage the feat, but Valentina did it effortlessly. Had she wished, she could have adopted the distinct zero-gee body language of one raised on Luna or Mars. It was failure to master such subtleties of body language that exposed far more agents than verbal slipups or inconvenient physical evidence.

At the end of the umbilicus connecting ship and port, she followed a flashing stripe color-coded for baggage claim and Transit Authority. She collected her single bag and towed it toward an official who was speaking with the passengers and checking off something on a belt unit.

"Your name?" the official asked.

"Valerie Amber." It was a persona she had established several years before, complete with records. It would stand up to a fairly rigorous investigation.

"And your occupation?"

"Student." It was the most plausible of covers. Students were everywhere, enrolling in courses for a term, then moving on to another school or instructor, working when they ran out of funds. For many, it was just an excuse to travel, which was an education in itself.

"Passing through, or do you wish to settle here permanently?"

"Passing through."

"Enjoy your stay." That was it. No customs search or stamping of passports. Her baggage had been searched when she had left Lunar orbit, not for contraband but for explosives or toxic chemicals that might endanger the ship and its inhabitants. Other than that, nobody cared a great deal what a traveller might be carrying. At an office labeled Inprocessing she paid a minuscule facilities deposit to cover the air, water and public restroom facilities she would be using. Payment would be deducted according to length of stay. Anything else she required, she would be charged for.

Along with a crowd of other new arrivals, she pondered a three-dimensional chart of Avalon. It was color-coded, with blue for open chambers, yellow for tunnels, green for tube-car passages and so forth. It was confusing, because Avalon had never been planned as a habitat. It had been one of the earliest mining operations in the Belt, and the tunnels and chambers were long-abandoned mine galleries. People had moved into the larger chambers, and access tunnels had been cut to connect them. It was a bewildering labyrinth, so Valentina purchased a small holographic facsimile and earset to keep from getting lost. When she activated the holo, a flashing white dot would show her where she was.

The Hall of the Mountain King seemed as good a place as any to start, so she caught a tube car. It was crammed with workers headed for their jobs, spacers

just off their ships and students doing whatever it was
students did. The Belt settlements had nothing like the
luxurious space of the Lunar or Martian colonies. An
old, established habitat like Avalon could be as crowded
as an Earth city, not because of population but because
of limited space.

As they moved toward the asteroid's outer periphery,
the car swung on its gimbals in response to the growing, spin-induced artificial gravity. Some of the travellers took anti-nausea pills from belt dispensers. To those
unused to gravity, its effects could be distressing. As
she stepped from the car, Valentina affected the slightly
wobbly gait of one to whom even the Lunar gravity of
HMK was an unaccustomed experience.

She passed through a low, rough, stone arch into the
main chamber. The access tunnel opened onto a wide
terrace about midway up the layers of tiers surrounding
the major open area. The plan was amorphous, with
many smaller canyons opening off the major gallery.
Most of it was crammed with commerical establishments.
She keyed her holographic guide for a quick orientation. Near her, many others were doing the same. The
flicker of holos was the trademark of new visitors. To
Valentina, the place was only mildly bewildering. Some
of her fellow travellers had never before seen an indoor
space so large.

"The Hall of the Mountain King," said the voice from
her earset, "has grown over the years into the largest
man-made, non-Lunar habitat space in existence. At
any given time, several hundred businesses are located
here. There are travellers' accommodations and entertainment facilities, eating establishments, places of worship and a few private residences. Besides the main
chamber, there are side galleries such as the Grotto,
the Bat Cave, the—"

Valentina let it drone on until she was sure she had
the layout of the place firmly fixed in her mind. Then
she shut off the holo and stepped out onto one of the
spindly catwalks that connected adjacent tiers and other
catwalks in no particular order. The term seemed espe-

cially appropriate since a good many cats shared the walks with the humans.

Few people spared her a glance. Even young men, after a flicker of interest, looked elsewhere. Her drab clothing, severe hair style and lack of cosmetics suggested that she was from one of the more severe religious settlements, possibly the neo-puritans. The prim, humorless set of her mouth reinforced the impression. She did not move with undue speed. She had definite plans and goals, but her persona required a certain aimless quality—that of a student who was not quite committed to a certain course.

Sometimes Valentina wondered whether her meticulous planning was worth the trouble. Chances were, nobody would notice her anyway, if she merely took the trouble to disguise her beauty. However, the urge to stay in persona had been drilled into her early, at a time when the Intelligence schools had hired the finest acting coaches to instruct the pupils. Now it was all but impossible for her to drop the character she had constructed. She could switch from one to another with facility, but acting naturally was all but unthinkable.

She stopped at a booth that offered shrimp tempura. From the earliest days of self-sustaining life off-Earth, shrimp had been a principal source of protein. They grew in pestiferous abundance in the salt-water tanks throughout the Belt. Everywhere around her vegetation grew. In the tunnels, on the tiers, even on the catwalks, vines, bushes and dwarf trees grew from planters. They aided in atmosphere production, produced food and softened the harsh functionality of asteroid life.

As he ate, Valentina watched the people around her. The Earth origins of spacers could be tricky to read, but most of those on Avalon seemed to be Caucasian or Asiatic in about equal numbers, with a sprinkling of people from everywhere else and innumerable mixtures. There were a few eccentrics who had chosen cosmetic treatments that gave them the appearance of no known race. Clothing was mostly functional, although there were some who wore very little of it. There seemed to be a fad for garish jewelry among the young.

There was a lot of exuberant advertising in every possible medium. Most of it was holographic, but some used archaic lettering, a rarity on near-illiterate Earth. Chinese banners of scarlet cloth bearing gold calligraphy were stretched on the fronts of some shops, and one establishment had revived flashing neon in glass tubes. From what Valentina could make out, the lower levels of tiers were devoted to selling necessities and equipment, the middle range to luxuries and services, and the upper tiers to entertainment.

It was nothing particularly enthralling to her, but she reminded herself to rubberneck. In her current persona, she was the Belt's equivalent of a hick in the big city. The brief preliminary scan told her that she should modify her persona to something more worldly. It had served its purpose.

At intervals along the tiers, small side-tunnels led to public restroom facilities. Valentina located one and paid a small fee for a private booth. She maneuvered herself and her bag into it and found tht it had sparse shower facilities and a holographic mirror. She switched on the mirror, undressed and went to work on her appearance. She unbound her hair and, with a few deft cosmetic touches, altered her appearance into something far more alluring. She did not bother with a full-strength vamp treatment, but now her eyes and lips were highlighted. The coverall she took from her bag was as functional as the other had been, but it had a shiny finish and was tailored to emphasize her figure rather than disguise it. When she left, she was the object of a good many appraising looks, not all of them from males.

On the thirty-fourth tier, amid the entertainment section, she found a hotel in the middle price range. She chose it primarily because its hand-lettered sign listed the symbol for infonet services among its facilities. Instead of having a front wall, the tiny lobby was separated from the tier terrace by a living fence of close-planted bamboo. A tiny woman in a kimono came around the reception desk and bowed. In the primarily zero-gee Island Worlds, the custom of bowing had fallen out of use, so someone in this place was a traditionalist.

"May I help you?" she asked, straightening.

"I need a room with infonent services," Valentina said.

"Of course. Please come this way." Behind the desk was a corridor. Sliding partitions lined the walls at intervals and the woman opened one. The room was small, about three meters square. To Valentina's surprise, it was floored with *tatami*. On an impulse, she took off her boots before entering. At this level the gravity was somewhat less than one-third Earth normal, but she could feel the pleasant texture of the weave.

"We have a *tatami* craftsman here on Avalon," the woman said. "He contracts with one of the grain firms to grow the reeds. I know of no other settlement that has them."

"They're exquisite," Valentina said. "I've never seen reed mats before."

"This is your first visit to Avalon? Welcome, then. I hope you enjoy your stay. All four walls and the ceiling have holo display." She indicated a plate with pressure points marked in symbols. "These are your service and infonet controls. The folding spa unit has bath, steam and sauna capability. For an extra charge, we have masseuse service."

"I'll take it. I'm still on ship's time and exhausted. This will be perfect."

"Then I'll let you get some rest." The woman took a small exchange unit from her obi and Valentina thrust her credit crystal carrier into its slot. The woman bowed her way out and Valentina found herself alone for the first time in weeks. The ship had not been luxurious and she felt the urgent need of a bath. She hit the spa control and undressed as the unit inflated.

At full inflation, the spa was a transparent capsule shaped like an oversized shoe. She stretched its top

opening and stepped in. With only her head exposed,
she alternated sauna and steam until she streamed with
sweat. Then she let the unit fill with water. She thrust
her shoulders and arms out of the unit and while she
soaked she ran through the series of holographic wall
displays. The room disappeared and she was in the
midst of an ocean, then in rapid succession a desert and
a forest, then a long series of terrains, landscapes and
seascapes. Last of all were starscapes with various moons
and planets. They were all familiar, artificial environments designed to relieve the claustrophobic conditions
of life in space.

She dried with an airblast and deflated the spa. She
contemplated getting into the infonet to begin organiz-
ing her operation, but gave it up when she realized how
weary she really was. She pushed the bed control and
it unrolled from its niche in the wall. The bed was a
thin foam mat, all that was needed in the light gravity.
She collapsed onto it face down and signalled for a
masseuse. A few minutes later the masseuse arrived.
She was of Scandinavian coloration, seemed to be barely
out of her teens and was strong as a horse. Valentina
gradually relaxed under the girl's expert ministrations.
As the tension was kneaded out of each muscle, her
eyelids grew heavier. She was asleep before the girl
left her room.

She awoke thoroughly refreshed, but uneasy at how
much she had let down her guard. It had been years
since she had simply gone to sleep in the presence of a
total stranger, without setting up the most elementary
security. Why should this place lull her into such a
trusting state? She vowed not to repeat the error.

She left the hotel to find breakfast. In the absence of
day and night, Avalon operated around the clock. For
the sake of convenience and thousands of years of human conditioning, there was a twenty-four-hour "day"
divided into three shifts. Which shift was used for what
was entirely the choice of the individual. Roughly one-
third of the population was sleeping at any given time.

After breakfast, she returned to her room to begin

serious work. She keyed the infonet and requested information on the alien artifact. Of hard data there was dauntingly little. She ran over the news stories and found nothing she did not already know. The object had been found on Rhea during an exploration expedition conducted by McNaughton & Co. The discoverer was one Derek Kuroda. It was duly delivered to the immense scientific station of Aeaea, where it still resided.

Periodically, Aeaea released reports of its experiments on the ellipsoid, but so far the scientists had accomplished nothing, save finding negative results almost as exciting as the positive kind. There was a long list of experiments that had turned up nothing. Valentina could understand little of that part.

From the announcement of the discovery, scholars throughout the solar system had clamored to be allowed onto the study team. Aeaea was a private company, though, and allowed only a few supremely prestigious scientists who were not among its personnel to examine the object. There was no mention of Sieglinde Kornfeld. That in itself meant nothing. Her passion for secrecy was notorious and she might be working on Aeaea under a news blackout.

Popular response to the discovery had been, predictably, mixed. Many decried the right of Aeaea to sole access. Others declared that the thing was some sort of holy relic and should not be studied at all. Another school considered it dangerous and favored putting it on a ship and firing it out of the system.

There had been a brief flurry of interest in the popular media with all the usual wild extrapolations and pseudo-scientific explanations. Astrologers had had a field day. Interest had quickly subsided, largely because the Rhea Object was so prosaic. Had it had some bizarre shape, or been very large, or covered with alien writing, it might have been more interesting. Best of all might have been a pyramidal shape, or Mayan glyphs or some discernible connection with Stonehenge. It was difficult to work up much enthusiasm over something that resembled a glass paperweight. It seemed to be utterly inert. No voices came from it; it performed no miracles. Its major distinction was its fantastic density, and that was a quality that came across poorly on holographic reproduction.

Valentina switched off the set. So much for public information. Now it was time to extrapolate. She keyed the walls for a star display *sans* planets. In an instant, she was sitting on *tatami* adrift in deep space, in total silence. Holographic display had reached such perfection that it was in no way discernible from reality except to the touch. If she reached out a few feet, her fingers would touch the solid wall. She knew that intellectually, but to all the senses, she was in space. She had always preferred this holo environment for meditation.

The available information had contained nothing new. She had little interest in the object itself. That was not her task. To get her hands on it, and on all the information, public or otherwise, that had been gleaned, required access to it. She began at the first, with the discovery. What interested her now were the anomalies. What was *not* being said? What was being left out, sidestepped, glossed over? There she might find the key.

First, there was the discoverer. The find was being treated as a McNaughton discovery, because it had been found during one of that firm's explorations, and it had been a McNaughton ship that had delivered the object to Aeaea. Why was the discoverer, Derek Kuroda, being slighted?

A team of high-powered physicists and other scientists had been assembled to study the thing, most of them Aeaeans, but some from other places. Why was the most illustrious physicist of them all, Sieglinde Kornfeld-Taggart, not mentioned? It might be her passion for secrecy, but there might be other reasons. Was she dead? Was she conducting her part of the study from a distance? Was she in some part of the system so remote that she had not had time to reach Aeaea yet? It was not unthinkable. Even with the development of the Ciano-Kornfeld antimatter drive, there were parts of the system that could require months to reach. But she had reliable information that Sieglinde had been on or near Avalon just days before the discovery. Intuitively, Valentina felt that the key to her problem was here. She suppressed it and left it for her subconscious to work out.

Back to the discoverer. She called up all the information she could find on Derek. He was younger than she had expected. His resumé listed excellent academic credentials. His background was in the sciences and he had requested a place on the first expedition to be put together upon development of the superluminal drive. He had had a great deal of physical preparation for planetary environments and was qualified to work for limited times at up to 1.5 Earth gravity.

With her professional skills, it was not difficult for Valentina to gain access to the Academy's restricted files on young Derek. Here his record was not so sterling—repeated absenteeism, a fondness for carousing and brawling, occasional insolence toward his superiors. It was not highly unusual among students in the rough-hewn Island Worlds society, but not to be expected from the scion of one of the most illustrious Founding Families.

McNaughton records showed that Derek had been employed by them only briefly. He had tendered his resignation immediately after delivering the Rhea Object. He had not even stayed for the few days left until payday. That seemed totally out of character. A quick search turned up information that his solo ship, *Cyrano*, was on a payment schedule. It was up-to-date, even since Derek had left his employment. There was no record of his securing further employment. This meant nothing in itself, since the Confederates were notorious for their cavalier attitude toward record-keeping, especially if it might end up in government files and tax accounting.

As for Sieglinde, Valentina didn't bother to try. The woman had managed to erase nearly all traces of her former life and what could be learned since was restricted to what she chose to release to the popular media and her copious scientific publications, none of these being very useful in researching her private life. All that was known was that she had been born on Mars, her parents had died in the Barsoom City riots, and that she was probably the greatest genius of the age.

She had married into the Taggart family, part of the Kuroda-Sousa-Taggart-Ciano extended clan, and had four living children. Her husband, Thor Taggart, had died under mysterious circumstances while testing an experi-mental drive unit.

There were linkages and connections everywhere here and Valentina spent some time sorting a few of them out. Young Derek was a Kuroda, and apparently some-thing of a black sheep. Sieglinde was related to that clan by marriage, although there were indications that she was not greatly loved by the Kurodas or Taggarts. As strange as she was, she was far more likely to be on good terms with the unbelievably eccentric Cianos. It was possible that the connection was coincidental. After all, the Island Worlders ran to large families and the older clans numbered many hundreds of members. But Valentina did not believe in coincidence.

So here she had young Derek, He had made a fabulous discovery but had handed it over to the McNaughtons. Granted, his contract stipulated that he had to do exactly that, but if she read him right, he was not the type to let such trivialities stand in his way. He ran off without collecting his pay. His debts were paid up. A thought occurred to her and she broke into the McNaughton files for Derek's mamaship. *Cyrano* had been low on fuel when he had left. A query turned up the information that he had had barely enough to reach Avalon.

She ran a scan of Avalon's docking records. He had arrived fully fueled. Where had he been in the interim? How had he payed for the fuel? A broad smile spread across her face as it came to her.

"You clever little bastard!" she said in reluctant admiration. "You found two of them, didn't you?" With such a find, where would he go? Where but to his relative, Sieglinde? So that was why she hadn't showed at the most exciting study in history. She had an egg of her own.

Valentina shut off the holo and infonet and sat back, satisfied. It had been a good morning's work. She was ready to act now, and the place to start was with Derek Kuroda.

FIVE

The bar was called the Black Hole, and it opened off the next-to-uppermost tier of the Bat Cave. Its entertainment offerings were fairly sedate compared to some of the rougher spacer establishments. The clientele ran largely to students, younger ship's officers, and local business types.

Derek sat at his usual corner table, putting on a fair imitation of well-lit bonhomie. The others at the table were enjoying his company and doing most of their drinking at his expense. The table and chairs were scarcely needed in the light gravity, but they were traditional and gave scale and a certain cohesiveness to a convivial gathering. There were some parts of the human psyche that refused to respond to the possibilities of life off Earth. Working accommodations had infinite variety but bars looked like bars everywhere.

"Confess, Derek," said the girl to his right. He turned and looked at her, making the movement slow and deliberate, pausing a second to let his eyes refocus. She was a da Sousa, a distant cousin, and she worked on a passenger ship. Her hair lay back along her scalp in sleek waves and a tiny ruby gleamed from her left nostril, accentuating her sharp, unpretty features. Her looks were correctable, but many spacers stubbornly refused to employ cosmetic surgery.

"Confess what?" he said, slurring slightly.

"Where you're getting the credit for all this glad-handing. You're notoriously the brokest Kuroda of your generation. Then you find the alien what'sit, which the McNaughtons promptly appropriate before firing you—"

"I quit."

"Whatever. Anyway, suddenly, you're a gentleman of leisure. I'm not complaining, mind you. I'm taking advantage of your largesse, after all. But there haven't been any large robberies recently that I've heard of. What is it? Something scandalous, or at least faintly disreputable?"

Esmerelda. That was her name, he remembered. He'd known her when they were small children. Even then, she had talked too much.

"Like I said, Esme, I sold my story to a big Earth media syndicate. They paid big."

"For a story about how you stubbed your toe? Granted, it's not easy to do in low-gee like that, but it's nothing to pay for." She keyed a new holo display over the table and realistic tropical fish flickered colorfully amid their drinks.

"Hell, no. I made up all kinds of lies. There were the six-toed footprints, the wreckage of a ship shaped like an Egyptian scarab beetle, the glowing writing that appeared in the vacuum over the green egg, warning me to repent and stop eating so many sweets—" He broke off as everybody snatched up their drinks. A cat had charged onto their table and was trying to catch the holographic fish. Someone changed the display to a platter of glowing coals and the cat left.

"And they believe all you brought back was the paperweight?" Berkeley said. He was a young man little older than Derek who worked for Port Authority and wore a perpetual affected air of boredom. He turned to Esmerelda. "What's a paperweight, anyway? That's what the Earth commentators are always calling it."

"It's a necessity where you've got paper, gravity and wind. Haven't you ever been to Earth?"

"No, and I never will," Berkeley said. "Have you?"

"Sure. I went down once to see if my gravity conditioning really worked. I felt like hell but I managed." She shuddered. "It was the big spaces and the bugs and animals and all the people that got to me. And the oceans! The holos don't give you any idea how they *smell!*"

Derek wished they would leave. Somehow, carousing wasn't nearly as much fun when you had to do it. He'd put together a small team of people he'd known since his early school days, and that had been fun, but the hanging around in bars and gambling establishments had palled quickly.

A chime sounded and Berkeley got up, washing down a sober-up pill with the last of his drink. "End of second shift," he said, "time to go to work. What a bore. I wish they'd outlaw something around here so we could have smugglers again. I hear they were fun to outwit."

As Berkeley went through the screen that shut off light from the terrace outside, he stepped aside for someone. Derek saw the woman as he was exhaling and for a few moments, he forgot to inhale. Even in the dim light she was stunning, with tawny hair and huge eyes. It was obvious she was new in Avalon, and her unfamiliarity with the gravity gave her a slight, delicious awkwardness.

Esmerelda followed the direction of his gaze. Her eyes, set a bit too close to her long nose, narrowed slighty. The woman stood blinking while her eyes adjusted to the dimness. He grunted as Esmerelda elbowed him in the side.

"Pull your tongue in, Derek, it's unseemly to slobber all over the table. Where's your taste, anyway? She looks like a tarted-up Earthie to me."

"No Earthie walks like that," Derek said. "And I'll pass my own judgment of desirability, if you don't mind."

She stood. "You're welcome to her. I have a gaggle of tourists to nurse. If you plan to move in on glamor queen there, I'd suggest you take a sober-up first. You're cross-eyed and your breath could set off atmosphere alarms." She whirled and left in a low-gravity stalk while he made an elaborately obscene gesture toward her back.

He looked around and saw that the woman had seated herself at a nearby table, its holoset displaying a miniaturized volcano erupting on Io. Such low-level lighting was unflattering to most women, but it did not detract from this one's beauty.

Feverishly, Derek sought a way to approach her. She looked older than he, but not that much older. He reminded himself that he was pretending to be a rake, a playboy and hell-raiser. How would such a person go about this? Should he continue his drunk act? Best not. Surreptitiously, he sprayed a breath-freshener into his mouth. What else? He was presentably dressed, his hair was impeccable. His problem, as he pondered it, was lack of experience with glamorous ladies from nowhere. Dare he just go over and introduce himself and risk acting like a lout?

When Valentina had walked in, she had pretended to spend a few seconds adjusting to the change in light. She had used those seconds to scan the room, spot Derek, and do a quick study of the young man and his companion. Body language said the two were not close friends. Derek was also pretending to be drunk, for some reason. It was useless to speculate on that now. There was a brief, even-so-slightly acrimonious exchange, and the plain-featured girl left. That was convenient.

She saw that Derek was fidgeting. As she had intended, he had been smitten the moment she walked in. It almost seemed a pity to take advantage of such inexperience, but a professional used every tool that came to hand. She looked over the surroundings. The bar was typical, sparsely populated at the moment, but it would probably fill nearer the end of this shift. A girl took her order. In the Belt, humans performed many of the lesser tasks given up to robot labor on Earth. One of the walls was a holographic display in which a troupe performed a nude zero-gee ballet with consummate grace amid underwater lighting effects. In this place, she thought, it probably passed for sophistication, if not outright decadence. She let Derek sweat for a while.

He nerved himself up to go over and say something like, "May I buy you a drink?" when she took it out of his shaky hands.

"Aren't you Derek Kuroda?"

He looked up. It was her. For a moment, her question puzzled him. Then the answer burst into his mind. "Yes, I am."

She smiled, and all the blood drained from his brain down to the vicinity of his gonads and their environs. "I saw you on the holos, after you made the discovery. I hope you don't mind me coming over here like this, a total stranger."

"Oh, not at all! Have a seat. Can I order you something?" Desperately, he tried to think of something witty to say, something devastatingly disarming. His brain seemed to have turned to toxic sludge.

"I hear Avalon has wonderful Chablis," she said.

"The best!" he insisted. He despised Chablis. "The very best. Margaret!" The waitress came over, yawning. "Bring this lady a Chablis."

"Any particular brand?" Margaret asked. "Or do you want the plonk we have on tap?"

"Never!" Derek said. "A Chateau Orecrusher '72, from vineyard 4D, third level up, next to the infrareds."

"Jesus, Derek," Margaret said, wrinkling her nose, "that's the crummiest Chablis ever made." She turned to Valentina. "Lady, you want a good one, try Chateau Sauve-Qui-Peut '69. They were trying out the new sugar-enhancing bacterium that year, and the radiation level was a bit higher because of the supernova of '69 or something. Anyway, they've never been able to repeat the circumstances and it's the best Chablis ever."

"In that case," Valentina said, "I'll try it."

Derek shrugged. "Not my specialty, I'm afraid."

She smiled and his heart lurched. "Actually, I don't know a thing about wines. I'm a student."

"A student of what?"

"Journalism. I intend to be a freelance reporter for

one of the holo networks. That's how I spotted you. I spend a lot of time following the reports about your discovery. One of the things I wanted to do when I got here was to interview you, but I wasn't expecting to just run into you like this. I want to hear all about it. The discovery, I mean. I just can't understand why you, the discoverer, went so unnoticed."

"It's a cruel world. The McNaughtons wanted credit for the find and I was under contract to them."

"So you quit because they wanted to hog all the glory. I think that was a fine gesture." She hoped she wasn't laying it on too thick. Just because he was young didn't mean he had to be dumb.

"Actually, there was more to it than that." He knew he was being flattered and decided that he liked it. "I didn't like working for McNaughton."

"I'd heard the McNaughtons and Kurodas didn't always get along together."

"It wasn't that. Sometimes I don't get along with my family either. McNaughton's gotten to be a big corporation with a bureaucracy all its own. Most of the lower-level people were all right, but the upper management were always sticking their noses in, demanding reports and paperwork and standardization of procedures and stuff like that. Hell, if I'd wanted to live like that, I would've moved to Earth."

"I can see how you'd feel disillusioned." She blinked at him admiringly. "Listen, I don't want to seem pushy, but would you be willing to give me an interview? I'd like to get the real story. Not just about making the find, but about how McNaughton manipulated it. I think your side of it should be public."

"You think so?" Actually, she didn't really seem so much older than himself. Three or four years at the most. "I'd have no objection."

"What would be a convenient time?"

"Let's see, what shift are you on?"

For a moment she didn't understand what he meant, then she remembered the peculiar local time system.

"This is my second shift since I woke up. I just arrived on Avalon yesterday. I'm still adjusting to your time."

"Fine. We're both on the same timeframe, then. I'm free for the rest of this shift. Where do you suggest?"

"Your ship? That always makes a good setting for an interview with an explorer. I hope it's here. I don't have equipment to simulate it."

"No problem. It's at the South Pole Dock." He looked up with annoyance as three men pushed boisterously into the bar. They were dressed as commercial spacers and were well into their voyage-end celebration. As they took a table and ordered, he turned back to Valentina. "Would two hours from now be all right? I have a few things to take care of." Actually, he needed to clean up the mess in *Cyrano*, which had the characteristics of bachelor accommodations throughout history.

"That would be perfect. I have to go to my place and get my equipment ready. It's an old secondhand holo outfit without much editing capability, but I can make do." She glanced at the three roistering spacers, realized she recognized one of them, and paid them no further attention.

After a few last-minute instructions on how to find *Cyrano*, she left the bar. Immediately, she took a catwalk to the tier opposite. In the Bat Cave, the distance separating them was only about fifty feet. She pulled up the integral hood of her coverall to disguise her hair and pretended to inspect the goods in the glass window of a luxury shop, keeping her attention on the reflected entrance of the Black Hole. After a few minutes, Derek came out and made his way toward a droptube. Within seconds, one of the spacers came out and followed. It was the one who had seemed familiar. She did not bother to follow the two. Instead, she concentrated on the gesture that had prodded her memory.

As she made her way back to her hotel, she thought it over. It was the way the man had picked up his glass. Faces meant nothing. Surgical clinics routinely reconstructed faces. Coloring, hair texture, even height could be manipulated. Tiny mannerisms were far more revealing. He had cocked his wrist inward and jerked out his elbow before tilting the glass up. He wasn't one of the big ones, but she knew she had seen that one before.

Just as she reached her room, she had it: Alexandrov. Two years before, Carstairs had slipped her into a party hosted by the Russian embassy in London. She was there to leech onto the Burmese Minister for Opium, but Carstairs had pointed out Alexandrov, who was a colonel in Russian intelligence.

Now what the bloody hell, she wondered, was a Russian doing here? Obviously, he was on the same sort of errand she was. Surely Carstairs hadn't held back something? No, unlike some superiors, Carstairs never sent his people out without a complete picture of the situation.

Why would the Russians be involved? The Soviet Union was all but moribund, its client-states long since broken away, its huge Islamic South joined with the Moslem states of the Middle East and little left save Great Russia to bear the torch of discredited Marxism. What was their interest here? It might be their all but reflexive urge to meddle and snoop. But it might be something else. Like the British and the Americans, the Russians dreamed of a return to their former position of world dominance. It was possible that someone in their intelligence apparatus saw in the Rhea Object a path back to power. If so, might Alexandrov have reached the same conclusion as she about Derek? Or were they just covering all possible bases?

Sometime soon, she was going to have a little chat with Comrade Alexandrov.

While Derek frantically tidied up *Cyrano*'s living quarters, he tried to think rationally about the woman. She'd said that her name was Valerie Amber. It sounded like a fake name, but that was nothing unusual. People changed their names all the time. Still, it was too convenient, this gorgeous creature appearing from nowhere and taking such a flattering interest in him.

Deep down, he knew he was being had. On further thought, being had didn't seem to be such a bad idea.

He knew he was in for trouble. If Ulric found out he was cozying up to a stranger who might well be an Earthie agent, he would probably have Derek expelled from the Clan. Worse, he would certainly cut off payments on *Cyrano*. It was a thorny problem, and it would do no good to consult with Ethelred. Being a computer, Ethelred had no grasp of interpersonal relationships. A certain electronic disdain was about all Ethelred could manage.

He checked for neglected food wrappers and overlooked laundry, readouts that had missed the disposal slot, tangles of hair pulled from his comb, or any other incriminating evidence of human occupancy. Certain that all was immaculate, he sprayed the interior with a commercial air freshener. On long solo voyages, you got so you didn't notice how the place smelled. Other people noticed.

A furry white blob shot past him, closely pursued by Carruthers. The two furballs disappeared into the tiny laboratory whence came a series of shrill squeaks. Derek hoped the sounds signified a kill, but you could never tell unless the cat bore the carcass back in triumph.

"Ethelred, get me Port Maintenance."

A bored-looking functionary appeared in holograph. "May I be of service?"

"When I arrived, there were no mice in my ship," Derek lectured. "I just saw my cat chasing one. How did it get aboard?"

The man looked, if anything, even more bored. "You got some way to tell an Avalon mouse from any other kind?"

"No, but I know there were none before I got here."

"I got no way of knowing that. For all I know, you arrived here with a whole cargo of 'em. Do I blame you for every mouse on Avalon? They got ways of getting onto ships. They ride on cargo pallets and hide in provision crates. They climb up chemical pipes and they squinch themselves in under those little thingies on top of gas bottles. Sometimes they just walk in through the hatches. Are all your hatches closed?"

Derek turned around, saw that his main hatch was two inches ajar, and turned back. "Hell, yes, they're closed."

"I think you need a better cat. You got any more problems? I got plenty."

"Take care of them, then." Derek switched off the holo. He longed for the days of aristocracy, when you could have insolent functionaries horsewhipped. Of course, he was assuming that he would have been one of the aristocrats. He turned to close the hatch and saw that there was a man standing in it, pointing a gun at him.

"Hell, aren't mice bad enough?"

"Mice?" the man said atonally.

"Actually, I was expecting somebody a lot prettier." Derek had a gun. Unfortunately, it was back in his sleeping quarters.

"Just step back there to the pilot's seat and make yourself comfortable," the man said, pushing his way through the hatch. "If I see your hands move toward any controls, I'll shoot."

Derek sat. "I wouldn't do any shooting if I were you. My internal security systems are pretty merciless."

"You don't have any internal security on this ship."

Damn. How had the man known that? "How can you be so sure?"

"I've gone over the latest data in the owners' files."

"Like hell. I'm the owner."

The intruder shook his head. "Bank of the Belt is the owner. You just make payments. Now quit playing games. I want some answers about that thing you found on Rhea. Specifically, I want to know what else you found. If I'm satisfied by your answers, you just might live."

"I'll do my best not to upset you," Derek assured him. "What do you want to know about it?"

"First, a little precaution." The man reached into a side pocket and fished out a small disk. Balancing it on a thumbnail, he flipped it coin-fashion at Derek's forehead. It struck with a faint splat and struck there.

"It's a truth detector. You haven't had any special conditioning to get around it, so you'd better stick to the truth. I'll shoot a little piece off you for each untruthful answer, and I'll let you wonder about which piece will go next. It stimulates the memory."

Derek made a mental note to keep his gun where he could reach it. Also to keep the hatches shut. The damnedest things came walking in. "All right, shoot. I mean, fire away. I mean—"

"I know what you mean. You're lucky I don't take your colloquialisms literally. First off—" he glanced at a wrist-set readout "—how accurate is the information disclosed thus far by Aeaea about the Rhea Object you turned over to them?"

"I didn't turn it over to them, McNaughton—" The muzzle of the pistol switched from his midriff to a point at the top of the bridge of his nose. "As far as I know, it's accurate. They didn't make public any data that contradicted what my own instruments had found. Of course, they have much more sophisticated instruments of analysis."

"That is the kind of cooperation I want. To continue: What else beside the egg did you find?"

"I didn't see any alien artifact that was un-egg-shaped." Jesus, he thought, I could've phrased that better. The holos made it look a lot easier to think fast at gunpoint.

"Ah-ah-ah, Mr. Kuroda, that won't do." He lowered the muzzle back to Derek's midriff, then lowered it farther. "You aren't exactly lying, but then, you aren't telling the whole truth. So, I won't shoot off your whole—" He stiffened, his eyes crossed, and he collapsed to the deck.

Valerie stood above the inert form, a long needle in her hand. She released it and it slipped back up her sleeve. There was a look of intense disgust on her face. "I guess this means I don't get the interview, huh?"

Things were happening too damned fast. Derek didn't

know which was worse—the surprise, the embarrassment, the sheer disorientation, or what. "Next time," he said finally, "I keep my gun with me."

"It wouldn't help," Valerie said. "He was a pro. Not in my class, but a pro. What that means is, if you started out with your gun in your hand and he had his back turned and his weapon anywhere in reach and you tried to shoot him, he'd manage to get you first."

"You know," Derek said, "I can't think of a single day in my whole life that's given me so many blows to my ego."

"The day isn't over yet, Derek," said Ulric. He came in through the all-accommodating hatch. The gray old man wore his black armorcloth singlet and carried a pistol that looked a lot more lethal than the one the somnolent agent had carried.

"Hi, Ulric!" Derek said. "I want you to meet my friend Valerie. Val, this is—"

"Shut up," said François. He was behind Ulric, and had a weapon that looked even deadlier. "I can't believe that you've been allowed to work in Clan security. You're so dumb—"

"Don't talk to me," Derek said. "Talk to your superior here, who appointed me to my present—"

"Shut up, both of you," Ulric said. "It's this lady that concerns me now. Your name, please, and no prevarications."

"Valentina Ambartsumian."

"Hey, that's not too far from the name you gave me," Derek said. "If I had a name like that, I'd shorten it, too."

"Will you be quiet?" Ulric shouted. "I've been following this lady's progress in our fair asteroid since she arrived. She's an Earthie agent, recently operating on Luna."

Valentina was appalled. How had the man known that? Her training and cover was the best to be had. She didn't think she could have been detected by some slipup, like Alexandrov. Far more likely, there was a traitor in Carstairs' operation. Treachery was one of the great human constants.

"If she's an Earthie agent," Derek said, "then why did she nail this one?" He nudged Alexandrov with his toe. The body shifted in the faint gravity. "By the way, is he dead?"

"Paralyzed but conscious," Valentina said. "He'll come out of it in a couple of hours."

"Excellent," Ulric said. "The fact that you removed him as a threat in so professional a fashion is the main reason I'm being so civil. My first impulse was to shoot you."

"Let's not rule that out as an option," François said. "She may still be armed. I say we search her."

Derek turned to her. "You're not going to commit suicide, are you?"

"What in the world for?" she asked.

"I thought spies and secret agents carried poison around in case they were captured."

"How melodramatic. No, that may be true in wartime, when an agent may have secrets that the other side shouldn't learn, or just to avoid torture. I don't have any information that would do my superiors any harm and I doubt that you employ torture."

"More's the pity," Ulric said. "By way of precaution, young lady, would you please remove the device with which you dealt with this man?"

Valentina pulled back her sleeve and unclipped the sheathed needle. It drifted to the deck and lay there looking absurdly harmless.

"She could have implants," François insisted.

"No, Gretchen says there's nothing under her skin that didn't grow there." He turned to Valentina. "Gretchen was your masseuse."

Only her superb self-control kept her from flushing. "So for all your talk of an open society you're as spy-ridden as any Earth government."

"Not at all," Ulric said. "We may believe in complete individual freedom, but we're not stupid. Besides, this had nothing to do with the Confederacy, or with the Avalon government. I set it up myself using Clan manpower and that of allied families."

"With Derek as bait?"

"For this operation, yes. I knew it wouldn't be long before Earthie agents came after the Rhea Object, and Derek, as the discoverer, would be the focal point of some attention. It looks as if I netted two on the first try."

"I wasn't expecting to play such a passive role," Derek said.

"You'll learn," said Ulric. "This business isn't over yet."

"Well, what do we do now?" Valentina demanded. "You have no legal right to take me prisoner, but I don't suppose that bothers you."

"Not at all. Do you ever feel constrained by legalities?" He turned to Derek. "Set course for the lab." He turned back to Valentina. "As a matter of fact, we're going just where you wanted to go, but at a great savings in time. We're going to see Sieglinde."

"It's going to be a little cramped in *Cyrano*," Derek reminded him.

"That's all right," Ulric said. "We're all friends here."

SIX

Aeaea was unique among the Island Worlds in being totally artificial. Over the years it had been constructed of whatever materials were convenient. The original structure, now invisible beneath layers of metal and ultraglass, had been built in Lunar orbit using mooncrete as the primary building material. The founders had moved it into trans-Martian orbit to have freedom from government interference and privacy from their competition. Most of Aeaea's output was pure, abstract technology.

The immense tech station tried to steer a neutral course between Earth and Confederacy, but that was difficult when most Earth dwellers perceived *all* offworlders as enemies. Even the Earth-dominated Lunaires and Martians were regarded as little more than semi-rebellious "colonials" to be exploited. Still, the Aeaeans regarded all parties as customers and the rest usually had to go along, because their services were necessary and because no one really knew the extent of Aeaea's power. So far, its security remained unpenetrated.

Aldo Vecchio knew that he was a crack in Aeaean security, but he had not thought about the fact in a long time. He was a senior nuclear physicist in Aeaea, with twenty years on the staff. He had been born on Mars, and had been hired into the Aeaean nuclear physics department shortly after receiving his degree at the University of Tarkovskygrad.

Aside from his work, there was only one thing Vecchio cared about—his sister, Nilze. His adored younger sister suffered from a rare congenital disease, and the disease could only be treated, at great expense, on Earth. It might have been possible to treat her in Aeaea, but she had rejected the strange, sterile environment of the tech station, certain that she would wither and die there.

Treatment was available on Earth, in their ancestral Italy, but at great price. His salary was generous by Earth standards, but he had known that he could not support her treatment for more than a year or two. On one of his semiannual visits to his sister, a man had approached him with a solution to his problem. In return for clandestine, unspecified services at a future date, Nilze would be cared for in a beautiful nursing home near the equally beautiful city of Florence. The Italian government had preserved Florence and its surrounding Tuscan countryside as an irreplaceable cultural treasure.

He had sought assurance that none of these activities would jeopardize a human life, especially his own. He was assured that he would be involved in nothing so drastic, merely industrial espionage of the quasi-legitimate sort that went on all the time. His conscience somewhat mollified, Aldo complied. Ten years later, the IOU was called in.

Aldo closed up his lab and made his way to the plush senior scientist lodgings in one of Aeaea's newer sections. There was always a certain satisfaction in returning here. The address was a high status symbol in Aeaea's complicated hierarchy. It had taken him seven years to gain such a position. He had almost forgotten his old debt.

As he entered his apartment, he saw the message light flashing on his communication console. The flash-pattern indicated that it was from off Aeaea, and he wondered who it might be. He went to the console and punched in his personal code. As the message appeared above the console, he paled. It had come at last. "I will be arriving in Avalon in two weeks and staying at the Omni. I would like to see you if you can get some vacation time. Your Uncle Donald."

He closed his eyes for a moment. It was a shock, but he did not seriously consider defiance. His sister's life and comfort were too important to him. Resignedly, he booked a passage on a regular Aeaea-to-Avalon run of the liner *Horai-Maru*.

Two weeks later, he checked into the Omni, one of the asteroid's luxury establishments. He had no idea whom he would be contacted by. Undoubtedly, it would not be the man who had "recruited" him, a faceless man of a type common to all governments and most large institutes and businesses. Vecchio was not even certain whether his "employer" was a government or a private enterprise, and he had been careful not to ask. Since it had happened on Earth, it was probably the former. However, it was not outside the realm of possibility that one of the other asteroid tech stations had wanted a mole in Aeaea. He dismissed such thoughts from his mind.

As he awaited his contact, Vecchio pondered the timing of the summons. Coming when it did, it probably concerned the Rhea Object. On Aeaea, it was the subject of all conversation, even among those who were not assigned to the project. If so, his caller would be disappointed. Thus far, they had discovered nothing of much use to anybody. To scientists, of course, this lack of response to tests was as exciting as the no doubt shattering discoveries that would inevitably be made. Exploiters, however, would want something more concrete and immediate.

The small room's console announced a visitor. Aldo took a deep breath and touched the entrance control. The door slid back to reveal a burly man, hairless and pale. Something struck Aldo as strange about the man's looks, but he refused to speculate on what it was.

"Buona sera, Signore Vecchio. I bring you greetings from Signorina Nilze."

"Come in, please." Like nearly everyone offworld, Vecchio had spoken English all his life, but on Mars he had been raised in the small Italian community. His own family was from Trieste, and he recognized the man's accent as Slavonic, possibly Serbian.

"I am Josip Mihajlovic. For our purposes, I am from Trieste, and our families back on Earth are old friends for many generations."

"As you wish," Aldo said, with a sinking feeling. The man's name, although undoubtedly false, was not unthinkable. Trieste had a sizable Yugoslavian community. In the turmoil of World War II, Croatians had attacked their traditional enemy Serbs, many of whom had fled there in the aftermath.

"Please take a couch." Aldo indicated a spindly structure with a sling of thin cloth. "May I get you a drink?"

"That would be excellent," the man said in English. "Gin, if you don't mind." The English was flawless. If he had not spoken Italian, Aldo might not have guessed his origin. He went to the compact bar and drew gin for Mihajlovic, chianti for himself. To the Serb, this obviously took care of the amenities.

"I am here to learn what I can about the Rhea Object," said Mihajlovic. "My employers do not believe that Aeaea is making public all that they have learned about the thing."

Aldo released a tiny sigh of relief. "I can assure you that they have. So far, we know nothing save that it defeats all our attempts at testing."

The Serb shrugged, a thoroughly Earthly gesture. "No matter to me. If I can confirm this, perhaps they will be satisfied. The fact remains, they do not trust the official version."

"How shall we effect your entry into Aeaea?" Aldo asked. "Have your employers taken care of that?"

"Oh, yes. I am a lab technician from the International Institute of Theoretical Physics, in Trieste. Since my degree is a minor one, I've taken advantage of the recent relaxation of restrictions declared by Mr. Carstairs so that scientific personnel from Earth can come out and take part in the study on Aeaea. Naturally, as a man who has always yearned for an opportunity to come here, I began to pull family strings to get you to take me on as a temporary lab technician."

"Aeaea is difficult when it comes to—"

"As a senior staff scientist, you have authority to hire some assistants at your own discretion. Island Worlders will always acknowledge family obligations as legitimate motives. I assure you that I shall pass the security check. Great care has gone into creating my background."

"Let us hope so," Aldo said. "I risk my career by sponsoring you."

"You would risk a good deal more than your career by betraying me," the Serb said coldly. There was something in the man's attitude, in his burly, forceful presence, that said he was something more than an industrial spy.

"I shall be most careful," Vecchio assured him.

Like most overtly egalitarian societies, that of Aeaea had a subtle but all-pervasive status system. Housing was its most noticeable gauge. When Vladyka, alias Josip Mihajlovic, finished in-processsing at the tech station, he was taken to an area of Spartan accommodations where workers, technicians and low-ranking scientists lived. He congratulated himself on his easy penetration of Aeaea, although it was Shevket's foresight in planting a mole here years ago that had made it possible.

"Welcome to the peons' quarters," said a man who wore a pink coverall. There was some sort of color-coding to the uniforms, but Vladyka hadn't learned it yet.

"So some are more equal than others, eh?"

"You ever encounter a society where that wasn't true?" The man's accent was Lunar, possibly from one of the old U.S. colonies.

Vladyka thrust his single bag into the cubbyhole that was to serve as his sleeping quarters. "Are Earthies second-class citizens as well?"

"No, because you're not a citizen at all. Earthies are more like fourth-class aliens. Loonies like me get third-class status."

"I'll be lab-teching for a senior staff scientist. Is he first class?"

"Pretty high up. But the top of the heap here are the ones who were born on Aeaea. You won't see many of them. The quarters they like drive other people crazy and some of 'em don't even look human. They go in for all kinds of optical and electronic implants to help in their researches. Hell, I saw one a few days ago drifting through one of the labs stark naked and I couldn't tell if it was a man or a woman, there were so many gadgets attached to it."

It was a stroke of luck to find someone so talkative. It made sense, though. This man was a foreigner here and he wanted a sympathetic listener. "Back home," said the Montenegran, who was masquerading as a Serbian, "we keep hearing that the people out here are mutating into something inhuman. I thought that was just the alarmist media, but maybe there's something to it."

"I've been all over the Belt and on most of the inhabited satellites, and there's some pretty strange people living on some of them, but I never saw anything as weird as the native Aeaeans. Some of 'em are third generation, though why anything that looks like them wants to reproduce is beyond me."

They were in the middle of a shift so there were few workers in the quarters. "I take it you're off-shift right now?" Vladyka queried.

"I don't go on for another four hours."

"I have a couple of shifts to get myself oriented. That means finding a bar. Show me where to find a drink and I'll stand you to one."

"You'll get along fine here. My name's Gorshin. I work in hydroponics. That's what the godawful pink uniform means. There's places where people'd get the wrong idea, they saw you wearing a color like this. Just pull yourself up this tube here and we'll be in concourse B, where the good bars are. Where'll you be working?"

"In Aldo Vecchio's lab. Something to do with the Rhea Object." He pulled himself up a tube with fluorescent walls, an easy and efficient process in the faint, spin-induced gravity. The concourse above was nearly tubular, more of a flattened ovoid, and had clearly been something else at one time. Nothing was wasted in space, and concourse B might once have been a particle accelerator or plasma generator. Doorways of varying shape opened off the concourse. Most of them seemed to be commercial establishments.

"Concourse B's a commercial zone," Gorshin said. "It's one of the places anyone has access to. Most of Aeaea, you have to have the right clearance to get into." It seemed that the tech station had nothing like the chaos of Avalon. The signs were discreet and always set to the left of the doorway. If there was some significance to this regularity, Vladyka couldn't imagine what it might be, except as confirmation of Ugo Ciano's famous characterization of the founders of Aeaea as "a buncha anal retentives."

Unlike the workers' quarters, the concourse was thronged. A great many of those present were not dressed in any of the local uniforms but many wore the white coverall favored by laboratory scientists everywhere. The two men entered a bar imaginatively titled "Bar #5." It, too, was crowded.

"Is it always this jammed?" Vladyka asked. "I had always thought of Aeaea as mostly automated with a small staff."

"Usually it's a lot less crowded. People've come here from all over to work on the Rhea Project, just like you." They punched orders on the top of their pedestal-type table. The artificial gravity was too weak to bother with chairs. The drinks appeared within seconds, sealed in film so thin they looked like mere blobs of liquid. They took thin straws from a dispenser and poked them through the film.

As he sipped, Vladyka eyed the crowd in the bar and

those passing by outside. Somewhere here, he was certain, he would find Sieglinde Kornfeld-Taggart. She would be in disguise, of course, but he was confident he could find her. He was confident he could do anything he wanted, including killing Sieglinde and stealing the Rhea Object. Self-doubt was for losers and defeatists.

"Has any progress been made on the famous green egg?" He noticed that the egalitarian spirit did seem to extend to the bar. It was crowded with menials, scientists and what appeared to be media people, indiscriminately mixed.

"Working in hydro-P, I don't have much to do with it. But it's all anyone's talked about for weeks, and from what I hear they haven't turned up a damned thing."

Vladyka knew this was the official story. He was equally certain that the true story was something else entirely. Naturally, the Aeaeans would pretend that they had discovered nothing. Even a senior staff scientist like Vecchio would not be let in on the real discoveries. After all, Vecchio was not native-born, not even an Island Worlder, but merely a Martian immigrant. He knew that no government, no corporation made free with its secrets. The whole concept was laughable.

"I suppose security must be tight," he suggested.

"No more'n usual," Gorshin said. "Like I told you, a lot of this place is limited access, but that's mainly organization, not security. In Third Quadrant there's a bunch of labs and manufacturing facilities that's off limits to all but a few. That's where they work on the items they don't make public till they got the patents nailed down tight."

So, that was where the real work on the Rhea Object was going on. It was probably where he'd find Sieglinde as well. "Let me buy you another." He saw a tall, thin man enter, silver hair and Roman profile unmistakable from a thousand holo broadcasts. "Hey, isn't that Professor Schmidt-Fong?"

Gorshin glanced idly at the man. "That's him. All the

big ones are here—Matsunaga, Gordon, Moreau-Goldstein, Yau, you name 'em. Physicists and chemists, mostly, but the top ones in almost every field're here."

"What about that woman who was so big in the last war who's supposed to have been the one that perfected the antimatter drive? Cornfield or something?"

"Sieglinde Kornfeld-Taggart." Gorshin shook his head. "She hasn't showed up that I've heard. Way I hear it, she's not on real good terms with the ones that run this place."

So even here her presence was being kept secret. He spent another hour in general conversation, wanting to gain a reputation as a friendly, generous sort. Surly loners were always regarded with suspicion. He had been given a directory upon in-processing, and when Gorshin left for his next shift Vladyka consulted it to find an information center.

The facility he found was built like a miniature amphitheater, with ascending rows of stands surrounding a fairly large holo tank. The place was intended for visitors and new arrivals, to give them some degree of orientation in a habitat that was unlike any other.

The room dimmed and a brief history lesson began, detailing Aeaea's beginnings as a moon-orbiting station owned by a handful of entrepreneuring scientists and engineers, its early successes and expansions, its eventual removal to the Belt. A series of cutaways revealed how the structure had grown, from the original cylinder of mooncrete, through the metal and ultraglass additions of the next half-century, then the huge expansion during the war, when Aeaea had been contracted to develop Ugo Ciano's antimatter drive engine. More labs and living quarters had been added over the subsequent years, but the presentation ended with the status quo as of several months previously. After that, the display was open for individual queries.

As Vladyka had suspected, the area Gorshin had called the Third Quadrant had been skirted in the presentation. He queried the display about it in a general way, so as not to arouse suspicion in any eavesdropping, but he learned little. The name itself was obsolescent, referring to a section of the original mooncrete structure. First, Second and Fourth were now administrative and residential sections, all lab functions having long since moved into more modern quarters.

The old structure was a logical place to locate the station's most secret operations. In the earliest days of Lunar exploration it had been discovered that excellent concrete could be made from minerals found abundantly on the moon. It was far cheaper to launch mooncrete from the lunar surface than to bring metals and other costly materials from Earth. Also, mooncrete could be molded into thick walls and bulkheads, reducing chance of damage from meteoroids and exposure to radiation. Since the scientists and engineers were not working with pre-formed sections and members, they could easily design an enclosure to fit the latest development in any given project.

Without seeming obvious, Vladyka studied what little was available on Quadrant Three. Due to the thickness of the walls, he would have to get in through one of the entrances. They were small and no doubt very secure. This was going to be interesting. But then, he thought with deep satisfaction, had it been easy, they would not have sent Daniko Vladyka.

SEVEN

"Whose ship is that?" Ulric pointed to one of *Cyrano*'s screens. It revealed a vessel shaped bizarrely like a Chinese lantern, docked near the Ciano lab next to a school vessel. A throng of students were reembarking from the rock by way of a transparent umbilicus.

"That's the *Johann Gutenberg*, Chih'-Chin Fu's ship," Derek said.

"Wonderful," Ulric said. "I thought we'd only have to deal with one lunatic. It seems there will be two."

"Three," François corrected. "Don't forget Crazy Roseberry."

"Am I to believe," Valentina said, "that you don't hold these people in the esteem their accomplishments led me to anticipate?"

Her wrists were still bound with a strand of micro-monofilament. It was not especially tight, but a hard jerk could cut her hands off.

"I really don't give a damn what you believe," Ulric said. "It's what you know that concerns me. But, to answer your question, I have always questioned that woman's sanity. Not her genius, mind you—just whether all her hatches were secured. She's given us all ample reason to doubt."

"She's the greatest—" Derek was cut off by a glare

from Ulric. All too aware of his delicate position with the family, he prudently shut up.

Cyrano docked in the small, airtight harbor and they prepared to disembark as the dock repressurized. With his pistol, Ulric indicated that Valentina should be the first off the ship. She moved stiffly. They were all cramped after the trip in the tiny ship and she had the added handicap of bound hands and feet. A man in improbable robes greeted them as they descended to the floor of the dock.

"What an unexpected pleasure," said Fu. "So many people to emerge from so small a vessel. Young Derek I know, and Mr. Ulric Kuroda I know by reputation, but you, young sir—"

"François Kuroda." The bullet-headed young man nodded curtly.

"And this charming lady I know by surveillance. Valentina Ambartsumian, I believe?"

"I see no point in denying it."

"Why should you? After all, we're all friends here. Come, let's trade these dismal environs for more comfortable surroundings. I have prevailed upon the estimable Mr. Roseberry to open Ugo Ciano's own lounge for us."

"I have to see Sieglinde," Ulric insisted.

"All in good time. She is closeted in her laboratory, as she has been for quite some time. She insists upon her privacy, and failure to comply with her wishes can be life-threatening."

Ciano's lounge was, predictably, an odd place. The walls were water tanks full of colorful tropical fish. A floor-to-ceiling rack held hundreds of bottles. Derek took one and read the label. It said "Wild Turkey." All the bottles were identical. Despite the slightness of the gravity, all the furniture was nightmarishly Victorian— heavy, dark wood upholstered in overstuffed scarlet leather or velvet. The floor was covered with artificial plastic grass, of the type that once floored Earth sports stadia. The whole room was filled with junk defying categorization.

"He came here to *relax?*" Ulric said.

"A man of interesting tastes," Fu said. "I find in him a kindred spirit."

"I can imagine. Look, I don't have time to waste. I need to—"

Fu broke in smoothly. "Then perhaps we could employ this interval constructively while waiting for Sieglinde to grace us with her presence." His hand disappeared into his robe and reemerged with a small handset. He began tapping its tiny plates with the tips of two-inch fingernails. "Miss Ambartsumian, be so kind as to tell us if you see anyone you recognize. These are Earth agents who have been working off-planet in recent years. Some we know well, others we only suspect."

"Do you really think I'll tell you anything of value?"

"I believe so. For one thing, I will know the instant you see someone familiar to you."

Could he really be that sensitive? She decided that he probably was. The man had practically invented the art of physiognomical analysis. Even her training and control probably wouldn't fool him. She shrugged. "Go ahead."

"I should point out that none of these work for Mr. Carstairs. Since your loyalty is solely to him, you'll do him no disservice by aiding us in this." In the air between them appeared several human forms in sequence. Each appeared, rotated and disappeared after a few seconds. At one, he stopped the display. "You know this one?"

"I'm not sure." It was a male, burly, pale and hairless. She considered him for a moment. "Darken him a bit. Give him bristly, black hair and a droopy mustache."

Fu's fingers danced over the handset. Besides the additions she asked for he gave the man a heavy beard-shadow. "Better?"

"Damn!" she said, softly. "*He's* out here?"

"Who the hell is he?" Ulric demanded.

"He's a Montenegran peasant named Daniko Vladyka. Thinks he's God's gift to the intelligence profession. A real killer, ruthless and very ambitious."

"Who does he work for?" Fu asked.

"Mehmet Shevket." She didn't quite spit.

"That's a name we've heard too much of lately," Ulric added. "Where'd you find him, Mr. Fu?"

"He is elusive, but he once made the mistake of sneaking into Armstrong by one of the old smugglers' routes. That brought him to my attention, although subsequent monitoring of his activities on that occasion turned up nothing of great interest."

"He was probably just establishing contacts," Valentina said.

"So I surmised. More recently, he has been operating near Avalon in a ship named *Ivo the Black*. He has used a number of names."

"There's no law against that," Derek said. He was tired of being ignored.

"There ought to be," François said. "How the hell can we keep track of people if we don't make them stick to one name at a time?"

"Turning into a budding little fascist, aren't you, François? Next you'll want ID tags, passports. Why don't you just vote Earth First at the next elections?"

"Y'know," François said, "there's an ancient and little-known martial art called pistol whipping. Why don't we—"

"Why don't you both cut out the adolescent chest-thumping?" Ulric suggested. "You're both too old for it, physically, at least, and the rest of us find it offensive."

A wall slid up, fish and all, and Sieglinde entered, dressed in a white coverall, her eyes ringed with blue smudges. "Hello Ulric, François." She nodded to them and crossed the room to Derek. "You didn't take long."

"It was pretty much as you figured," Derek said. "Though why I'd draw them all like a magnet I'm not certain. By the way, there's a Russian trussed up in my EV suit locker."

Her eyebrow went up half a millimeter. "Do you always keep Russians in there?"

"We had to put him someplace," Ulric said, "and the ship was cramped. You two are talking as if you'd planned it all, Sieglinde."

"I told Derek what to expect. Also that I wanted any agents that attached themselves to him brought here."

"I gave him somewhat the same instructions." He glared balefully at Derek from beneath white eyebrows. "I'll speak with you later."

"I needed to get my ship and fuel paid for. I tried to make everybody happy. What's wrong with that?"

"Why," Sieglinde demanded in a chill voice, "is this woman tied up?"

"She's dangerous," Ulric told her. "Carstairs' personal agent. You know she has to be the best. No sense taking any chances."

"Untie her. Now!" Her order cracked out with such authority that the three Avalonians scrambled to do her bidding. "It is inhumane, besides being an insult to my security systems. Nobody's managed to lay a hand on me in more than fifty years. Did you really think this child could harm me?"

"Actually," François said, "it was us we were worried about."

"As well you might. You're safe here. That's better. So," she withdrew her attention from the others so thoroughly that they might as well not have existed, "you're Anthony's special agent. I suppose he sent you to find out about the Rhea Object?"

"Yes. I was supposed to infiltrate Aeaea, but I deduced that Derek had found more than one and that you were conducting an independent investigation."

"Very good. Did you have orders to steal it or kill me?" She might have been talking about the ambient air pressure.

"No, just to learn what was being discovered about the thing. My boss doesn't trust your scientists to be totally open, I'm afraid."

"It's been a century since any Earth politician told the truth about anything," Ulric said. "I can understand why they distrust everybody else."

Sieglinde ignored him. "I think I'll have a few words with Mr. Carstairs."

"You'll have to go through your Earth ambassador,"

Valentina said. "Even I don't have a direct line to him. I have to report to a secure computer program and it can be days before I can get him on a secure line. It may be a shorter wait now, since he's given my current mission top priority."

"Why wait?" Sieglinde said. She took a handset from her belt. It was one of the mysterious items she had designed and nobody else could figure out. It was a perfectly transparent, unmarked rectangular plastic plate. Her fingers traced across it and she turned to the antiquated robot beside her. "The usual."

While they waited, the rest gave it orders. Presently, a fish tank wall raised and a miniature locomotive rolled in, bearing drinks on a string of tiny flatcars.

"The late Mr. Ciano," Fu said, "had a decided taste for the baroque."

They were all silenced when Anthony Carstairs appeared in holograph in the center of the room. He looked surprised and disgusted at the same time. From the direction of his gaze, the only one in the room visible to him was Sieglinde. He collected himself quickly. " 'Allo, Linde. To what do I owe the honor?"

"I need to have a few words with you, Tony."

"Always glad to oblige. Where are you? Luna?"

"No, I'm in the Belt, near Avalon."

His expression sharpened. "You've always dealt straight with me, Linde. Why're you lying now? There's at least a ten-minute transmission delay between here and there. We can't talk like this, with no time lag."

"A little experiment of mine in superluminal communication. I just got most of the bugs worked out."

"Blimey! Finally got it licked, did you? Congratulations."

"It only works for short distances so far, but I'll have it perfected soon. It's a convenience, but it's not what I called you about. I have your agent here," she turned. "What is your name, dear?"

"Valentina."

"She says her name is Valentina."

"Bloody hell. What shape's she in?"

"She's quite all right. Tony, if you wanted to know about the Rhea Object, why didn't you just ask me? You know I'd tell you the truth."

"Christ, woman, I thought the damned thing was on bloody Aeaea! I wouldn't trust those buggers to tell me the seat of my pants were on fire if I could smell the smoke! I take it you've got your own paperweight to study?"

"Sieglinde!" Ulric barked. "You can't talk like this over a transmission!"

She turned to him with a face like iron. "Ulric, I'll ask you for the last time not to insult my security procedures. They're the tightest known to humanity."

"Eh?" Carstairs said. "Linde, who's the bugger I can't see from here?"

"Just a relative. He thinks my secrecy protection can be pierced."

"Hell, don't I just wish! You spacers and your damned families. I suppose you have a great gaggle of 'em up there?"

"Just a moment, let me adjust the set. Tony, meet Derek, who discovered the artifacts, Ulric, a distant kinsman in the Kuroda clan, François, likewise—"

"Jesus, Sieglinde," Ulric protested, "you can't do this! It'll ruin—" She ignored him.

"The rest I believe you know. The only other inhabitant of this place is Mr. Roseberry, who's off taking care of something or other."

"G'day Mr. Fu, Val. Old Roseberry, eh? So you're in Ciano's old lab? Good place to work on it, I suppose."

"Don't forget the Russian in my EV suit locker," Derek reminded her, earning a warning glare from Ulric.

Carstairs smiled broadly. "So you're keeping Russians in lockers these days, eh? I never used that one on you even in my best propaganda speeches during the war."

"We'll get to him presently. The point is that you, and we, and all of humanity have a big problem. The Rhea Objects came along at exactly the right or exactly the wrong time, depending on your viewpoint. It struck me that, instead of all this sneaking around and double-dealing, it makes a lot more sense to get together to discuss this."

"Right you are, Linde. I just let my naturally sneaky and duplicitous nature get the better of me." He reached out of sight, apparently into a desk drawer, and pulled out a bottle of Scotch and a glass. "Think I'll have a dram, since you're all indulging." He poured a gill and tossed if off, then poured another and sat back in his chair. "Now, by problem, I imagine you're referring to Mehmet Shevket and his merry band?"

"Exactly. One of his agents has already been spotted. Miss Valentina kindly identified him for us."

"I told her to watch for them." He cocked an eye toward Valentina. "I suspect he's a bad 'un, Val?"

"One of the worst. A Montenegran pig named Vladyka. You remember him."

"That I do. Distinguished himself for brutality in the Malaysian insurrection. It made him a natural for Shevket's personal following. Do you have him located now?"

"He has, unfortunately, escaped our observation for the moment. We have no such all-encompassing surveillance systems as you have on Earth."

Carstairs snorted amusement. "It's the system you've picked, you live with it. But take my advice: When you find that bugger, kill him."

"I have every intention of doing just that," Ulric said, barely restraining his temper.

"Good for you," Carstairs said. "Now, Linde, shall we get down to the meat of this little get-together? I have about three hours clear before I have to meet a whole delegation of people from Tasmania or some such place. I'm told I can't brush them off."

"That should be adequate," Sieglinde said.

"Respected cousin," Ulric said, with great formality, so as not to give traditional grounds for offense, "does this seemingly slapdash procedure truly constitute a maximum-security conference? It seems to me that this business could be all our death warrants."

Carstairs chuckled. "Tell him, Linde."

"Esteemed *junior* cousin," she said as formally and a good deal more pointedly, "there is one other person in the building in Greenwich, England, where Anthony's office now resides. This is a clerk-type person, male, approximately thirty-four years of age, one hundred seventy-two pounds weight. From his heartbeat I know that he's not eavesdropping."

"His *heartbeat?!*" Ulric's voice became a near-squeak.

"Exactly," she confirmed. "I can monitor a great deal of what he's doing, how he's feeling. I can't really tell you what he's thinking, but I can get a good lead on what his intentions are. Believe me, he's now involved in drudgery."

"It's quite true," said Chih'-Chin Fu. "With modern techniques of electronic surveillance, brought to their highest pitch by this lady and my humble self, it is quite possible to make such statements."

François turned on her. "You can do this and you don't make it available to us? Do you realize how valuable this thing is to our security?"

She glared back at him with eyes far colder. "I know exactly how valuable these techniques are to any who want to monitor other peoples' thinking. That's why I'll never turn them over to you or anybody else—family, government or other!"

"Hear, hear!" Derek said.

"Got the family sorted out, love?" Carstairs asked. "Must be a problem, all this blood relation stuff. Don't know what I'd do if I had to let all my cousins and such into my confidence."

Sieglinde sat back and sipped her amber drink. "You'll never understand, will you, Tony? We disagree on almost everything, but I'll trust my life to Ulric. I have in the past. Same with François or Derek. We're all family. They're bound to support and help me, and I'll do the same for them. It doesn't matter if we hate each other's guts. We'll give each other the support we need."

Derek looked at Ulric. He couldn't believe it. The man was blushing. This subject actually embarrassed the fearsome Ulric Kuroda!

"That's correct," Ulric said.

Carstairs smiled ruefully. "Then you've retained something the rest of us've lost. No matter. Let's get down to business. The subject under discussion is Mehmet Shevket. Do we all agree that this bugger's a prime pain in the arse?"

"Agreed," chorused Sieglinde, Fu, Ulric, François, Derek and Valentina.

"Then let's come up with some decent tactics to deal with him. First of all. Valentina?"

"Yes?" she said.

"From now on, you're to cooperate with this lady. We are now establishing a coordinated intelligence operation. Linde's going to be occupied with her green egg for quite some time to come, I presume, so will you be directing operations at that end, Mr. Ulric?"

"That's correct," he said, eyeing Valentina dubiously.

"Splendid. Through Linde's magical bug-proof communications I'll keep you abreast of my dealings with General Shevket. There is, of course, the likelihood that I'll be assassinated. In that case, you're on your own, because I don't know anybody down here you could trust."

"You seem to take the prospect of assassination calmly," Sieglinde said.

His face twisted and he refilled his glass. "Live like I have the past half-century and it becomes a bloody welcome alternative to watching this planet stumble from one catastrophe to the next. War, the ecology, the population—I've fought 'em all. But the world won't survive Dictator Shevket."

"Why not just kill him?" Derek suggested.

Carstairs emitted a barking laugh. "You think it hasn't been tried? Not by me, mind you, but there've been plenty of attempts. He got to his present eminence by treading over a lot of corpses. Fanatics from resistance movements, hired guns, jealous rivals, they've all had their innings. He's yet to be nicked. I'll keep alert for an opportunity, but don't count on any results."

"Ordinarily," Sieglinde said, "I don't approve of assassination, but this man sounds like a good candidate for it."

"He's a bloody butcher," Carstairs affirmed, "and about fifteen different kinds of pervert. Not that that's so uncommon, it's just that he has the sort of charisma that gets a lot of people enthusiastic about him. Man on horseback, you know? Think he's going to be their savior, God knows why."

"What's his interest in the Rhea Object?" Derek asked.

"Same as everybody's," Carstairs said. "He figures it for a weapon or a power source, and in any case, he doesn't want you to have it. Speaking of the thing, what've you learned so far, Linde?"

"Enough to treat it with respect. Have you been keeping up with the reports from Aeaea?"

Carstairs shrugged. "Not my field. And I hope you'll understand if I don't have perfect confidence that they're telling us everything."

"You have my assurance that what they've released so far is reliable. They first put it through an angular momentum test and determined that all the mass is concentrated in that opaque area at the center. The mass in that opacity is a ton per cubic centimeter, which makes it about fifty thousand times as dense as gold. The mass of the translucent envelope is negligible."

"I think I follow you so far," Carstairs said. "But what's keeping that much compressed mass confined?"

"That's what we're all trying to find out. There's no external electric or magnetic field emanating from it, and it seems to have no definable temperature of its own. The Aeaeans dipped it in molten lead, and the surface temperature seemed to reach equilibrium with its environment instantaneously. They switched it to liquid helium and it reached extreme low temperature just as quickly.

"The central part is opaque to all electromagnetic radiations, from gamma-ray to radio. Lately, they've been getting desperate. They tried to get through the envelope with chemical agents, extreme heat, extraordinary pressure, high electric voltage, even laser beam. So far, it's been unproductive."

"Damn!" Carstairs said. "Being a bit rough on the thing, aren't they?"

"I agree. In fact, I consider some of their more extreme measures to be foolhardy. We're dealing here with matter under inconceivable compression. If that pressure is released in any manner except the intended way . . ."

"Blooey," Carstairs finished for her. "What are the chances they'll blow up Aeaea?"

"Very slight. They're being amazingly unimaginative, even for that bunch. At this rate they won't accomplish anything no matter what they try."

"Are you doing any better?" he asked her.

"Somewhat. It's too soon to say for certain, but I have an experiment in progress that may tell us just what it is and how it works."

"I know you don't like to make any pronouncements until you have all the evidence," Carstairs said, "but do you have any hunches or educated guesses about what the bloody things are?"

She looked at the others in the room, then back to Carstairs. "I'm fairly certain that it's some sort of fuel pack for an interstellar vessel. And I think it's depleted. Dense as the matter in it is, I think there was originally far more of it. If certain conjectures are correct, it might have been over a billion tons per cubic centimeter."

For several hours after the conference with Carstairs, Sieglinde brought the others up to date on her work, explaining some of the more abstruse details of her exotic new technology. *"New to us,"* she hastened to add. *"Somebody else had it, maybe a long time ago."*

Something kept nagging at the back of Derek's mind. He hadn't specialized in physics in college, but anyone whose life depended on spacecraft had to know something about the subject. He worked up his courage and hit her with a question.

"Hey, Aunt Linde, I'd have thought that a superluminal conversation would play merry hell with the principle of cause and effect in physics. How's it work?"

Her look was pitying. "Derek, when you went to school, were they still teaching that garbage?"

"I'm afraid," Ulric said, "that quite a few physicists still hold with that view. I was wondering the same thing, in fact."

She sighed. "It's one of those problems science is riddled with. Somebody makes a mistake that looks plausible. Years later it still has currency because it's an *old* mistake. Somehow, the musty smell of age adds credence. All right, let's tackle it. Back in the twentieth century, a physicist came up with the concept of tachyons. You remember what tachyons were supposed to be?" The rest all shook their heads solemnly.

"Okay, a tachyon was a mythical superluminal particle. Get that—not energy, but a particle. It was a sort of vehicle for energy, if you can imagine that. Anyway, the way they were visualized was completely incorrect. Can you imagine information travelling faster than instantaneously?" They all shook their heads dutifully.

"Right. So, the fastest a tachyon can travel from point A to point B, separated, say, by one light-year, is instantaneous. An event occurring at point A, let's say it's the primary star exploding as a supernova, could be transmitted to point B instantaneously through indeterminate n-dimensional space, or by tachyon, if you prefer the mythical superluminal particle." She mused for a moment. "As a scientific blunder that sounded awfully reasonable at the time, I suppose aether or phlogiston were roughly equivalent in earlier times."

"Aether?" Derek said.

"Phlogiston?" said François.

"Never mind. Anyway, the person receiving the message will learn immediately about the supernova occurring at point A instead of waiting a year, staring at the sky. That doesn't mean that the receiver heard from the future. It doesn't mean that the sender communicated with the past. No, there was no violation of the law of causality when I spoke with Carstairs. There will be none in the future through use of my superluminal transmitter."

"Damn!" François said. "If we put this thing to use in the stock market, it'll be like we have a telegraph and everybody else has runners!"

"That's about what I'd expect from you," Derek said disdainfully. "But, if we could use this on the horse races and ball games down on Earth, the bookmaking advantages—"

EIGHT

Vladyka had spotted the woman on his third off-shift. He had finished tidying Vecchio's lab and had gone to Concourse B. Since his arrival, he had spent his off-shift hours in the entertainment facilities, striking up conversations with as wide an acquaintanceship as possible. It was seldom difficult. After an initial reserve at his obvious Earth origins, the Island Worlders almost invariably relaxed and grew congenial. Vladyka had an ingratiating manner, and most of the Belt inhabitants were easygoing and gregarious. Although they differed widely in lifestyle, they had little suspicion of strangers. To Vladyka, they seemed almost childishly trusting. He came from a land where the denizens of the next valley were usually enemies, and had risen in rank through a system in which treachery and murder were the surest means of advancement.

The first establishment he selected for the evening was called Bar #3. He had learned that the tediously predictable names were the result of their former use as numbered laboratories. When they had been rezoned for commercial use, some niggling regulation had required that they keep their former designation. It was no wonder, Vladyka thought, that the other, more freewheeling Island Worlders thought the Aeaeans were so strange.

As usual, he picked a table with a good view of the bar, the entrance and some of the concourse outside. Within minutes, he acquired several drinking companions. Two of them he already knew; the others he made fast friends by buying a round of drinks. As usual, the conversation was dominated by the Rhea Object.

"You put in your bet yet?" asked a ship captain. He nodded to the back of the room, where a holograph of the Object surmounted a display dominated by large red letters spelling, "What Is It?" Below were listed a multitude of possibilities and the day's odds. Gamblers could place bets on any of them, or introduce a new possibility with a minimum bet. Total sums bet already were in the hundreds of millions. Speculations varied widely. Some thought it was not an artifact at all, but a natural phenomenon. A few suspected a hoax. One had bet that it really *was* a paperweight. The odds-on favorite, though, was that it was some form of power source. The captain was arguing just that point.

"Stands to reason," he said. "Why the hell else would you cram that much mass into that small a space unless you planned to release it in a controlled manner for propulsion?"

"It's a tempting thought," said a chemist's assistant, "but how do you get it out of there without destroying the envelope? And how would you keep it under control? I think it's something left over from a collapsar. We've always wondered where the matter went when it got so supercompressed. I think it just squeezes down," he made a squeezing gesture with both hands to demonstrate, "and when it won't squeeze any more, it pops out in some other part of the universe, maybe in some other form. I think that's what the green egg is." He spoke with the conviction of one who was neither physicist, mathematician nor astronomer.

"All neatly packaged in a nearly massless envelope?" said a woman who wore the charcoal-gray uniform of the astronomical section.

"We know we're dealing with something totally new," the chemist's assistant said. "We have no idea what goes on in the heart of a collapsar. Hell, how do we know it doesn't wrap its remains neatly before ejecting them through hyperspace or wherever?"

Vladyka had no interest whatever in the fundamental nature of the egg, so he refrained from all such speculations and arguments. He was about to steer the conversation in some other direction when he saw the woman walk into the bar. Something clicked in his perception. She seemed fortyish, reasonably pretty, and had dark-brown hair. All that could be the result of surgery, of course, but other things were more revealing. She moved like one who had spent many years in space, but she retained the indefinable awkwardness of one who had not been born there. The Kornfeld woman had been born on Mars and had spent at least her first sixteen years there. There was something in the woman's attitude as well. She wore the uniform of a low-ranking scientist, but her bearing was that of a highly assured savant. Most of all, he trusted his instinct. He knew his instinct was infallible and his instinct said that this was Sieglinde Kornfeld. She was looking for a table space in the crowded bar.

"Come join us," Vladyka called. "I think we can wedge in one more." He made a space so that she would be next to him.

She smiled and inclined her head at an oblique angle, the zero-g equivalent of a bow. "Thank you. It's always mobbed of late, with all the new people in on the Rhea Object study."

"Is that what you're on?" Vladyka asked.

"No, I'm from Serendip."

The Montenegran wondered what this could mean. "I thought I knew them all, but I never heard of that one. Let's see, Serendip was the old name for Sri Lanka, wasn't it? Is that your home asteroid?" The custom of naming the asteroid worlds for islands was an old one.

She smiled, displaying a small dimple slightly to the

left of the tip of her chin. He was almost certain that the Kornfeld woman had such a dimple. He'd have to check his records. "You must be new around here."

"Just been here a few days." He packed it with all the affability and charm he could muster, which was considerable.

"It's the department where serendipitous ideas are tested for potential—commercial, military, scientific or anything else." She ordered a Martian Chablis and Vladyka insisted on paying.

"These Aeaeans continue to amaze me," he said. "They give bars numbers and stick a name like that on a research department." Actually, the whole thing sounded phony to him. It was probably a blind constructed to hide her real work—studying the Rhea Object in private and hiding her findings from Earth.

"They're weird," she agreed. Her wine materialized and she tested it. It seemed to pass inspection. "Martian wines are much better than the ones they make out here."

"Is that where you're from originally?" he said slyly.

"No, I was born on Phobos Station." He thought the answer came too hastily, as if she had revealed too much. "I'm a third-generation Phobian. My grandparents were among the founders."

"Mars and its satellites were Russian back then," Vladyka said. "Is that where they came from?"

"No, they were French, hired for the Russian project. My name is Giselle Pellier. Does that sound Russian?"

"I'm glad to hear it," Vladyka said, "I'm a Serb, and we don't get along with Russians so well. My name's Josip Mihajlovic. Shorten it to Joe." It did his ego good to know that he could so easily charm a woman of such wide experience whose suspicions were legendary. But then, he reflected with satisfaction, if any man could do it, it would be Daniko Vladyka.

The astronomer turned to Giselle. "How are you betting?"

"Alien weapon. Imagine the explosive power those things must have."

"I've been imagining that all too clearly," said the chemist's assistant. "I don't like the way they're experimenting with that thing right here in Aeaea. Suppose they do succeed in cracking the envelope? Aeaea would just cease to exist."

"Along with any ships parked nearby," said the ship captain, sourly. "I don't know why they don't work on it somewhere else. They could build a lab not far from here and experiment with it to their heart's content and risk only the minimum number of lives."

This hadn't occurred to Vladyka before. What if the damned thing weren't here at all? In Quadrant Three the scientists might be pretending to work on a hunk of glass while the real work went on in a much safer environment. This would take some consideration.

"I'm sure they're taking all necessary precautions," Giselle said. Her accent was just faintly French, as if she had been raised in a household where the language was still used. He always admired good cover work by a fellow pro. And she looked a good many years younger than her true age. Of course, with modern medical science and cosmetic surgery, anyone could look almost any age, at least until they reached their seventies or eighties.

"How can they know what precautions to take?" the chemist's assistant demanded. "This thing is utterly unique."

"It's a bit pointless worrying about it, isn't it?" Vladyka said. "We're here and it's here and if it goes boom, there's not a damned thing any of us can do about it, is there?" Noticing that they looked a little gloomy at this, he decided to lighten the mood. "The tricky question is, if they do blow this place up, there's a major problem."

"What might that be?" Giselle asked.

He pointed to the display at the back of the bar. "Undoubtedly, somebody's bet that that is exactly what's going to happen. If it does, how is he going to collect?" That got a laugh, and he called for another round and paid for it, further increasing his popularity. He played on them expertly, steering conversation away from serious subjects, ingratiating himself with them, especially with Giselle.

For her part, Giselle was amused by him, but fascinated at the same time. He was good-looking, in a rough sort of way. He had a certain charm, although she thought he might have been more attractive had he spent more of his attention on her, and less on the others at the table. It was painfully apparent to her that his bonhomie was intended to curry favor with his companions. Well, she could understand that. He was a stranger here, and so was she, although she had been working on Aeaea for several years. She knew how lonely a new arrival could be.

She did wonder why he had chosen her as a prospect. She had no illusions about her desirability. Age no longer meant what it used to, and beauty could be bought from a good clinic. She knew she could hold her own, but there was a niggling part of her mind that insisted on saying, *why me?* She was aware that those men who had been attracted to her in the past had been charmed by her conversation, her wit, any number of qualities that served to reinforce her adequate physical charms. She had preferred such men. This Josip looked like the type who would pursue nubile young creatures with ripe bodies and rudimentary minds. There were enough of those about—daughters of the staff people, girls off the innumerable family-ships that handled so much of Island World freighting. Yet he had targeted her. It brought her up short, that she had unconsciously settled on the word "targeted." She began to give him some serious thought.

She was a highly trained metallurgist, but recently her duties had been broadened. A few months before she had been called for an interview by the head of Aeaean security. She had been enlisted as a part-time security agent. The Rhea Object Project had brought droves of non-Aeaeans to the Island World, and the authorities were worried about industrial espionage.

The problem was nothing new, but the influx of outsiders increased the chances of espionage greatly. Giselle was charged with keeping an eye on the non-Aeaeans. It was nothing that might be considered true spying or surveillance, but more a matter of noticing any behavior that seemed to be suspect. Island Worlders had such a detestation of government surveillance that this was as far as the Aeaean security forces were willing to go.

She decided to go along with him, at least to a limited extent. He might be one of the people the security forces were apprehensive about. Of course, it might simply be her body he was interested in. That was not a totally discomforting thought. But she was not utterly unrealistic. He might well be an agent sent to work his way into Aeaean operations. Romancing a staff scientist was not an unreasonable way to go about it. Whatever his motivation might be, it seemed worthwhile to play along.

While the others were deep in a conversation about a major new find of high-grade titanium ore, Vladyka turned to Giselle.

"Not to be pushy or anything, but do you have any plans for dinner? I don't know this place very well yet. Maybe you could show me, for instance, where a good place for dinner might be."

Whatever he had in mind, he wasn't wasting any time at it. She, however, wanted him checked out first. "I'm sorry. I teach a class in about an hour. It meets every third day."

He could tell she wasn't being truthful, which was a good sign. Kornfeld was noted for her caution. "How about tomorrow, then?" He smiled his best smile.

She hesitated a moment. "I believe I'm free for that shift. If you like, we could go to Rubinoff's. It's one of the better places if you like Russian food. Does that conflict with Serbian prejudices?"

"Not at all. I'll even eat Turkish food. All cuisine is innocent until proven guilty. Shall we meet here?"

They made arrangements and she left. The next day

she reported to the security office for her weekly briefing. The head of security told the operatives of several spies nabbed in the previous few days. He displayed life-sized holograms of suspected spies they were to be watching for. There were dozens of them, but the security chief, an Avalonian named Genovese, singled out one for special attention.

"This one," he said, "has just been reported as working in the Belt. He is from Montenegro, and his real name is Daniko Vladyka. We're showing him here with and without hair." Giselle felt a tingle of excitement. The hairless version looked somewhat like the man she had met the day before. That meant little, as features could be easily altered, but these holos, taken when the man did not know he was being imaged, expressed something of his personality.

"This is one to be ultra-careful with," Genovese droned on. "He's no mere industrial spy. He has been identified as an Earth agent. Of course, I realize that we are at peace with the Earth authorities," that drew some dry chuckles, "nevertheless, an informant has spilled the information that he has in the past been a successful assassin and torturer. Should he appear here and try to appropriate the Rhea Object, he wouldn't hesitate to kill."

She almost called for his attention, but a self-conscious fear of embarrassment stopped her. It was, after all, just a suspicion. There must be thousands of men similar to this one. Suppose she had him hailed into the security office and questioned, and he proved to be perfectly innocent? She decided to wait until she had better grounds for suspicion.

Vladyka left the bar certain that he had found the right woman. All the signs had been there. Even the restaurant she picked had been characteristic. Kornfeld had been raised on Mars and that planet still retained much of the culture of its early Russian settlers. The question now was how to handle the snatch and interrogation. True, his orders concerning Kornfeld had just been to kill her, but he was now certain that the Rhea

Object wasn't on Aeaea, but in some secret lab not far away.

He pondered the implications of that. If it wasn't here, why was the Kornfeld woman here? Because, obviously, it was being studied here by remote. It only stood to reason. The ship's captain had said it: Why would they risk such potential danger? Obviously, ranking scientists like Kornfeld weren't about to risk their valuable lives so close to the thing. The risky operations were being carried out by expendable technicians while the big shots monitored the work through instruments. Now all the loose ends were tied up. As always, Vladyka was pleased with his own impeccable reasoning.

Now, how to carry out the interrogation? He had brought along a portable interrogation kit, equipped with drugs and instruments for eliciting information from reluctant subjects. They required privacy for use, and this assignment could be tricky. Sieglinde Kornfeld would be no ordinary subject. He didn't know what kind of anti-drug treatment she might have, but he had some of the very latest pharmaceuticals in his kit and she couldn't have immunized herself against all of them yet.

His first order of business was to arrange for a private location, never an easy task in the Island Worlds. His own ship would have been ideal, but he had been forced to come to Aeaea by commercial transport to avoid jeopardizing his cover. That also meant that he had to arrange for a getaway. It was tricky, but he loved his work.

First, he arranged for a room at a hotel in the older part of the station, where the inner walls were still of concrete. He knew that screams were the sign of a sloppy interrogator, but here he would lack the leisure for artistry. He allowed himself eight hours from their meeting to the finish of the interrogation. She shouldn't be missed by her co-workers for several hours after that. For the room, he used an alternate identity and paid cash.

Then he arranged for passage on a Terran ship, using

yet another identity and again paying cash. It was all laughably easy, due to the Island Worlders' sloppy security and reluctance to demand rigorous ID searches. The next day, he transferred his belongings to the hotel room. He was now ready for the evening.

When she arrived, he was at a small table in the lounge with a bulb of Chablis opposite him. "See," he said, "I didn't forget."

"How thoughtful." She smiled, revealing the dimple again, and he mentally castigated himself for failing to check his records for it. Ah, well. Even dimples could be faked.

He made it a point to be especially charming. This was always a good policy, as it softened up the subject for what was to follow. As they walked into the restaurant, he had a moment of doubt. Suppose someone here actually came from his part of Earth? Might that someone note that his accent differed subtly from that of a Serbian from Trieste? Then he relaxed. It would make no difference. No one was looking for him. His cover was thorough. Nobody even knew that Daniko Vladyka was anywhere off-Earth.

During their meal, which she ordered for them, he noticed a certain nervousness in her chatter. Was it passionate anticipation? No, her breathing was wrong for that. It might be discomfort at keeping up her assumed identity. Whatever it was, the hour was getting late, and he had an interrogation to conduct, an elimination to perform, and a ship to catch.

He put his hand lightly on hers. "Giselle, I'm from Earth, where we have a little privacy to compensate for our numbers. It's always so crowded here. Wouldn't you like to go somewhere and talk without so many people around?"

Her hand moved slightly, but she didn't pull it away. "Ah, well, if you'd like to go to my apartment, it's rather a mess, but I'm rooming with only two other women. One of them might be away."

"I have a better idea. I have a room at the Hotel Andalucia. Real privacy. Doesn't that sound better?"

Now she was growing frightened. Even an Earthie shouldn't be so precipitate. The vodka-induced fog cleared swiftly from her brain. Something nudged her memory. Wasn't Serbia near Montenegro? Or was it Romania? Geography wasn't her strong point, but there was no way she was going to be shut up alone with a man who might be a professional assassin.

She pulled her hand back. "Cheri, this is a little too sudden. I know things are different on Earth, but here we move more slowly."

Damn! Quickly, he composed himself. The last thing he wanted was a scene here. But he had anticipated this possibility as well. "I am sorry. Of course I don't want to press you. What do you say we meet tomorrow for dinner and I choose the place. Is that leisurely enough for Island World sensibilities?"

She smiled again. Perhaps she was overreacting. "That would be fine. Meet at the same place?"

"And the same time. Until then." He gave a courtly bow, which was a difficult operation in the low gravity. She left and, after waiting a few moments, he followed her. In some area where there were relatively few people about, he would give her a swift injection. Nobody would think it outlandish to see a man helping an inebriated woman home. Many people were allergic to sober-up pills, and in any case, most people averted their attention from such an embarrassing sight.

Giselle's suspicions were almost allayed when she noticed that she was being followed. She had stopped before the holo display of a jewelry shop, and as she turned, she saw a man in the uniform of the physics section stepping suddenly into a doorway. It is not easy to make a swift change of direction in low gravity. She was sure it was Mihajlovic. She had no idea why a spy would be so determined to corner her, but she decided that she had ignored her instincts too many times. She walked on as if she had noticed nothing, but she raised the transmitter she wore on a finger.

"This is Giselle Pellier. I am being followed by a suspected infiltrator. I am approaching subsector G from

H in Sector Beta. Would you put a tail on both of us?"

"Acknowledged. Will comply immediately." She felt unutterably relieved.

Vladyka noticed the instant she raised her hand. Inexpertly, she was trying to disguise the fact that she was speaking into a transmitter. Immediately, he faded back. He had no trouble spotting the two security men who emerged from side corridors to fall in behind Sieglinde. It was certainly the Kornfeld woman. Would a mere staff metallurgist have Aeaean security at her beck and call?

He stepped into the first drop-tube he saw. He took turns and tubes at random, keeping to dense crowds, of which Aeaea had a sufficiency. As soon as he was certain that he wasn't shadowed, he bought a civilian coverall and donned it in a dressing room. He next found a pay restroom that featured privacy and set about altering his appearance with the cosmetics in his belt pouch.

Fifteen minutes later he emerged. His skin was dark, his eyes were green and his features had been subtly changed. He didn't have a hairpiece in his kit, but in space, hairlessness was so common that it hardly counted as identification. He moved like a native Island Worlder. No one, not even the Kornfeld woman, was going to identify him by sight. He decided to abandon his belongings in the hotel room. Unfortunately, he had given her the name of the place.

He found a holo theater and settled down to wait out the next few hours in the dimness. There were no alarms, no uniformed men rushing about looking for the intruder. Either they assigned him low priority, or it was another example of these people's lax police procedures. In a similarly closed environment on Earth, even such an expert as Daniko Vladyka wouldn't have remained at large for more than a few minutes. There were snoops everywhere, and anyone entering a facility like this would have a locater implanted. Well, it wasn't his job to clue them in on how to run a police state.

He was perfectly relaxed as he passed into his ship. Nobody questioned his ID, not even the bored-looking security people at port control. He was disappointed, but far from discouraged. He had located Sieglinde Kornfeld, something nobody else had been able to do. What he had to do now was to find out where the Rhea Object really was. Where the green egg was, Kornfeld would show up sooner or later. He would take a circuitous route back to his ship and put his team on the problem at once. No matter how quiet and secretive they tried to be, such a project would have to leave tracks. As sloppy as these people were, those tracks shouldn't be difficult to find.

NINE

The invitation took Larsen by surprise. His dealings with Mehmet Shevket had always been on an official basis. They had never mixed socially. The majority of Shevket's cronies were in the military, while Larsen's were denizens of the political and business worlds.

The old-fashioned card lay on his desk, its flowing black script embossed on the costly, cream-colored paper: "His Excellency General Mehmet Shevket requests the honor of your company at his lodge in the Camargue." There followed date and time. It seemed that there was to be an intimate gathering for relaxation and socializing at the general's beautiful country estate. The smell of conspiracy drifted like perfume from the card. Larsen liked that smell. Conspiracy was the fabric of his life. He keyed his social secretary. "Send a formal acceptance to His Excellency."

From the air, Shevket's estate looked merely picturesque, a Gothic fantasy of curtain walls, towers and buttresses. He had bought the ruined chateau and had restored it to his own taste, discarding its original name and calling it Kara Kum. Its archaic defenses masked modern, sophisticated security systems. As the executive hoverer descended, Larsen could see small herds of animals fleeing in panic. Shevket had appropriated a huge parcel of land for his self-bestowed fief, had depopulated much of it, and had stocked it with game animals. A passionate hunter, he enjoyed pursuing the beasts on horseback, killing them with arrow or spear.

The craft settled on the flat roof of a tower and Larsen descended its carpeted ramp. Shevket was there to greet him, resplendent in his customary black leathers. This time he wore a scarlet scarf to match the coral handle of his dagger. The two men shook hands as the hoverer lifted away.

"How good of you to come," Shevket said.

"Very kind of you to invite me. I confess it took me by surprise. We've never met on this—basis, shall we say?"

"No time like the present. I think, if we're to work together, we must get to know one another better. And I have other guests here I would like you to meet—people who will be important in our future activities."

So this was the reason for the invitation. "I look forward to meeting them. This is a lovely estate, General." They walked to the tower's parapet and looked over the unearthly Camargue landscape. It was low and swampy and looked like nothing that belonged in Europe.

"Do you know why I like to own flat land?" Shevket asked. "It's because, from a height, I can see so much of what is mine." He laughed, and Larsen realized that it was the first time he had heard such a sound from Shevket.

"Reasonable, but hardly humorous, General."

"Not humor, but pleasant anticipation. It just occurred to me that someday we'll need homes in orbit, to see all we own. Come," he gestured grandly, "dinner will be served soon. Allow me to show you my chateau." They stepped into a small elevator.

"Tomorrow," Shevket said as they descended, "we shall go hunting on the heaths. My stable is peerless and I've brought in some magnificent beasts for the hunt."

"I'm afraid hunting isn't one of my favored pastimes," Larsen said. "And I have never ridden a horse and have no interest in such primitive locomotion. I fear your no doubt lavish indoor delights will have to suffice."

Shevket's look was superior. "As you wish. As my honored guest, you shall have the best I can offer." The door slid open. "And now we have arrived in the great hall."

They stepped into a chamber of disorienting vastness. At first glance it appeared to be a typical baronial hall, until the eye began to pick up strange details. The walls met at odd angles. Above, the beams of rough-hewn wood slanted and met in ways that did not seem structural. Peculiar catwalks crossed the open area, going from nowhere to nowhere. Light from high, slit windows slanted across the hall, and it took the eyes a moment to adjust to the fact that it was coming in at subtly differing angles, unlike real sunlight. It was definitely unsettling.

"It is, ah, unique, General. Rather like Piranesi's *Carceri*."

"You recognized it. Congratulations. My designer is enamored of that artist, as am I."

"A most unusual choice, but effective." Piranesi's enigmatic series of drawings had always struck Larsen as depicting torture dungeons, where shadowy figures flitted on sinister missions amid surroundings of demented architecture that dwarfed human scale.

A Romanesque arch carved with grotesque figures led to an art gallery that further revealed Shevket's taste for the lurid. The works on display ranged from classical to modern, but the entire collection positively vibrated with blood, death, sex and domination. Many were unabashedly pornographic. There were battle scenes by Gericault, harems by Ingres, slave markets by Gérôme. There were holosculptures so shockingly violent that Larsen paled. Even more upsetting was Shevket's unself-conscious delight in the collection.

The tour of the art gallery at an end, Shevket excused himself to make some last-minute arrangements for the evening's banquet. A servant guided Larsen to his suite. There was no sign of robots in the chateau, only human servants. They went about their duties silently and all of them, male and female, were of striking beauty.

Like most Earthmen of his generation, Larsen was unaccustomed to menials. Aside from the occasional waiter such as those in the U.N. palace, he had encountered few in his life. The world viewed service work as exploitation, and most people preferred living on the edge of starvation with government welfare to accepting menial employment. Where had the Turk found these exquisite creatures?

The one assigned to him was a young woman with olive skin and chestnut hair. Her flowing scarlet gown was of some sheer fabric, almost transparent. A light chain of chromed steel closely encircled her neck. As he noted it, Larsen remembered that all the servants he had seen so far had been wearing such chains.

"What is your name?" he asked.

"Natasha." Her voice was barely audible, her eyes downcast.

"Do you live nearby?"

"I live here."

She was certainly unforthcoming, but her accent was reasonably cultured. "Is seeing to the comfort of the guests your specialty, or have you other duties as well?" He wasn't sure how a household with human servants operated.

"I am yours while you are here." That seemed an odd way of phrasing it. To his utter astonishment, she knelt and remained in that pose, hands on knees, head lowered.

"You mean you are to take care of my quarters and see to my needs?" Her pose was so alluring that it ruffled the self-composure in which he took such pride.

"I am yours to command as you will, while you are here," she said.

"I see. How very—archaic." This was something unexpected. He should have been shocked, but there was very little that could shock Aage Larsen. He examined his reactions and decided that the situation was quite pleasurable. It could be that Shevket was setting him up, but for what? Political blackmail? Larsen was un-married. The popular press was well controlled and a liaison with an attractive young woman would do his reputation no harm among the people that really counted.

Gently, he touched her hair. She made no move to draw away. Larsen had always been contemptuous of men who could not keep their sexual urges under control. Such preoccupations seemed to him to be trivial and adolescent compared to the pleasures of power. He wondered what made this different and he decided that it was the woman's obvious posture and attitude of submission. It was as if this relationship were ordained by nature.

Whatever the explanation, he had no intention of acting on any hormonal impulse until he had some clearer idea of what Shevket's scheme was. Quickly, he changed clothes and renewed his cosmetics. Satisfied with his appearance, he left the room and descended a wide staircase to an elegant salon. Here the decor was Louis XIV. How typical, he thought, that Shevket's choice of setting always ran to things regal and dynastic.

There was a sizable gathering in the salon. All the guests were male, most of them in uniform. There were some exceptions. Larsen noted a pale, thin, almost languid young man in tight trousers, his arm draped over the shoulders of a servant boy as if for support, a fishbowl-sized glass of maroon wine in his free hand. Nearby stood a cold-faced man dressed like an executive and wearing the sort of light-filtering spectacles favored by media people. Larsen remembered vaguely that the variable filters on the spectacles somehow aided holographers in their work.

Shevket strode superbly across the room to greet Larsen. Everyone in the Turk's path managed discreetly to step out of his way. Larsen had a freakish impression that water would have parted before the man, allowing him to cross dry-shod.

"Come, Aage, meet my other guests. Here is Colonel Manuel Murieta, of the Earth Land Forces."

"Honored, your Excellency." He clicked his boot

heels as he held out his hand. His uniform was similar to Shevket's, but of green leather with crimson facings. The man was dark with a drooping black mustache.

"I'm sure you've met Under-Admiral von Gruenwald?"

"At several functions," Larsen said, shaking hands with a tall, thin man in the rather old-fashioned uniform favored by the space forces.

"I am delighted to see you here, sir," said the Teuton. His head was clean-shaven and Larsen thought the man looked incomplete without a monocle. "It's good to know that some of the civilian political sector are in agreement with the general's vision."

Larsen let that pass without comment. "The general is a remarkable man." Such noncommittal but inarguable statements were a politician's stock in trade.

Shevket introduced all the military men first. Larsen quickly noticed a pattern: None of them were of the highest rank. Most were colonels, some mere majors or captains. Larsen knew his history, and he knew these ranks to be the classical breeding ground for coups. In any corrupt system, the highest ranks were given to the cronies of the ruling powers. Those high generals in turn give the next lower positions to their own favorites. They never retire from their lucrative postings, and a mass of younger officers are left knowing that the field grades are as high as their careers will ever go. Unless, of course, they conspire to oust the old appointees.

"This," Shevket said, introducing him to the man in the filter spectacles, "is Julian Norwich, the media specialist." He pronounced it British-style, as "Norrich."

"I think I've studied some of your work, Mr. Norwich. Didn't you write *Popular Media in Political Life?*"

Norwich allowed his face to show pleasure. "I did. I trust you liked it?"

Shevket broke in. "It should be required reading for anyone with political ambitions."

"I agree," Larsen said. The work had been devoted to the belief that propaganda was the ultimate reality of political life, that objective reality meant little or nothing. Everything in Larsen's political career supported the thesis.

"And this," Shevket brought the languid young man forward, "is Cesar Favre, poet extraordinaire."

Extraordinaire was hardly the word for it. Larsen had heard of Cesar Favre, leading light of the Neo-Decadents. He was all the rage among the artistic set. They affected to despise popular media such as holography and called for a return to the earlier arts, including poetry. Favre's reputation for degeneracy was the wonder of those people who still bothered to read.

"I have heard wonderful things of you," Larsen said.

"A diplomatic way of saying you haven't read my work." Favre's hand seemed to be performing a sexual act with Larsen's own.

"On the contrary, I've read most of your published works. I found *Dialogues of the Cannibals* quite powerful, but I thought *The Feast of Vlad Tepes* perhaps a trifle shrill. There is such a thing as straining a metaphor to the breaking point." He was rewarded with a look of surprise in the young man's washed-out blue eyes.

"What a wonder! A politician who reads! Most of the critics who delight in savaging my verses don't do as much."

"If you two would excuse me," Shevket said, "I have some things to attend to." He spun on a shiny heel and strode from the room.

"Isn't he magnificent?" Favre said. He took a sip from his huge balloon glass. Larsen caught a pungent scent of some drug. "I'd thought that such men were an extinct species." His eyes grew vague and he twirled his fingers in the servant boy's hair.

"How so?" Larsen asked, fascinated and repelled in equal measure.

"How long has it been since we've seen a true superman who looked like one? The great monsters of recent history have been godlike only in their deeds. Hitler, Stalin, Mao, Napoleon," he gestured limply with his wineglass, "they were all such commonplace-looking men. Mussolini was all style, no substance. Kemal Ataturk came the closest, but his arena of operation was too small. Where are the truly spectacular and flamboyant *übermenschen* of the past? The Alexanders, the Ramses Thirds, the Ashurbanipals, the Tchaka Zulus? We live in an age of small events and small men."

This was certainly an original interpretation of history. "Well, perhaps things shall look up soon."

"Oh, I do hope so," Favre said. "Life shouldn't be so dull and respectable."

"You seem to have ably surmounted the obstacle of respectability, Monsieur Favre." Larsen seriously thought that, should the boy step aside, the poet would collapse bonelessly to the floor where he would then melt through minute cracks in the polished parquet.

Favre surprised him by showing a flash of humor accompanied by a rather engaging smile. "We have both risen above the handicaps of our origins, your excellency. I have defeated the spectre of bourgeois respectability, you of bourgeois morality and niggling scruples."

"You do me a disservice," Larsen said. "I am well known for my compassion and humanitarian ideals."

The poet raised his glass in ironic salute. "I acknowledge a superior performer, sir. Never could I have spoken such a line with a straight face."

"Each of us acts in accordance with his gifts." Larsen kept his face carefully composed.

For the first time, Favre laughed. It was a pleasant, musical sound. "I confess, when I saw you in the holos, I thought you the dullest sort of politician. I was appalled when I heard that the general had invited you to this affair. But now I find that I like you. Now I understand why the general esteems you so highly. As I alluded a moment ago, Hitler himself was an ordinary looking man of little personal presence save when on the speaking platform."

"And you," Larsen said, "are not the talented but shallow aesthete I had thought, despite your strenuous efforts to convey exactly that impression."

The two men smiled honestly for the first time, and they shook hands again. This time the gesture was sincere.

"Dinner is served!" shouted a handsome young servant of powerful physique and voice. The well-lubricated crowd of men flowed into the banqueting hall. Larsen was relieved to see that it was not the nightmarish great hall, but another room nearly as large, with a lower ceiling, lit by genuine torches burning in cressets.

Larsen had a fondness for theatrical trappings, and he occupied the first few minutes of the banquet analyzing its components. He was seated near the head of the table, next to Shevket. The table itself was made of age-blackened wood, scarred and dented. The torch-light and candlelight provided a ruddy illumination that encouraged a crude, masculine conviviality.

"Welcome, gentlemen," said Shevket, the fires striking dramatic highlights from his shiny uniform. "Tonight, we have much to speak about. But before all the talk, let us feast as men should feast. Food and drink now, words later." He resumed his seat amid approving cheers.

The servants began to bring in the first courses. Others circulated with pitchers of various wines and beers. Larsen noted that they all wore the chromed chains around their necks. He had a disturbing but intriguing feeling that these were not mere servants, but slaves. How could this be possible? One thing was certain: If any man could accomplish it, it would be Mehmet Shevket.

The food was delicious but robust. There was a profusion of wild game, imparting a carnivorous atmosphere that plainly suited the men assembled there. Larsen noted that no meat dish was served that made any attempt at disguising its animal origin. It was all entire beasts, birds or fish, or recognizable parts of such. There was a clatter of vessels, a gnashing of knives against plates, the clamor of loud voices. Whatever else these men might be, Larsen thought, they were certainly not elegant.

There was something both stimulating and oppressive about the profusion of colorful uniforms, the impression of strength and barely restrained violence. Most of these men had gained their rank by killing dissidents and rebels in great numbers.

Tiring of the spectacle of militant gorging, Larsen raised his eyes to the wall opposite him. Even there, the atmosphere remained consistent. Ancient weapons sprawled across the wall—halberds and axes, swords, maces, fans of spears arranged behind shields. Intermixed with the lethal steel were the skulls of animals, crested with horns and antlers.

After an hour of guzzling and eating, during which Larsen had merely sipped and nibbled, the last trays were borne away by the silent servitors. The conversation died down to a mutter as men fed to repletion tried to regather their faculties.

Larsen turned to the man sitting next to him, Favre. The poet had spent most of the meal talking with the man on his other side, a young and very handsome captain in the Greek service. Larsen noted that Favre had drunk much and eaten little.

"I am curious," the Dane began, "about your poetic antecedents. In your work I find of course hints of Rimbaud and Verlaine, certain touches of Merimée, and naturally your own individual style. What other poets have influenced you?"

"D'Annunzio," Favre said, "and Mishima. I discovered them young and never forgot their work."

Larsen had never heard of them. "I fear that my scholarship is not that detailed. I am unfamiliar with the gentlemen."

Favre showed a trace of animation. "They were poets who understood the dark corridors of our minds, the places where joy in power and carnality reign. There was another named Lawrence—"

Shevket stood and the muttering of conversation died away.

"My friends! My honored guests! Tonight we are assembled to speak of important matters—serious matters that will affect all of history to come." His words, delivered in a penetrating voice, began to pierce the alcohol-induced fog enveloping his listeners.

The general easily dominated the room, standing to his commanding height, his aura of power and authority wrapping him as perfectly as his uniform. "It is time for a social experiment that has long outlived its time to be discarded. I speak of our worldwide system of feeding useless mouths and dignifying the worthless bulk of our population by pretending that their lives are sacred and somehow of inestimable value. We have never truly acted as if this were the case, and I propose that we cease even the pretense."

Men straightened, glancing at their fellows for sign of reaction. Even in this gathering, these were strong words. By force of habit, Larsen took a quick reading of expressions. There was much astonishment, but no dismay.

"At the risk of being accused of oratory, I shall share with you my thoughts on the situation in which we now find ourselves, and how we got here." He paced back and forth at the head of the table, a huge scarlet banner draped behind him. He had their total attention now.

"The principal folly of both classical capitalism and the somewhat later myth of communism/socialism lies in their rejection of any heroic, action-oriented role for man as an individual or in the mass. Instead, they have reduced him to a purely economic unit." He pronounced "economic" with a sneer. "To the communist he is a worker. To the capitalist he is a consumer. Neither role could ever be satisfying to any but the most spiritless." Larsen saw heads nodding. Thus far, Shevket had said nothing these men disagreed with.

"Even the profession of soldier," he gestured to his own uniform, to the many others lining the table, "is to be undertaken only as an onerous duty. Its participation in sanctioned violence is to be tolerated but not enjoyed, and its only reward is the stingy approbation of the noncombatant populace." His voice rose sharply.

"The concepts of glory, honor and duty have been discarded as archaic and nonproductive.

"It is against this pallid interpretation of man's place in society that we must rebel. That all men *should* rebel! We must rebel not merely in opposition to a moribund economic and social order, but in defense of our very sanity! Man did not evolve from cud-chewing vegetarians, but from hunters. The highest, the best among us are still killers and carnivores."

This was bizarre, but Larsen felt it strangely stimulating. He saw that the men around him were likewise enthralled. He had never considered Shevket anything but a dangerous brute, to be used but never to be anything more than an implement. There were depths here he had never suspected.

"Now, we find ourselves mere herdsmen of our fellow men, and I use the term 'men' advisedly. Of course, there is nothing wrong with the pastoral life. Herding was the first step in our development after hunting. But no one ever raised cattle and sheep and other animals for the satisfaction of knowing the beasts were taken care of. No one wanted to give the animals a chance to attain their 'full potential.' They were to be eaten, or shorn, or skinned or worked or ridden!" With each word he pounded on the table for emphasis. His eyes held an almost demented ferocity. "They were to be used! Beyond the demands of personal, family loyalty, or duty to a comrade, that is the only sane reason for taking care of another being, human or otherwise."

Approval was more open now. Men were nodding and smiling, making curt comments to one another, as if to say that this was what they had been thinking all along. Larsen noted two whose attitude differed: Favre the poet was gazing at Shevket with rapt admiration, almost worship. There was something repellently erotic in his glazed gaze, his flushed complexion, in the way the breath came quick through his half-parted lips. The other was Norwich, the media man. He watched the others at the table with the calculation of one attuned to audience reaction. Larsen realized that he probably wore the same look himself. As in in acknowledgement, Norwich gave him a conspiratorial look and nodded slightly.

When the muttering died down, Shevket went on. "I need hardly remind you that people will not rebel spontaneously. The mass mind is too dim to comprehend that anything is wrong. The problem and the solution must be presented to them by those who have the vision to encompass the catastrophe and the charisma to attract and compel a following. By my words, do not think that I speak of establishing some kind of 'people's government.'" He charged the words with irony. "It will not be necessary to gain the support of all or even a majority of the population. A few sheep dogs can handle any number of sheep." Amid applause he raised a tankard and took a long swallow of ale. He set it solidly on the table and wiped his mouth with the back of his hand. Larsen wondered where he had learned his gestures. Every move he made seemed to ingratiate him with the men present.

"This degenerative process cannot be reversed by anyone who conceives of power and its exercise as it has become traditional in the so-called democratic nations; by currying the favor of an indulged and pampered electorate by promising yet more indulgence, more pampering. It goes without saying that this is a legitimate path to power for someone who has no intention of honoring scrupulously his campaign promises. Still, power thus gained remains too dependent upon the apparatus of election. Far more desirable would be the elevation to absolute power of a man swept upward upon a wave of mass enthusiasm by those who are ready to shake off their assumed mantle of gentleness and passivity!"

The hearers were actually cheering now. Larsen wondered whether their exultation, fueled by alcohol and oratory, would survive a night's sleep. He decided that it might. There men were plainly being offered power and high position in a new world order. If they continued to believe in Shevket.

"What has always stood in the path of such a movement?" The Turk spread his hands questioningly. "Principally, it has been the imposition of a myth which has suppressed the superior human being and offered instead the spectacle of the inferior led by the mediocre. For natural aggression, it has substituted passive spectatorship. It has cast up entertainers and athletes as political experts and models for the young. This is not merely insanity, it is suicidal insanity."

He placed his palms on the table and leaned forward. "I propose that we change all this. What will the price be? Freedom? Who has any of that vague commodity? Much of the world's population has never had it and will never miss it. The supposedly democratic West extolled the virtues of this freedom and accomplished nothing.

"In this illogical system, man finds himself assured at every turn that it is his birthright to conduct and express himself in perfect freedom as an individual. He is, through growth and education, to determine his wants and his capabilities, and by a sober evaluation of each to conduct his life upon a course of fulfillment and happiness, insofar as that course does not interfere with the rights of his fellow man. Such was the inspiring, conventional interpretation of the rights of man within the framework of Western democracy, as promulgated by the American and French revolutions. But how closely does this pleasant vision conform with reality and human nature?" He knew he had them now. Every face at the table was rapt with attention. They might not be thinking through all he said, but that was not necessary. Sufficient that they sensed power for themselves in his words, and the conviction that he was the master of his theory.

"The fact is, it fails utterly at almost every turn. Called upon to exercise personal responsibility for every important decision of his life, the average man finds himself smitten with terror. Most will seek guidance through some exterior authority. It may be a parent or other authority figure, a church, even a newspaper or holo horoscope. It is no puzzle that seers and fortune-tellers have never lacked for an audience, even among those thought to be enlightened. It is another way of shirking responsibility for one's own life. Leave it to the gods or the stars or whatever. Anything is better than self-determination.

"Likewise with the supposed fulfillment of the self-guided life. Most lead aimless, nonproductive lives of utter dependency upon state handouts. The few that work find themselves locked into dead-end jobs with no purpose except maintenance of a minimum standard of living, and no prospect of anything better. They would be as well off under almost any political-economic system, and it is highly unlikely that any amount of education or access to opportunity would improve their lot one iota. The fact is that the average man is a drone, has always been a drone and will always be a drone. What, then, is the value of this much-touted freedom?"

He took another pull at his ale, this time amid utter silence. "The one thing all of us here at this table know is that men must fight. If their leaders give them no enemy to destroy, they will waste their aggressive energies in futile rebellions and hopeless insurgencies. I propose that we give our people someone to fight. We all know the enemy. It is those who were too cowardly to face life on a declining planet and instead found for themselves a place less demanding. Now these space-dwelling parasites insult us with their material wealth, implying that *we* need *them* in order to survive!"

Amid indignant murmurs he turned his attention to the men who wore the uniform of the space services. "I mean, of course, no disparagement to the officers and men of our space forces. On the contrary, theirs is the most dangerous and demanding duty in all our military establishment, since they must serve in an environment more hostile and unforgiving of error than the open sea. But the planets and satellites are there for conquest and exploitation. They were never meant to be refuges for those too spineless to live on the motherworld!" At this the cheering was ferocious. These men had spent their careers without a chance at a decent war. Most of the senior service officers had made their reputations during the Space War. These men had burned for such an opportunity since first donning the uniform.

Larsen marveled at the way Shevket played his audience, like a virtuoso performing on a perfect instrument. He knew that the Turk had attracted a considerable following with his hard-line opinions among the holo audience. Of course, he had never expressed such extreme views in public, but might he sway a truly mass audience with some genuinely violent oratory? That was probably what Norwich the media man was here for.

"Our time draws near," Shevket resumed. "If we do not act quickly and seize the moment, it will be past retrieving. I declare here the foundation of the Victory party. It is a word that sounds good in any language: la victoire, Sieg, Qahir. However one expresses it, it is a word to stir the soul. Who is with me?"

As one man, they stood and cheered. Larsen stood as quickly as the rest, knowing that should he fail to do so he would lose out forever if Shevket prevailed. Knowing as well that, should this prove a flash in the pan, as had so many other movements, no one would remember that he had been here save those that could be easily eliminated. But he found himself genuinely stirred. Nothing in his previous career had held out the promise of such satisfaction. The cold pleasures of power as he had wielded it in the past seemed colorless juxtaposed with the despotic delights promised by Shevket. To command men for the pure joy of seeing one's will obeyed! That was an experience worth devoting some real effort to.

"Are there any questions?" Shevket asked. "This is a momentous occasion. Surely you have some doubts you wish me to address."

The men milled uncertainly. Cheering with a crowd was one thing. Standing forth as individuals was quite another. Still, these men had not gained their rank through lack of personal assertion. The young Greek captain who had been conversing with Favre leaned on the table and looked to his left, at Shevket.

"My General, what of Mr. Anthony Carstairs and the hierarchy of the Earth First Party? They have dominated this planet for a generation and they will not relinquish power easily."

"Leave Carstairs to me, Captain Nicopoulos. As for the rest of that party," Larsen appreciated how the use of the simple adjective "that" separated all those present from it, "it is a useful structure, and may be left largely intact once we have imposed our own people in all positions of real authority." It was a pertinent point, and Larsen wondered whether the Greek captain had been primed with it.

"You by now realize," Shevket continued, "that we are all now part of a conspiracy. Do not be afraid of the word. All of the great turning points of history have begun with a conspiracy. Only losers are remembered as conspirators and plotters. The victors are known to history as founders and visionaries. We are strong. We shall become numerous. And only faintness of heart can stand in our way. We shall forge the single world state that Earth First always promised and never delivered. That world will return to the natural order of mankind: There shall be leaders, there shall be followers, and there shall be serfs. No longer shall the strong serve the weak!"

When the cheering and shouting died down, he went on more conversationally. "In the course of the next three days I will interview each of you individually. You will be briefed on your new duties. Soon I shall have other men like you here for their preliminary indoctrination, but you shall always be the first." He raised his tankard. "To victory!"

When Larsen returned to his room, the girl was still there. This time she knelt by the bed and she had discarded the scarlet gown. He undressed and crawled between the cool sheets, his mind turning over the possibilities of the evening. She started to climb in with him but he stopped her with a gesture. "No, I have no further need of you tonight." Wordlessly, she picked up her gown and left the room. He settled back in the bed and said to himself, "After all, being seduced twice in the same evening might be overdoing it."

The next morning he showered and shaved and dressed with his usual fastidious care. Exiting the room, he found Natasha awaiting him outside the door. He wondered whether she had stood there all night. She guided him through the corridors to a terrace where a lavish breakfast buffet had been laid. He contented himself with French rolls and coffee and made small talk with a few of the uniformed men. Not many were awake at the early hour and those that were showed bleary eyes despite the anti-hangover drugs they had taken.

Breakfast finished, Larsen strolled in the well-kept grounds for a while, then returned to the chateau. Inside he saw few people save the ubiquitous servants in their chromed collars. A sound of clicking metal drew him to a cavernous room full of athletic gear and floored with thick mats. In its center two men were fencing with sabers. They were anonymous in their masks, but he knew the larger of the two had to be Shevket. The smaller man was swift and powerful, a perfect counterpoise to the Turk's strength, imperturbability, and precision. Larsen knew nothing of swordplay, but he found these two superb athletes fascinating to watch.

Abruptly, Shevket abandoned his defensive style and loosed a flurry of high-line attacks. It ended when he slid past his opponent's guard and the lightweight fencing foil landed with a resounding smack on the leather top of the other's mask. "Touché!"

"Bravo!" Larsen called out, applauding.

The two men unmasked and Larsen was astonished to see that Shevket's opponent was none other than Cesar Favre, looking nothing at all like the indolent aesthete of the previous evening. With his sword, he gave Larsen an ironic salute. "You have learned my guilty secret. I love battle as much as the general.

Unlike him, I prefer the safe kind. I have yet to defeat him with any sword."

"Have you had breakfast, Aage?" Shevket asked.

"I have."

"Excellent. If you find it convenient, I would like to speak with you for a while in my study."

The Dane raised his eyebrows slightly. "Is this to be my interview?"

Shevket smiled, showing a mouthful of predator's teeth. "No, you of all people need not be interviewed. I just wish to go over some important matters with you. Norwich will be there as well."

"Lead on." The two took their leave of Favre and walked through the tapestry-hung corridors to Shevket's private quarters. Larsen had to hurry a bit to keep up with the general's long stride, and he suspected that Shevket took unnaturally long steps in order to put others at that disadvantage.

The study was lined with shelves of old-fashioned books in cloth and leather bindings. Larsen scanned them, expecting to find the collected works of the Marquis de Sade, but was disappointed. He did find the political equivalents of those works, along with a great many military volumes and books of art. A servant brought in a tray of drinks and a few moments later Norwich joined them.

"Gentlemen, help yourselves and have a seat." Shevket took his own advice and took a glass of white wine. Larsen took a Bloody Mary and sat in one of the room's comfortable, overstuffed Victorian chairs.

"Last night," Shevket said when they were settled, "I primed some of my best prospective supporters. Now we must speak of a mass media strategy to raise our new party into a position of dominance. You are aware that I do not see it as a party of the people or any nonsense of that sort. Nonetheless, we must have mass support at first. That means whipping up enthusiasm and *that* means using the media."

"I am happy to see that you understand that, General," said Norwich. "Earth First has all but forgotten the importance of proper media coordination in achieving political ends. Decades in power have lulled them into thinking they got there and stayed there through some sort of cosmic predestination. Actually, they accomplished it through extremely subtle and adroit manipulation of the media, especially the popular holos of the day. Of course, we have far more effective techniques at our disposal now."

"You said you had mapped out a preliminary campaign," Shevket said. "Please outline this for Mr. Larsen and me."

"First, allow me to sketch some of the techniques used in the past to raise individual men to power and to sway large numbers of people." From a side pocket he took a small, flat box perhaps three by six inches, less than half an inch thick. This he placed in the center of the floor.

"This is our latest unit, not yet available to the public. In it I've set a program, which I can control with this unit," he held up a smaller handset with control plates, "for purposes of explanation. From time to time I'll talk over the program to tell you what is happening, but when these programs reach the public, they will be non-interferable. That means that the viewer, although we prefer the word 'experiencer,' will be aware of nothing but the program. Shout in his ear and he won't hear you. Step before him and he won't see you."

"Amazing!" Larsen said.

Norwich smiled like a proud father. "It's what we've been searching for since the beginning of communication—total control of the audience." He fiddled with the handset. "To begin, nothing quite so dramatic. Before the age of mass communication, let us say prior to the early twentieth century, there were only two ways for a candidate for office, a demagogue, or a mere rabble-rouser to influence the body politic. These were the written word and the spoken word. Then, as now, few people knew how to read or bothered to if they knew. The principal way to whip up passions was still, as it had been since earliest times, oratory. With the advent of radio, it became possible for millions to hear the spoken word at once, but this had its disadvantages. People sitting in their own homes did not get the mob feeling of being in a mass audience. The poor sound reproduction of the crude speakers destroyed much of the nuance of the human voice. The British Prime Minister Churchill was one of the few who was able to sway people by the power of his voice over the radio.

"The early motion pictures had no sound, so their effectiveness was limited to depicting powerful visual images. A good deal of this was seen in the First World War when all sides involved made films depicting their enemies as ravaging barbarians. These were unspeakably crude, but the audiences of the day were not visually sophisticated and the efforts proved quite effective.

"Still, the main political instrument of this period was the mass rally. I will now show you some images from the time. These have of course been cleaned up and enhanced to make them easier on modern senses." Lifelike images sprang to life in the center of the room. The rest of the study faded and its place was taken by holographic crowds. The quality was not what it would have been had the scenes been holographed in the first place, but they were astonishingly realistic, the off-key color and movement just sufficient to give an impression of great age.

"This is wonderful!" Larsen said.

"Wait until you see what is to come," Norwich promised. "Now, here in one of the earlier films we see Vladimir Lenin addressing a crowd. Note how important the tight packing of the crowd is. You will see that throughout most of these oratory scenes." In the holo, a baldheaded man in archaic spectacles harangued a crowd. The film had been a silent but a Russian voice had been perfectly lip-synched and the crowd noises were believable.

"Here we have the infamous Herr Hitler."

"A much-maligned man, in my opinion," Shevket said.

"Um, yes. In any case, he may have been the greatest master in history of the art of harangue. I'm afraid you have to be German to appreciate it, though. This scene shows one of the famous Nuremberg rallies. You will notice that, besides compelling speeches, these people made great use of pageantry. The next scene is the American President Roosevelt. Again, he was more of a radio personality. This was the last great age of political oratory, because next came—" the holo switched to an image of a plastic box with a glowing window "—television. It was dreadfully crude in its inception, but its effect was astounding."

"Difficult to believe people would actually sit for hours and watch those tiny monochrome images," Larsen said.

"And yet they did," Norwich resumed. "Oh, there were flashes of the old style in the middle decades of the century. There was a black American named King who did rather well with the spoken word. He was a preacher and the churches were practically the last schools of oratory still left.

"You see, television did two things: It shrank the images to what you see here, reducing the statesmen to puppet-show scale, and it robbed them of their audiences because, once they were accustomed to television, it became impossible to get people to leave their homes in large numbers for anything but sporting or entertainment events.

"Politicians tried to adapt. Actually, many were not displeased with the new medium. Addressing mass audiences in city after city was a grueling, exhausting routine, as you may well conceive. Instead, they took the lessons to be learned from the burgeoning advertising business and resorted to short commercials to get their point across. In fact, they hired advertising people for this purpose. It was at this time that they began to learn the importance of such concepts as image, manufacturing those pseudo-personae as they were needed. The television medium encouraged laziness, and politicians of the developed nations were pursuing a lazy electorate. Selling them sloth, you might say."

"And with great success," commented Larsen, drily.

"No question of it. Now, having given you this wholly inadequate preparation, allow me to demonstrate how our new technology is going to make General Shevket the most wildly adored leader since, oh, since Hitler, or perhaps Juan Peron." He switched off the images still parading through the room.

"In modern political life," Norwich went on, "say for the past century or more, the element of crowd spirit has been lacking. As in the early days of television, people still prefer to huddle close to their holoscreens. I propose to change all that. You see, in the course of my studies, I ran across a memoir—am I waxing too pedantic?"

"No, please go on," Larsen urged. "You understand that, above all other things, I love to hear about the methods by which power may be wielded. I find this all fascinating." Shevket nodded as well.

"Excellent. As I was saying, I ran across the memoir of a very early cinema director, a man named DeMille. He relates how, during the screening of a new comedy— these screenings took place in small rooms before a small audience, perhaps the director alone—he became convinced it would be a fiasco. It failed to make him laugh. He was sick to think of all the money he had wasted on the project. Aides urged him to preview it in a theater anyway, and he did. To his great surprise, the audience roared with laughter throughout the film. To his greater surprise, so did he. It was then that he realized that *we almost never laugh alone!* From that time forward, he would only screen a comedy in a theater full of people.

"Thus it is always. We laugh harder at comedy, weep more copiously at pathos, cheer more fiercely with the hero's victory, shiver more violently at horror, when we are in the presence of others who feel the same emotions. Each spectator feeds and multiplies off the others. This mob feeling has been largely lost except in sports and street riots, which are often very similar events. It has been totally lost in political life. Until. With this rather sprawling and disjointed preamble—"

"No," Larsen hastened to assure him, "this has been fascinating and instructive."

"Thank you. Now, for the meat of the matter. What you are about to see is an actor giving a prepared speech in Mongolian. We chose that obscure language because, for demonstration purposes, it is not the content of the speech but the experience of the event that counts. Imagine General Shevket in place of the actor, giving a rousing speech that is of great interest to all listeners. Say, for instance, that he is raising them to a war frenzy."

The room faded once more. Then, as if dawn were swiftly spreading light over the scene, Larsen found himself seated in an immense auditorium, in a seat near the front row. The realism was astounding. He could hear the babble of conversation on all sides. He felt the breeze and he was certain that he could actually *smell* the people, the fresh-cut wood of the speaking platform, the viands people were munching as they waited.

Silence fell, then there was a blare of martial music. A uniformed man strode to the front of the podium and launched into a speech. His gestures were broad, and although Larsen could not understand the words, he felt the stirring force of the oration. Gradually, the people around him growled, cheered, waved fists in approbation, in anger—whatever emotion the orator wished to arouse in them. Subtly, the speaker seemed to grow taller with the passion of his speech, until he towered like a colossus above the crowd. People leapt to their feet, shouting and screaming. Helplessly, Larsen did the same, cheering along with the rest. In mid-cheer, he found himself in Shevket's study, with both men looking at him. Their expressions were sober, not mocking.

Pale and shaken, Larsen sat back into his chair. "My god!" He took out a handkerchief and mopped his sweaty face. "What is this thing?"

"It's the future," said Shevket.

"To be more precise," Norwich added, "it is a quantum leap in communication. This is to previous holography what holography was to television. Everyone who sees such a program will perceive himself in that seat near the front and below the orator, the most effective position. You saw your reaction to a stranger speaking a language you don't understand on a subject of which you are ignorant. Imagine a person and a speech more relevant."

"But," Larsen all but stammered, "how did I feel the breeze? And the smells!"

Norwich shook his head. "Imaginary. The aural and visual images were so realistic that your mind supplied the rest. I think that, at last, we have finally surpassed Chih'-Chin Fu's mastery of the medium."

"That old wizard!" Shevket spat. "Do you suppose he could use something like this out there to whip up the population?"

"Most unlikely," Norwich said. "In the first place, the settlers in space are not accustomed to large numbers. They have entirely lost the instinct for mob behavior. Secondly, they're just too damned busy. The electronic media have become the lazy man's substitute for real life. There are damned few lazy people out there, General."

"What's to keep Carstairs from using this?" Larsen asked. "The mind boggles at the thought of a fifty-foot-high Anthony Carstairs whipping up the planet to skin us alive."

"Carstairs," Norwich told him, "is a most impressive man from close range. He has little presence before an audience. That is why he has always worked in the background, using a succession of public cat's-paws. Besides, my company has entered into a contract with the general and the Victory Party. For the next five years, the party has exclusive rights."

"A fat lot of good that will do if Carstairs decides to break the contract," Larsen said. "He can invoke planetary security, you know."

Shevket said coldly, "Let me take care of Carstairs."

After Norwich had left, Larsen refreshed his drink and turned to the general, who was gazing out a window over his estate. "That was most impressive," said the Dane. "Perhaps the most impressive thing I've ever experienced, but I still have some questions."

"Ask them," said Shevket.

"Was this really the first pack of hungry young officers you've lured to your castle for purposes of seduction?"

Shevket gave one of his rare, musical laughs. "You mean, are you truly one of the party's inner circle? Did I invite *you* to the founding assembly? The answer is yes. Of course, there will be more. I will need many more military officers under my sway, and others in government, both local and global. But this is a start. From now on, these meetings will be all but continuous. But you, my friend, will be my right hand in this new order."

"In what position?" Larsen asked calmly.

"Chancellor. I shall be generalissimo. In the first years of the world-state, I expect to be fully occupied with war. Too many leaders of the past have come to grief trying to juggle military and political functions at the same time. As chancellor, you shall have supreme political power. You shall also have all those state and ceremonial functions that you enjoy and I find so tedious. I shall control the military, the intelligence, and the police. How does that strike you?"

It was a dizzying concept, but Larsen knew better than to show it. "It leaves you with the whip hand."

Shevket raised a hand, from which his horsewhip dangled. "As you can see, that is my right. What is your answer?"

"I accept."

"Splendid! Let's drink on it!" He poured them full glasses, the glasses clinked, and they drank.

Larsen lowered his glass. "Tell me something. Why Favre?"

Shevket grinned. "Doesn't look like a man of heroic action, does he?"

"No, but then, that's a pose. What astonishes me is that you want a poet in your organization at all."

"Ah, but he shall bring us the intelligentsia." Shevket went to a window and sat on its low bench.

"One would think the intelligentsia would be the last group to flock to our banner. I would anticipate their unremitting hostility."

Shevket waved a hand, causing the whip-thongs to sway. "They are sheep. Cesar's poems and recitals will extol the heroic spirit of the new man. Among the intelligentsia I shall be more than politically important. I shall be fashionable. Power is a subtle thing, Aage. Would it surprise you to know that, besides military and government people, I intend to cultivate fashion designers?"

"Nothing you do could surprise me at this point. Haute couture also has a place in the new order?"

"In its founding. People wear what they are told to by the fashion industry. I think that, should next season's designs feature a distinctly military look, a wholesome effect would result."

"This is most ingenious. Perhaps I've spent too much of my time in the corridors of power, among the movers and shakers. It seems that I've paid insufficient attention to the arts and to popular culture."

"I wish I could say that this is all of my devising, but I arrived at my plans by studying history. It was the poets and artists of the Italian Futurist movement that paved the way for the rise of the *fascisti*. Poets, artists, composers—they are romantic souls; they flock around a striking, dominant figure. Napoleon was surrounded by them."

"Some will protest," Larsen said. "They will lead demonstrations, marches, things like that."

"Very few. Mostly the young and untalented. The intelligentsia are great champions of liberty when it is fashionable and safe. I shall let it be known that it is most unsafe to defy me." He snapped the whip against his boot. "That is another symptom of our decadence. We have given these trivial people an importance they do not deserve. At one time, actors and other entertainers were not allowed to enter a respectable house through the front door. The proper employment of those persons is to flatter their betters. We shall reestablish that sensible state of affairs.

"As for the others, the literary types, the professors of the institutes of higher learning and such, they shall all fall into line. They fear force, and they all survive on government handouts. By proper manipulation of those two factors, we will bring them to heel."

"Obviously, this isn't something you just dreamt up. How long have you been planning this?"

"Since my days at military school. When I saw the mediocrity and incompetence not only of my contemporaries but of my superiors, I knew that the time was coming when a superior man could seize power by a bold stroke. I made it my business to learn not just the military arts but others as well: history, psychology—"

"Psychology? You must have attracted attention requesting such courses at a military academy."

"I didn't bother with the formal courses. Despite all the great heap of nonsensical drivel written and spoken about the human mind, the fact is that psychology is pitifully simple. Men respond reliably to certain basic stimuli. I know how to apply those stimuli. All the rest is tripe written to make a name for some drudge with a Ph.D."

"You haven't spoken of the industrialists yet. Earth First damaged them, but they are still there and they are still rich and powerful."

"What businessman doesn't love the prospect of a war? I shall have them eating out of my hand. I'll promise them prosperity, fat government contracts and booty from the conquered enemy. The economy has been a shambles for decades, so they know I can only improve things."

"But you can't trust them."

Shevket turned and glared at him. "Do you take me

for a simpleton? Of course I won't trust them. They are merchants. They make deals, they sell things. Given a good offer, they would sell us, too. These merchants have gained prestige because of their wealth. Once they were despised, beneath a warrior's notice. Soon it will be time to remind them of that."

"I can't fault your logic or your planning," Larsen said, "but your timing seems odd. This is all very precipitate. Why have you chosen to move at this time, and move so swiftly?"

For the first time, Shevket showed a tiny crack in his façade of confidence. "It's the damned alien artifact. After all my planning, to have such a wild card dealt me! When I get my hands on it, I must be in a position to make the best use of it. I had intended to begin making my moves a year from now, after dealing with Carstairs. As it is, I must strike now, and strike fast."

He stood and placed his visored cap carefully on his leonine blond head. "Well, perhaps it's just as well. Fortune favors the bold, and there will be more satisfaction in a world won by storm than in power gained by tedious plotting.

"Come along now, let's go hunting. I'll show you how to lance a boar from horseback."

"You must resign yourself to my absence. I prefer to let others take care of killing the meat. As I said, I find horses dangerous and unsanitary. I prefer more conventional transportation."

"Until dinner, then," Shevket said, again with his superior smile.

"Good hunting, General."

As Shevket walked out, he muttered, "But what *is* that damned thing?"

TEN

"Hey, look at this," Derek was in Fu's ship, *Johann Gutenberg*. Its interior somewhat resembled a genie's palace. The furnishings were fabulous, but few of them were real. Fu's holographic wizardy had led him into some bizarre practices, not least of which was altering the appearance of nearly everything in his ship. Air filters looked like gothic gargoyles, an EVA suit was disguised as a Chinese temple guardian statue, a food synthesizer masqueraded as a Ming vase. A visitor had to touch almost everything to find out what it really was. Some of the furnishings did not exist at all.

"What is it?" Valentina asked. She was by now accepted grudgingly by Ulric and wholeheartedly by Derek, although had she been ugly he might have had his doubts.

"It's a holorally for the Victory party. They're moving fast down there. Fu's people on Luna picked this up and relayed it to us. Isn't it unbelievable? How can people be swayed by something as crude as this?"

She drifted over to him and settled cross-legged in a low-grav seat on the carpeted floor, which was rigged to look like a giant tiger skin. The holograph wall showed a crowd hailing Shevket as he harangued them in his native Turkish. A code in the corner of the projection identified the locale as a stadium in Istanbul.

149

"Earth is a crowded place," she said. "Wide open and crowded at the same time. It makes people's reactions different. People out here have little feel for mob mentality. Down there, they're used to getting feedback from the people closest to them."

"It's more than that," said Chih'-Chin Fu, emerging through a holographic waterfall that screened his sleeping quarters. For some reason he had eschewed his customary Confucian scholar's robes and wore tweeds and puttees. He looked like an English country gentleman, except for his long white hair and beard and his three-inch fingernails. "It's a new technology, something that puts the viewer in the middle of the action with unbelievable fidelity and realism. It's a quantum leap beyond anything I've ever done. Several of my students have described it to me. They've gotten hold of a projection unit and it's being sent on, but it will be some weeks before it gets here from Luna." Derek had never seen the old man so agitated.

"It's probably just an area you never addressed," Derek said, diplomatically. "There was never any call for that sort of effect off-Earth."

"It still bothers me. I must be getting old, to let an entirely new technology be developed under my nose."

"Who do you think might be responsible?" Valentina said.

"Straight to the point as always, my dear. It wasn't any one person. These days, even I can't come up with any genuinely new devices on my own. Oh, I can come up with the concepts, but I have to assemble a team to develop the hardware. Let's see. Something this sophisticated, it would have to be Hololabs, S.A., or maybe Cheshire Labs. More like Cheshire." He stroked his wispy beard and cogitated. "I had a student once, who went to work for Cheshire. What was his name? Sandwich? Dunwich? No, oh, hell, what was it?"

"Norwich?" Valentina asked. "The ad man?"

"That's it!" Fu snapped his fingers, one of the few Earthie gestures he still retained. "Julian Norwich! Cold-blooded little bastard. Learned everything I taught him

faster than any other student I had, but I couldn't stand
him."

"Why?" Derek asked.

"Because of his concept of the medium." Fu always
talked about holography the way others talked about
their religions. "He had no interest in how to use it to
inform, to educate, to stimulate original thought. He
only wanted to use it to manipulate. No wonder he
ended up in advertising. He has the mind of—well, of a
low-grade genius when it comes to using the medium.
But he has the soul of a mouse. I'd be willing to bet
he's the one behind this perversion. He has the technical know-how to accomplish it and he's just the type
who'd suck up to the likes of Mehmet Shevket. If he's
high up in Cheshire Labs, and I imagine he is by this
time, he could have come up with this thing. It'd be his
dream come true. Damn!"

"Why are you so incensed?" Derek asked. "I'd think
the political implications here are a good deal more
alarming than the technological ones."

"Oh, I agree," Fu said. "It's just that this is the first
really revolutionary advance in holography in years,
and it's potentially the greatest teaching tool ever invented, and what's it being used for? To whip up mind-
less enthusiasm for a tin-pot dictator! Makes me want to
puke."

"How would you use it as a teaching device?" Valentina
asked.

He smiled at her beatifically. "I wish I'd had more
students like you." He turned to Derek furiously. "This
woman knows how to ask the right questions. Why don't
you?" He went on in a normal tone. "As nearly as I can
figure it, this thing works by a coherent light reflection
system of real complexity coupled with an advanced
sound system. It may be nothing genuinely new, just
immensely refined. If so, that means it's fairly compact
and automatable, like all modern systems. Derek, I
know you want to go into planetary exploration when
we have interstellar flight. Suppose, before you were to
set down on a planet, you sent in some probes using

this technique? You could get a real feel for the planet, some orientation to overcome the initial confusion, before having to commit your poor mortal body to the dangers of the real environment."

"Damn!" Derek said. "That would take a lot of the tension out of it."

"And I can guarantee you," Fu said, "that Norwich and his cohorts never let such a thought cross their minds. A million possibilities in this thing and they just want to use it to sell toilet paper or dictators or some other product."

A small dragon came flying through the room. Fu snatched it out of the air and began stroking it down the row of razor-edged spines that crested its back. It was his cat, equipped with a tiny holo unit that supplied the illusion, complete with scales, wings and fiery breath. It purred, emitting sparks and smoke.

Roseberry arrived, trailing a string of beer bulbs. "Well, that's the last of 'em off the place and good riddance." He referred to a load of schoolchildren he had just conducted through a tour of Ciano's lab. "It's all the same. The young don't have any appreciation of their heritage." He glared furiously and drew on a beer. Then a thought seemed to strike him. "Oh, by the way, Linde's come out of her lab. Looks like hell, but she has that look in her eye, the one she had when she whupped the antimatter problem back thirty years ago."

"Maybe now we'll find out what the egg is," Fu said. "Have they made any progress on Aeaea?"

"According to the latest reports, they haven't learned much. You know those people, though. They get as excited over their failures as other people do when they've accomplished something."

"You know what old Ugo used to say about them kind of people?" Roseberry asked.

"Yes," said Fu, "we know. Actually, it makes sense. Even a negative result is a result, and it tells you something you didn't know before."

"We got some other news from Aeaea," Valentina

said. "A man who was probably Vladyka was there for a few days, masquerading as a lab assistant. He got away from them without much difficulty."

"Bunch of bunglers," Derek muttered.

"Don't be too hard on them," she advised. "He's a pro. They're amateurs. Their security system is designed to detect industrial spies out to plunder their research before their patents can be established. Vladyka plays a more serious game. He won't hesitate to kill if it will facilitate his job, or to use torture to get answers. I want to go over their reports in some detail. Aeaean security questioned a number of people who had contact with Vladyka, if that's who it was. I can probably pick up something they missed."

"What has Ulric learned about that Russian who tried to capture you?" Fu asked Derek.

"Not much. He turned him over to Avalonian security, and they wanted to be all civilized about the interrogation. He wouldn't talk for weeks, and when he did, all he said was he'd been out here for years when he got the order to capture the ellipsoid. Like Valentina, he figured that I'd found more than one."

"So the *Althing* now knows that we have one of the Rhea Objects."

"Avalonian security and the Security Committee have agreed to keep it secret for now," Derek said. "But they want results soon. The important thing the interrogation turned up was that his orders came from the Russian government. He's not working for any U.N. office, nor for Carstairs, nor for Larsen and Shevket."

Fu stroked his beard. "How peculiar. The Russians, of all people." The once mightly Soviet Union had long since fragmented into a dozen or more minor nations, its gargantuan socio-economic theories and practices thoroughly discredited. Its failure to overcome the capitalist West by the end of the twentieth century, its failure to deal with domestic problems, and the inefficiency of its attempts to export revolutions to the Third World nations caused its prestige to shrink as, one by one, the satellite nations, then the subject states, broke away from the alliance. The Islamic south merged with the populous Middle East and Persian Gulf bloc; the eastern European nations allied with the West or formed blocs of their own as political expediency dictated. The more utopian visions of the early Marxists were co-opted by the U.N., and later, by the Earth First Party.

"Ah, well," Fu said, "I suppose all once-great powers long for a return to center stage. The Americans have been moping about it for decades. Perhaps the Russians think the Rhea Objects could recoup their fortunes for them."

"They could well do just that." They turned at the voice and saw Sieglinde coming through the dragon's mouth that was actually a doorway. She looked terribly tired. "I've finally cracked what they are. If anyone else could do the same, it's important enough to restore any nation to the limelight. Or put whoever has it into a position to dictate whatever he pleases." There were dark rings beneath her eyes, and she looked years older than when she had undertaken the project.

"Aunt Sieglinde," Derek said, "you look terrible. Have a drink, relax, and then tell us all about it."

She nodded wordlessly, too tired even to acknowledge him by speech. In such low gravity, fatigue did not cause people to slump, but the signs were unmistakable anyway. Roseberry handed her one of her customary concoctions of Steinhäger and lime. It seemed to revive her a little as she floated to a sitting position on the floor.

"Okay," she said at last. "First the general, then we'll get to specifics. Number one, it's a power source for a starship, probably discarded like a used up battery."

"Hot damn!" Derek exulted. "That means I just won five hundred from François. He was betting it was a weapon."

She looked at him wearily. "Nephew, your grasp of cosmic matters is truly astounding."

He looked abashed. "Sorry."

"To continue: I strongly suspect that these were power packs for small vessels, perhaps explorer craft. Most importantly, I believe I can duplicate them. With this technology, we can store and drain power such as we've only dreamed of. We can get the hell out of this system and visit many more within our own lifetimes."

"Fabulous!" Derek crowed.

Valentina was a good deal cooler. "That has been the aim of a great many scientists since the beginning of space flight. None of them have accomplished much. There are a good many who maintain that superluminal travel is an impossibility."

Sieglinde regained enough energy to shoot her a glare. "The same ones say superluminal communication is just as impossible. You've seen it demonstrated."

"And a wonderful accomplishment it is," said Fu. "Now, if you feel up to it, could you tell us what you have discovered about this amazing object? And bear in mind that we are not all accomplished physicists— certainly not of your caliber."

She smiled ruefully and sipped at her concoction. "Right. Thanks for reminding me. Here goes. The ellipsoid contains highly condensed matter that was originally a billion times denser. The envelope containing the matter is in effect a frozen form of the n-dimensional Ciano field that I've used for containing antimatter."

"Frozen?" Derek said. "How can you freeze—"

"Just bear with me," Sieglinde said. "We'll get into specifics later. I'll warn you that you'll need a good many more years of study to appreciate the details."

"We'll do our best," Derek said.

"There's nothing new about the Ciano field, of course. It's used in every antimatter drive these days. Nobody except me knows exactly how it's constructed, because of the tamper-proof seal placed *within* the finished product. The Aeaeans first produced antimatter engines commercially, and part of their fee was the use of my seal. They use it on their own products now.

"For some time now, I've been working on superluminal communication and superluminal transmission of matter through indeterminate n-dimensional space. Of late, some physicists have taken to calling it the Ciano-Kornfeld hyperspace."

"Often in tones of ironical skepticism," Fu added.

"What do they know? I'm right and they're wrong and I can prove it. You've already seen that I've been successful with superluminal communication, although it currently works only for a distance of several light hours. However, I've only been able to transmit matter through hyperspace within a Ciano field generator."

She sipped the last of her drink and Roseberry tossed her another bulb. "That's what I did with the ellipsoid. I placed it in a Ciano field generator—probably the largest in the solar system—and transmitted the matter in the core to a special container outside the ellipsoid but within the Ciano field. The dense matter was then at my disposal. The matter was in electron degeneracy; matter that dense had to be."

"I can't believe this!" Derek enthused. "The Aeaeans haven't been able to do anything with theirs in all this time with half the physicists in the solar system on the project."

She looked at him levelly. "That was the easy part. I got that done within twenty-four hours after you handed it to me. It only took a few more days to duplicate the ellipsoid."

"Duplicate it?" Derek asked.

"Shall I explain this or would you rather do it yourself?"

"Sorry," Derek said. "Go on."

"I had a pretty good idea that the core matter was much denser to begin with. Matter so dense could only come from one place—the collapsing core of a supermassive star or the core of a supernova. Depending on the mass of the collapsing core, it either becomes a neutron star or a black hole."

She took another pull at her drink and appeared to be on the edge of collapse.

"Linde," Fu said, "I think you are in need of anti-fatigue medication."

"That's right. The oldest kind. I need about twenty hours of uninterrupted sleep. First, I want to clue you all in on what I've found. I don't want to confuse my brain with any drugs, so if my delivery sounds a little jagged, just be patient. Let's see, where was I? Oh, yes, black holes.

"Contrary to the early theories back in the last century, a black hole doesn't collapse into a mathematical singularity point as some of the early theorists speculated. Instead, it attains the physical state called omega phase. The matter in omega state is much denser than the nuclear-degenerate matter in neutron stars. The fabric of conventional four-dimensional space, which naturally includes the time axis, is stretched to its breaking point at the center of a black hole but the compressed matter has nowhere else to go." She looked at them in turn. "Are you still with me?"

"So far," Derek agreed. Fu nodded. Valentina shrugged. Roseberry smiled at her proudly.

"Now, here comes the important part. What's gone before is theory. This is application—technology, if you will. If you provide an escape hatch through hyperspace, you can draw that virtually unlimited energy to a conjugate point in four-dimensional space. So, originally, the core of the ellipsoid was filled with matter in omega phase drawn from a black hole. The ellipsoid in my possession must have massed several billion tons when fully charged."

"I'm afraid," Valentina said, "that covert activity is my speciality, not physics. Somebody is going to have to translate this for me."

"I think Aunt Sieglinde is talking about as untechnically as she can already," Derek said. "Let me see if I can bridge the gap." At last, a chance to impress her! "Let's try an analogy. Imagine a two-dimensional world made up of a large plastic sheet. At point A is a black hole. At point B is Aunt Sieglinde's lab. The distance between the two may be several thousand light-years."

"A moment, Derek," Fu said. He took a handset from somewhere within his costume and his fingers did their magic. One end of the room turned into a holograph of the plastic sheet standing in for the universe. On it were point A and point B and it was covered with a crosshatching of fine lines. "The grid is for contour clarity," Fu explained. "Now, Derek, continue."

"Now, let's fold it over so that point A is just above point B." The hologram followed his instructions. "If you can go from point A to point B through three-dimensional space, the separation is virtually zero. Similarly, it's theoretically conceivable to take a shortcut in our four-dimensional space by going through hyperspace, but nobody's managed it yet because our technology's too primitive. The faster-than-light communication Aunt Linde's demonstrated is the first example of superluminal technology in history."

Valentina was a bit bemused at his use of the word "primitive." For many years, savants on Earth had been claiming that the pinnacle of technological civilization had already been achieved. But then, she thought, to people as forward-looking as these, the technology of the present would *always* seem primitive.

"Now, let's pour some heavy fluid into point A," said Derek, continuing his analogy. In the holo, the plastic bulged downward, the gridline defining a rounded cone. "The fluid is so heavy that the plastic sheet is near its breaking point. If it breaks through, it'll burst through three-dimensional space to get to any other point on the sheet that's been folded under it. So, you prick the plastic sheet with a pin and let the fluid go through the third dimension. Likewise, the highly compressed matter in a black hole can be brought to the laboratory here through hyperspace. How's that sound, Aunt Sieglinde? Aunt Sieglinde?"

Her nodding head jerked up. "Oh. Yes, a very good analogy. Incredibly crude, but it gets the idea across."

"Thank you, Derek," Valentina said. "I think I'm beginning to understand what this is all about." It would do no harm to flatter his ego. She turned to Sieglinde. "Does this mean that you're ready to test your hypothesis in your laboratory?" Derek and Fu winced slightly, knowing Sieglinde wouldn't announce a mere hypothesis. Apparently, she was too tired to be offended because she answered affably enough.

"It's not a hypothesis. I've already carried out an experiment on an uninhabited asteroid. Just for insurance, I picked one that was beyond Saturn's orbit at the time. I chose the black hole in Cygnus X-1 as the source. It took a while to locate it exactly in hyperspace as its astronomical distance isn't known with sufficient accuracy for my purposes. I created its conjugate point on the asteroid for less than a trillionth of a nanosecond. The test was done remotely, of course. The experiment was a success. The asteroid was obliterated. From the amount of energy that was released, I can now calibrate the time interval appropriate for safely transferring energy from a black hole. An appropriate time interval must be measured in the unit expressed in terms of Heisenberg's uncertainty constant."

"Uh, Aunt Sieglinde," Derek said, "I was under the impression that you've been back there in your lab all this time, not traipsing around all over the outer Belt. Never mind, I should've remembered nobody ever has any idea where you are."

"Invisibility is a great quality to possess," she agreed. "What all this means is unlimited energy for powering interstellar ships. With the aid of the time dilation effect as the vessel reaches relativistic velocity, a ship can reach her destination a hundred light-years away within a generation."

"When do we start?" Derek asked. "I'm ready."

"Not so fast," Sieglinde cautioned. "I still need to develop an effective shield to protect the ships from collision with interstellar particles. At a fraction of the speed of light, a pebble massing no more than a gram would pack the energy of a kiloton of TNT. It's a minor problem. I'll be testing a solution soon."

Derek turned to Valentina and Fu. "Who else would call that a minor problem? Aunt Linde—" But she had sagged sideways and was snoring gently.

ELEVEN

Carstairs read the reports on the latest U.N. council meetings, the figures on Victory party recruiting, the accounts by his spies of Victory party rallies worldwide. He was more than alarmed. For the first time in many years, he felt he was no longer in control of the situation. Everywhere he looked he saw Shevket and Larsen gaining strength. The nations that still retained some of their old wealth and power, once staunch supporters of Earth First, were flocking to Victory.

"Mansfield, come in here." He leaned back in his chair, elbow on armrest, chin in hand.

Mansfield was unsettled when he saw Carstairs looking so bemused. The man had always been dynamic and decisive. "Sir, I have the new reports on—"

"I just went over them," Carstairs said. "Sit down. We have some heavy planning to do, Greg. We're in serious trouble."

Gregory Mansfield had been executive secretary of Earth First party for twenty years. He knew his boss's moods and attitudes and what he saw frightened him. "Surely it's not all that bad, sir. We still have the support of a majority of the membership of the U.N." Carstairs glared at him and Mansfield knew there was a bout of the famous Carstairs sarcasm coming.

"Oh, splendid, Greg! Bloody comforting, isn't it? Nothing like having Lesotho and Brunei and Costa Rica on your side to shore up the old confidence, eh? Christ almighty, Greg, if El Salvador goes over to Shevket, we're doomed!"

Mansfield was silent for a few seconds, giving Carstairs a space to regain his equanimity. Then, "All right, Tony, you have a fight on your hands. Well, you had a fight on your hands thirty-five years ago and you whipped everyone who stood in your way. You built Earth First from a lunatic-fringe debating society to the most powerful political force the world has ever seen. Don't sell yourself short."

Carstairs smiled crookedly. "Oh, aye, but I was thirty-five years younger then. As I recall it, I was no spring chicken in those days, either. This barmy bastard Shevket's building a power base all over the world faster than I would've believed possible."

Mansfield made a contemptuous gesture. "Mob demonstrations, mass hysteria—what has that to do with real power?"

"On a world scale, nothing," Carstairs said. "On a national scale, it can mean everything. Talk to any of the various presidents and premiers and chancellors around the world. What do you think concerns them more, a tame Secretary General owned by Earth First, or a rampaging mob burning down their capital city? Our world state is still a fragile coalition of petty powers, Greg. We need two or three more centuries to create the real thing."

"But we have the U.N. forces," Mansfield protested. "They can call on our battalions to put down local insurgencies."

"Check the officer lists, Greg," Carstairs advised. "You'll note that the old ones, the ones who owe their promotions to us, have been retiring by the shipload the last couple of years. Those are rats with a nose for a sinking ship. Shevket's been suborning the younger officers, moving them into positions of authority. He has too many of them in his pocket now. And it's not just the armed forces. The bureaucracy is the same way. I suspect Larsen there. Oh, they're all good Earth First people on paper still, their dues paid up, but too many of 'em have been attending Victory meetings lately." He leaned back and sighed, an uncharacteristic sound of resignation coming from Carstairs.

"It's an old pattern, Greg, and I should've seen it coming years ago. Hell, it's not all that different from what we were doing when we got the Party going all those years ago. But we had ideals back then. We were going to save the world from itself. Well, in spite of what the Confederates claim, I will say we did.

"But Shevket and his toadies in the Victory party? All they want is pure power, for the joy of grinding their boots into the face of humanity." He shook himself as if getting rid of an evil dream. "Must be getting old. I'm being right gloomy these days. Here, Greg, have a drink." The robot bar, seldom used since Carstairs kept his own liquor in his desk, rolled in.

Mansfield made a selection and faced his boss. "So things are serious. What's our next move?"

"If I were you," Carstairs said, sipping from a bottle of Newcastle Brown, "I'd look into the prospects of an extended vacation offworld. I hear Mars is rather pleasant these days, what with terraforming so advanced. With a bit of cleverness, you could transfer enough assets to see you out in style. I'd give the same advice to our other loyal people, though God knows it'd be hard to figure out which those are."

Mansfield stared at Carstairs bleakly. He was a thin, gray man, older than his years despite longevity treatment. His condition was largely attributable to overwork, and most of that had been heaped on his shoulders by the man across from him. "I'll pretend I didn't hear that. You've been pretty rough with all of us, Tony, but never insulting. I threw my lot in with this planet long ago; I won't run like a whipped dog now."

Carstairs grinned, his old style showing through at last. "Good for you, Greg. That's what I thought you'd say. Still, I had to make the offer. And pass it along. I wouldn't ask any of our people to face what's coming for this planet."

Mansfield nodded minutely. "I'll do it. I think most will stay, though. It's a bit hard to overcome the effects of your own propaganda all at once."

"It's their choice." He waved to the pile of reports and the holograph projector. "I've been in power politics a long time. This shows all the signs of a win for Shevket." He held out a hand, forestalling protest from Mansfield. "I'm not saying it's certain, but from here on I'm going on the assumption that I won't beat the bastard in the U.N. or in the member states. He'll naturally think, since he has the military in his pocket, that it's all over, being as how brute force is all that counts when the gloves are off."

"From the sound of it," Mansfield said, "he'd be right."

"He thinks in simple terms, and the situation isn't all that simple. That bugger has a good many weaknesses, although he'd never recognize them, and I intend to exploit every last one of them. To begin with, though, we'll fight a long delaying action, make him take as long as possible to make his move."

"It seems to me," Mansfield said, "that we might be weaker at a later time. The time to strike is now, while we have a remnant of our strength left to us."

Carstairs shook his head. "No, it's too late for that. If I hadn't been so damned complacent about our power for all these years I'd've had both those snakes crushed long ago. But I let myself think I could always dominate them, that they were useful to me, that there'd always be time to deal with 'em later. Well, that kind of thinking's been the downfall of better men than Tony Carstairs. The stall, though, has another purpose. The fewer that know about it, the better. Does that bother you?"

Mansfield raised his eyebrows. "When did you ever need my consent to keep your own counsel? If your reasons are good enough for you, they're sufficient for me."

"Good. Now, there's something else about what's coming that's not going to be pretty. You're going to see me caving in to that Turkish pig and his Danish basset hound."

"That I find hard to believe."

"Oh, ask anybody who ever saw me in a knuckle bout back on the docks in Liverpool. I always let the other bastard think he'd won before I let him have it in the balls."

Mansfield allowed himself to smile. "That's the kind of talk I like to hear."

"Run along, Greg. I have some appointments to put into effect. And Greg—"

"Yes, sir?"

"If you or any of the others should be arrested, just say whatever they want to hear. I'll get you out one way or another. Shevket's not seen all my tricks yet, by a wide margin."

Mansfield nodded. "Right, sir."

When he was gone, Carstairs punched a combination into his holo communicator. A young man in space service uniform appeared, his face stricken with awe at the apparition in his own set. "Yes, your Excellency?"

"Son, tell the admiral that Anthony Carstairs requests a conference with him."

"Right away, sir!"

A few minutes later, a magnificently uniformed man appeared in holo projection before him. He had a dark, pleasant face marred somewhat by rows of tribal scars on his cheeks. "Admiral Augustus Mboya reporting. How may I be of service to your excellency?"

"Evening, Gus. Hope I didn't wake you. I have no idea what shift you're on up there."

"In ships we call them watches, not shifts, sir. But I was just engaged in a boring after-dinner conversation with my officers, and any diversion is welcome."

"Good. How goes the work on the new flagship?"

"On schedule, for the first time in my career. She should be ready to leave orbit in eight months."

"Excellent. Please have a complete set of plans sent

to me." He caught the admiral's look of astonishment. "Oh, I know I've never been famed for my enthusiasm for ships, but I take a personal interest in *Defender*. After all, five years ago it was me that—"

"Ah, excuse me, your Excellency, but hadn't you heard? She's no longer to be named *Defender*."

Carstairs' look sharpened. "No, I didn't know. What's she to be called?"

"*Conqueror*. The order came down just days ago. It's the most amazing directive, sir. It came from the Department of Defense, though. It renames almost all the ships in the Space Force. Not so bad with this one, of course, since she hasn't been officially launched yet. But ship people have an ancient superstition about changing the name of a ship." The admiral sounded agitated, and Carstairs wasn't certain whether it was about the order or because Carstairs hadn't known of it.

"What are the new names?" he asked.

"There are a great many of them. But the capital ships are getting names like *Genghis Khan, Cortez, Bonaparte, Thutmose the Fourth, Tchaka, Charlemagne, Attila, Julius Caesar*. It's quite a long list, sir. And rather disturbing to the crews of *Antares* and *Resolute* and *Dreadnought* and all the rest."

"I can imagine. Well, Gus, we'll look into it. Can't have our ships renamed for all the bloody-minded heathens of antiquity, can we now? Just send me those plans. And if you need anything, let me know. I'll cut through the red tape and see you get it."

"Thank you, sir," said Mboya, beaming.

Carstairs cut transmission and sat back, running a palm over the quarter-inch of gray stubble that covered his scalp. Everywhere he looked, things were far worse than he had thought. He refused to look about him for a scapegoat. He had nobody but himself to blame. He had grievously underestimated Shevket, allowed himself to think that the man's swaggering and his theatrical uniforms were evidence of a self-deluding poseur. Well, he thought, that's not a mistake I'll make again. Now it's war till we're down to knives and teeth. With his decision made, he had no further hesitation. It felt good to be back in action again, after all these years. He activated the code signal that would put him in touch with Sieglinde Kornfeld.

TWELVE

"The place has changed," Derek said. They had just arrived in Avalon for the big conference Sieglinde had called. HMK was crowded and bustling as usual.

"It looks the same to me," Valentina said.

"You weren't raised here. I can feel it. There's tension, apprehension, things like that. I can predict that there'll be a lot of talk in the bars, but it'll be quieter than usual."

"Why should anything have changed?" she asked. "The big announcement hasn't been made yet."

"Partly it's the new atmosphere on Earth, all the war talk. Plenty of people here remember the last one. Also, everybody knows Aunt Linde's here, and she's called an extraordinary session of the *Althing*. She's one of the few people empowered to do that, and it's been twenty-five years since she last exercised that right. And then there's the Rhea Object, and everybody knows it's all tied together somehow. Space people have a way of sensing things like that."

"When is the session scheduled?" Valentina asked. She leaned over a spindly railing and studied the milling activity below. Whatever anxiety these people were experiencing, it certainly wasn't affecting business. All the usual activities were going full blast.

169

"Tomorrow. But the family meeting is in six hours. We're to be there."

"When did I join the clan? I don't think even my talents would fool them for long if I tried posing as a Kuroda or a Taggart."

"You could try being a Ciano," he said. "Some of them are truly strange. Actually, you're going to be there because Aunt Linde says so. There'll be others there whose connection to the families is tenuous." He joined her at the railing and looked below. "I hope we stay here a while. I can't wait to see what it's like after Aunt Linde drops her bomb."

Valentina studied him. In the short time she had known Derek, he had grown more mature and serious, but he still had his boyish enthusiasms. "You love this place, don't you?"

He looked at her in astonishment. "Of course I do. I was born here. This is the greatest environment people have ever had. It gets a little rough sometimes, but we're free to do what we want."

"Cooped up in tiny, fragile ships or carving barren rocks into something marginally livable? I suppose it's freedom of a sort. But if you love it so, why are you so anxious to leave? All you've talked about for months is making the big jump."

He thought about it for a while. "Let's go to the museum."

That took her by surprise. "I didn't know there was one."

"Just follow me. And I'm not dodging your question. I think I can explain better there."

They took a tube car to the outermost level of Avalon, where the spin-induced gravity was strongest. The museum was a single, immensely long room. One wall was a continuous window open to the stars. Its door was unpretentious, a simple portal cut in the rough stone. Above the entrance, a holographic sign flashed the words *Museum of Man in Space*, in a multitude of languages, changing every few seconds.

Immediately within, a gold ball floated at eye level,

four whiplike antennae sweeping from it like a comet's tail. "Sputnik One," Derek said. "This is what it all started with. One little ball of metal and circuitry tossed out into orbit. Within just a few years, all this." He waved an arm at holos of the early vessels, most of them looking suicidally crude and fragile. There were holos of the pioneers and racks of spacesuits standing like sentinels along one wall.

"This is how we pushed out." He pointed to a huge floating display of the solar system with glimmering lights denoting the voyages and settlements and the chronology of their development. "Luna, the orbitals, Mars, the first Belt settlement, the Jovian satellites, the Saturnian satellites—always out, toward the edge of the solar system. And there," he pointed to dozens of glimmering lights headed outside the system entirely, "the Island Worlds already headed out under antimatter drive. And the Oort Cloud expedition, on its way now. Always outward. It's in the blood. We have to head out, find new places to live and work and explore."

"Not everybody wants that," Valentina said. "Not even a majority. There are a good many Island Worlders who will be content to stay here."

"There are always a few with the urge, though. Most people prefer to stay where they think it's safe; some only emigrate out of true desperation. But there are always some of us who have to see what's out there. It's always been that way. Otherwise, we'd all still be crowded in some little valley in Africa." He took her hand. "Come here, this is what I really wanted you to see." He led her past the last of the exhibits. Beyond was a huge, echoing space. The long window continued along the outer wall until it disappeared in the distance where the room followed the curvature of the worldlet's surface. The empty space was far larger than the part crowded with exhibits.

"It's empty," she said, puzzled. "Why do you want me to see this?" She wondered whether he was playing some joke on her.

"This is for the rest of it. The future. This is the

important part. We'll fill up every bit of it and then they'll have to excavate an extension."

For a moment she was too stunned to say anything. She had always thought the people here were the same as the ones she had left behind on Earth. They might have different customs and habits, but she had thought them to be motivated by the same things, mainly greed and fear and a desire to dominate their fellow humans.

"It's so different," she said. "Back home, everyone is either languishing for the past or obsessed with the present. The future means taking care of tomorrow's catastrophe. I never really believed that there were people who thought in terms of centuries, people who dedicate their lives to a future they'll never see. What's in it for them?"

"It's the urge," he said, smiling. "When the first of the Island Worlds made the big hop more than thirty years ago, using the antimatter drive, Sieglinde told them that she was working on the superluminal drive, but there were no guarantees. If she lived long enough and solved all the problems, ships with the new drive would catch up with them and fit them with the new engines. But there was a possibility, even a likelihood, that it wouldn't work out that way. There might be an insurmountable obstacle. The drive might never be perfected. They chose to go anyway, even though it would be the descendants of the great-grandchildren of those pioneers who'd reach a new solar system."

"Back home," she began, but he interrupted her.

"You don't have to think of it as 'back home' anymore, Val. Come with us." He still held her hand.

She stared at him, stunned. He looked so dreadfully earnest. She couldn't decide whether he was really heroic or just naive and childish. "Derek, I'm not a free agent. I can't just make decisions about my own future. I work for—"

"Carstairs' days are numbered, Val. He knows it. When he's gone, that planet will be no place for anyone who worked with him so closely, especially against Shevket."

"There's still Luna, Mars, the orbitals. I'm an expert, Derek. He'd never find me."

"It wouldn't be much of a life. When my interstellar ship is ready to go, I'm going to pack *Cyrano* in a hold, stock up on cat food for Carruthers and head out. Come with me."

"Derek," she said patiently, "we've been thrown together by forces neither of us has any control over. Don't mistake this kind of forced intimacy for anything more personal than it is. In the first place, I'm at least ten years older than you."

"Let's see," he mused, "what with the latest advances in medical science, we can both expect to live a century and a half. In that time, more advances can be made. Let's figure, barring misadventure, we might make it to two hundred. By that time, ten years will be one-twentieth of my lifetime. Hardly worth considering."

"Look, Derek, that 'barring misadventure' part is taking a lot for granted. There's still the matter of Vladyka to be addressed, and maybe a war, so let's not make any important decisions until the time comes, all right?"

"Okay," he agreed. "No decisions. That doesn't mean I won't keep trying to convince you, though."

"You're exasperating. But when I tell you to shut up about it, shut up."

"Agreed. Let's go get something to eat." They left the vast space that was empty of anything but promise.

The clan meeting was held in the old Kuroda great hall. The clan was an extended one, including a number of families, and there was no way for all the many hundreds of members to attend, but all families were represented. There were at least fifty present in the reed-matted room. Every physiognomy and form of dress known to the Island Worlds was present. Family unity was practically the only kind they all shared.

Derek and Valentina came in slightly late, earning a glare from Ulric, who sat at the head of the room near Nadia Kuroda, the current matriarch. They took seats well toward the lower end of the room, next to the wall. The room was stark and bare of any decoration save for a rack of ancient Japanese swords.

"Now that everyone seems to be here," Nadia said, "close the door." The heavy portal was shut and sealed with a hiss of pneumatics.

"This meeting," Nadia began, "the thirty-fifth since the clan left the motherworld, has been called by our kinswoman, Sieglinde Kornfeld-Taggart. It is the right of any member of the clan to call such a meeting when decisions must be reached concerning matters of great importance to the clan. At this time, please give Sieglinde your close attention."

Sieglinde sat to Nadia's right, and she launched into her speech without preamble. "We have reached another of the great turning points in the history of mankind. I have made a discovery that makes interstellar travel a practical proposition. At any other time I would develop it in a more leisurely fashion. However, events on Earth will not leave us that luxury. We have to leave the solar system, and we have to do it as soon as possible." There was an eruption of conversation, which Nadia silenced with a peremptory gesture.

"First," Sieglinde said, "I will tell you briefly what I have found. For the benefit of those without a specialized education, I'll stick to layman's terms as much as possible. Afterward, I'll conduct a special session for those among you who are physicists or mathematicians. This all began when our kinsman, Derek Kuroda, found two alien artifacts on Rhea."

"Two!" someone said.

"Yes, two. To continue—" For the next hour, she explained the events that had led from Derek's delivery of the object to the Ciano Lab to her experiments that proved its nature. She outlined the possibilities of the phenomenon, then allowed individual questions.

"Is there any indication of the nature of the aliens who left the things?" asked Salome Taggart, a writer for the popular holos.

"None at all, except that they are or were highly intelligent and they were a starfaring species."

"Any ideas as to the age of the things?" asked the professional Ibrahim Sousa.

"They could have been left there a hundred million years ago or an hour before Derek found them. As far as I can tell, they're quite indestructible to anything occurring naturally in the solar system, so condition means nothing. Of course, it also means that the aliens may still be around here someplace. If so, they're keeping to themselves."

"What makes all this so urgent," she went on, "is that the situation on Earth is deteriorating by the minute. The would-be planetary dictator, Mehmet Shevket, is rousing xenophobic hatred for the outerworlders to a fever pitch down there. He is using a new holo technology that makes his haranguing rhetoric enormously effective. It looks as if he is going to realize his ambition of becoming absolute ruler."

"How are you so certain of this?" Nadia asked.

"I've been in contact with Anthony Carstairs and he—" Instantly, people were on their feet and shouting.

"Oh, quiet down!" Ulric bellowed. "I was with her during some of her communications with Carstairs. He was the enemy during the last war. This time, it's Shevket and Larsen. Listen to what she has to say." Grumbling, the others complied.

"Carstairs tells me that Shevket has all but won. By now, even his assassination wouldn't stop the war. Carstairs will buy us all the time he can, but we must be prepared for war in one year, two at the outside."

Martin Shaw Taggart signaled for recognition and Nadia nodded. Like many of his family, the young man wore the uniform of Sálamis, the military world that formed the defense arm of the Confederacy. "My superiors have predicted an inevitable war within five years, although they've had problems convincing the *Althing* of that. How are you so certain that the time is so short?"

"Several reasons, some mine and some brought up

by Carstairs. Partly, it's the economic deterioration of Earth, which will be temporarily alleviated by a war. Then there's the hysteria factor, which is easy to rouse, but which can't be maintained indefinitely. I think the major factor, though, is the Rhea Object. They sense that it might mean great power once its secret is cracked, which it certainly does. They suspect that we are not telling them everything we've learned about it. They're wrong about the Aeaeans, but right as far as I am concerned. I'm not going to let them know about it until we're well away from here. Shevket wants to strike before we can exploit the thing fully and maybe make ourselves invincible.

"Carstairs says that they will need at least one year to mount an attack, because they can't start until their new ships are commissioned, crewed and tested. But expect it within a year after that. Does that answer your question, Martin?"

"It does, thank you. Good to see you back, Mom."

"I wish we could get together under happier circumstances."

"None of us," said Nadia, "wants to go through another war. The last one was terrible. This one will be worse. The Terrans have been improving their defenses in all the years since. Last time we bombarded them with a propaganda campaign that undermined the civilians' war spirit. This time, it appears that they have the advantage in that area."

"We want to avoid war," Sieglinde said, "and the best way to avoid war is to avoid the vicinity of a war. It is my urgent advice that we contract with the Aeaeans and a few other scientific-industrial firms to manufacture the drive units I am designing, that we fit these to asteroid ships, and that we vacate the system as soon as possible. I shall put this recommendation before the *Althing* tomorrow, but I wanted the clan to have the news first. Whatever the *Althing* decides, whatever the individual republics of the Confederacy decide, I want the clan to go!"

An uproar began that not even Ulric's leather-lunged

orders could silence. After half an hour, Nadia signalled and the outcry finally died down.

"I add my recommendation to Sieglinde's. You must all talk this over with your families, of course, but you must waste no time. Sieglinde will put at your disposal this new superluminal communication device to facilitate your conferences. She assures us that it is totally secure, and knowing Sieglinde, I believe it."

"That is the overwhelmingly important part of what I came here to say," Sieglinde told them. "Now, for those of you who have questions of a more technical nature, I'll answer them as best I can in the blue lounge."

A good third of the assembly flocked to follow her and Derek turned to Valentina. "Come on, let's go find our quarters. The real fun will start tomorrow, at the *Althing*."

She followed him through several labyrinthine corridors until they came to a suite that was much smaller than the Kuroda quarters, and decidedly odder. Valentina looked at the polished copper floor of the main room, the hollow, transparent furniture filled with colored smoke, the long tank full of live reptiles. "I think I recognize the décor. This must be where the Cianos live."

"Right again. The quarters are small, because there have never been very many Cianos, which is probably just as well for humanity. Right now my cousin Antigone is in residence. I saw her at the meeting, but she's a physicist, like most of the Cianos, so she'll probably be badgering Linde for a while."

Cautiously, Valentina lowered herself into a chair that seemed to be made of purple smoke. "Is that really how things get done out here? Family meetings where everybody has a say?"

"More or less. Avalon's a little concentrated, but really, the Belt culture is extremely dispersed. It was found that the family unit still works best in a frontier environment. Once the news gets spread, there'll be family meetings all over, then there'll be multi-clan meetings. The Roalstad clan, for instance, is closely allied with ours. They're mostly freighters, and the whole family practically lives full-time in their ships, but I saw Odin Roalstad at the meeting. He'll be on the horn to the family's ships right now and we'll have a joint get-together soon. Then individual colony and republic assemblies will thrash things out and tell their representatives at the *Althing* how they want to vote. It works pretty well, most of the time."

"It sounds inefficient to me, but when did anybody ever have an efficient—what the hell is that?" She pointed to a bizarre little figure that came through the door disguised as a Nootka totem pole. It was a small, humanoid robot, a stick figure with a featureless doorknob for a head. Over its head it held a tray of drinks and refreshments and beneath this burden it struggled and staggered as if bearing a great load under intense gravity. Occasionally it staggered sideways, but always it kept its balance and the tray stayed level. Finally it crossed the room and knelt abjectly before them, proffering the tray like a worshipper offering a sacrifice to the gods.

"This atrocity was designed by Stanislaus Ciano, one of Ugo's sons. He was rumored to be the only Ciano who possessed a sense of humor. He claimed he made it to test out a new gyroscope he'd designed." He selected a huge, skewered shrimp and bit into it. "Personally, I think he was crazy, like all the Cianos."

"I heard that!" said a voice from the entrance. The woman who came in wore a chin-to-floor cloak the exact color of fresh blood. Valentina remembered the amazing cloak from the meeting. It seemed to be made of some kind of watered silk that shimmered so luridly that she half-expected to see a spreading scarlet pool radiate from where the woman sat on the great hall's reed mats.

"Hello, Antigone," Derek said. "We've been quartered on you for the duration."

"Good," she said. "It'll be nice to have company. The rest never come to this part of the complex. I don't know why. And this is Valentina. Welcome to Castle Ciano." The two women gripped hands. Antigone had long, black hair, a white complexion and green eyes that showed white all around the irises. She took off her cloak and cast it across the room, collapsed into a chair and grabbed a bulb of Wild Turkey from the tray, holding it aloft. "To Ugo Ciano, wherever he is!"

"To Ugo," the other two chorused. The woman's slightly demented manner was so easy and natural that it took Valentina a moment to notice that she had been wearing nothing underneath the cloak. Derek seemed to notice nothing unusual, and Valentina did another of her numerous reassessments of the outworlders.

"Ugo Ciano has been dead for a long time, hasn't he?" she asked.

"Never proven!" said Antigone. "He tried out his new drive, there was a flash, and nothing was ever seen of him or his ship again. There are some of us who think he's still wandering around hyperspace somewhere." She sucked at the bulb of high-proof bourbon. "It's probably where he'd be happiest anyway."

"What do you think, Annie?" Derek asked. "Did Linde convince you?"

"It was a short session," she said. "Linde only answered a few questions before Nadia and Ulric hauled her off somewhere. Everything I heard her say checks out, though. I'm ready to head out. My bags are packed."

That, Valentina thought, probably didn't require much packing, given the woman's taste in attire. "Even if it means years cooped up in a ship headed for an unknown destination?"

"We live cooped up in ships all our lives," Antigone said. "Do you think I'd rather spend the next few years in a research lab dreaming up newer and better ways to kill Earthies? Be serious. The fact is, our lives won't change all that much, if we head out in big enough numbers. We've pretty well exhausted the possibilities of the asteroids."

"But to leave the solar system behind," Valentina said. "It's so final."

"Most of us," Antigone said, "never visit the planets or moons, just as most Earthies never visit other continents or countries. Almost anyone on Earth can live for years in a major city and never feel any great need to go anywhere else. You've seen the kind of facilities we have available to us in the major islands. There'll be plenty of work for everybody."

"That's another question," Valentina said. "Just what will you do? Mining has always been the major industry here, but you're leaving your biggest customer behind."

"We'll diversify," Derek said. "Earth never paid what our minerals were worth anyway. We'll be gearing up for planetary exploration. We'll have to start educating a lot of people in biological sciences since we hope to find life-bearing worlds. I'll need to go back to school for that. Oceanic studies, things like that."

"And," Antigone added, "we have to start doing some serious theoretical work on xenobiology and alien contact scenarios."

"What?" Valentina said.

"*Somebody* left those power packs behind."

"Oh."

"We'll stay busy," Derek said. "If the haul gets too dull for some people, we may develop a cold sleep process to cut the boredom."

"You people aren't afraid to think in big terms, are you?" Valentina said, disbelievingly.

"That situation on Earth," Derek said, "was brought about by people who refused to think ahead, or in any but small terms. If a lot of people were hungry, it was easier and quicker to take a surplus from the producers and give it away than to try to make the hungry ones productive. Why bother to educate people when it was so much easier to pander to their prejudice and ignorance and religious fanaticisms?"

"Not everyone is non-productive," Valentina protested.

"Just the vast majority," Antigone said. "And have the industrialists and the capitalists been any better? There was a time when they were willing to undertake long-term projects at a marginal profit, even operate at a loss for years, for the sake of accomplishing something great. For the last century, short-term, high-profit projects had been the rule. This year's annual dividend is all that counts. Few companies would be willing to wait two years for their money. Five years? Forget it.

"They fight the competition through more aggressive advertising, or government action, or cheap gimmickry. Anything but lowering prices, providing a better service or producing a superior product. The ideal is still monopoly. Supply and demand means nothing. If there is a surplus, the suppliers will conspire to create an artificial shortage to keep prices up."

"Carstairs crushed a lot of those conspiracies," Valentina said.

"He drove off a lot of honest businessmen as well," Derek told her. "Anyway, a system that requires the force and personality of one man at its head is no good. Now there are even more people, doing even less and demanding more. So, along comes Shevket. He's going to create some sort of slave state with perpetual war as its basis of prosperity."

"There's an old saying," Antigone said, "about people getting the government they deserve. I guess Carstairs' Earth First world-state wasn't bad enough for them. They'll deserve what they get this time, but I don't think I'll hang around to watch the final act."

Abruptly, she switched tracks. "We're going to have some work to do getting Sieglinde's drive units installed. Not only will the units be fairly large, but the accelerating thrust has to go directly through the center of mass of the asteroid. Any work going on in the rock during the journey is going to shift the center of mass, so there are going to have to be booster units to compensate."

Derek grinned. "I'm glad it's not my problem. Exploration is my specialty."

"Do you really plan to take some of the larger Island Worlds on this insane journey?" Valentina asked.

"Only the ones that vote to go," Derek said.

"I mean, isn't size a consideration? Surely only some of the smaller ones can be transported, like the ones that went out under antimatter drive."

"Linde wants to take Avalon," Antigone said.

"But Avalon's the largest of the inhabited asteroids!"

"It'll take a big engine," Antigone agreed.

I can't believe this, Valentina thought. I truly can't believe I'm sitting here with a boy barely out of his teens who seems to have developed a crush on me and a naked, whiskey-drinking woman seriously talking about taking an inhabited hunk of rock many kilometers in extent clear to another star system. It was as if she had suddenly been cast among an alien race.

"Let's see," Antigone said, reaching for a holo hand-set. "Here's Avalon." She called up a meter-long image of the rock, dotted with the lights of the ports, exterior operations and occasional windows. Near the narrower end Valentina could see the long window of the museum she had visited earlier in the day.

"Let's have a cutaway of the interior." A three-dimensional map of Avalon appeared, color-coded to display open spaces, tubes and tunnels, residential areas, industrial or agricultural areas, mining operations, ports and support facilities. As extensively worked as it had been, the vast bulk of the asteroid was still solid rock.

"Let me do a few calculations for a rough placement of the drive unit," Antigone said.

"Will it be internal or external?" Derek asked.

"Partially internal. It might simplify things if we installed it at the leading end of the rock and let the thrust blast back the whole length of the place, but that would take too long to install. Here we are." There was now an oblong outline of red and green dotted lines defining the shape of the drive unit. It took a large bite of rock near the South Polar port.

"Hey!" Derek protested. "We can't put it there!"

"Why not?" Antigone asked.

"That'll obliterate the Rabid Rockbuster. It's my favorite bar."

"This project is going to demand a lot of scarifices, Derek," his cousin assured him.

The next day they got ready for what promised to be an uproarious session of the *Althing*. As they were about to leave the Ciano quarters, Valentina turned to Antigone. "Don't forget your clothes."

"Oh. Thanks for reminding me." She took a dazzling rainbow cloak that draped a stuffed lion and wrapped it in graceful, low-grav folds.

The *Althing* was held in a huge, worked-out mine surrounded by rows of stands. When the *Althing* was not in session, which was most of the time, it was used as a sports arena. When they arrived, the spectator area was already jammed. All the delegates were present, at least in holographic form.

"What are those?" Valentina said, nodding toward a group of bizarre figures rigged with glittering instruments.

"Aeaeans," Derek said. "They rarely deign to show here, even in holo. They must figure this is serious. Their usual delegate is a little old character who looks normal."

"Here comes Linde," Antigone said.

Sieglinde was accompanied by a number of officials of the *Althing*. While they went through a brief ceremonial opening, Valentina studied the delegates and spectators. They were as colorful and polyglot as a U.N. meeting, but she noticed one major difference: nearly every one of them looked as if he was anxious to get away and go somewhere else. Unlike U.N. delegates, she thought, these people figure they have something better to do.

Magnus Roalstad, the blond-bearded Speaker of the Month, opened the session. "You will now hear a historic announcement from our illustrious Sieglinde Kornfeld-Taggart. No violence, please."

The uproar began immediately when Sieglinde reached into a bag and drew out her Rhea Object. The Aeaeans began to squall frantically. "Where did you get that!" yelled their senior delegate, a person of indeterminate gender whose head was encased in a lattice of silver rods and minute crystals. "We were supposed to have the only one!"

"From the same place you got yours," she said reasonably, "Derek Kuroda."

"Kuroda!" The Aeaean shrieked across the width of the chamber, "You said you found just one!"

"You told us the same thing!" yelled the McNaughton delegate, a man who closely resembled a gorilla.

Instantly, hundreds of holo projectors turned toward Derek and he stood isolated in a blinding beam of light. Renown at last, he thought, terrified. What historic words can I give them? Why didn't I anticipate this and rehearse something? He took a deep breath, squared his shoulders and tossed his long hair back gallantly.

"I lied!"

There was a tremendous uproar and he felt himself jerked backward. It was Ulric, glaring furiously from between frosty eyebrows and mustache. "Let's get you out of here, you young fool, before they tear you to shreds." Along with a team of family strongarms, Ulric hustled him outside the chamber and into a clan-owned bar that catered largely to ship's crews. There they could watch the proceedings in a large holo wall.

"Does everything get done in bars out here?" Valentina asked.

"Not everywhere," François told her. "But on Avalon, yes. Who wants an office when you can be comfortable instead? Besides, we're the biggest booze producer in the Confederacy, so it's good for business."

For the first two hours of the session, Sieglinde told the delegates of her discoveries. She used more detail than she had the evening before, and she was interrupted frequently. By the end of it pandemonium reigned.

"You know," Ulric said, "they're seeing all this on Earth."

"With about a twelve-minute delay," Derek said. "But then, how could we ever keep any of this secret now?"

In the holo, a delegate in a dazzling white turban had seized the initiative. "Professor Taggart, how do we know that these claims of yours are not just so much fantasy-spinning?"

"For one thing, Ali," she said, "I'm here in Avalon and you're in Deryabar, way the hell over on the other side of the sun, but we're talking without any time lag. That proves that I've cracked the superluminal communication problem, something most of my colleagues claimed to be impossible."

"Now that's impressed them," Derek said proudly. "They can't argue with that."

"They can and will," Ulric countered. "But I think they'll come around. This can't be ignored for long."

"How many do you think will vote to leave?" Valentina asked.

"Two-thirds," Derek said, confidently.

"Half," Ulric said. "Maybe as high as two-thirds, but I doubt it. Some are too attached to the system, especially the religious settlements. There'll even be those who actually want to stay and fight a war."

"But," Valentina asked, "can people just vote to leave the Confederacy?"

"Certainly," said François indignantly. "It's the first article in our constitution."

"It's hard to believe," she maintained, "that a nation would be sure to include a formula for its destruction in its very constitution."

"Didn't you notice the motto over the *Althing* entrance?" Antigone asked. "It says 'The state exists for the people, not the people for the state.' A good many of the asteroid worlds never even joined the Confederacy, although the texts on Earth would have it otherwise. They prefer a grand conspiracy of offworlders against the motherworld."

The debate in the *Althing* raged for hours. The group in the bar watched attentively for a while, then started playing poker. In the midst of a hand, Derek glanced at the holowall.

"Dealer takes two. How do you—"

"What is it?" Ulric asked impatiently. He held two pair, kings over jacks.

"Do we have a camera in there?" Derek said.

"Yes, why?"

"Get it back on that woman who was just talking, the one from Atlantis." The picture swiveled to the woman, who was now speaking to someone beside her. "There. Two rows behind her, three spaces to the left. Get a closeup of that man."

The picture zoomed and Valentina hissed. "It's him! Vladyka!"

Frantically, they left the table and rushed toward the *Althing* chamber. Ulric barked rapid-fire orders into a handset. François scooped up the table stakes.

Daniko Vladyka was in his element. He had come to enemy territory, and now he was going to kill his victim in the assembly of the enemy's leaders and then get away clean. It would be a work of art. He saw that the Kornfeld woman had changed from her Pellier disguise. She now more closely resembled the descriptions he had heard from witnesses.

The weapon he had chosen for the assassination was perfect—undetectable to any but the most advanced search. He was almost disappointed that no one had searched him as he had entered the chamber. Not even an elementary frisking! It was all too amateurish for words.

The aiming device was implanted in his right eye, so beautifully designed and perfectly miniaturized that he was unaware of it until it was activated. The laser generator was located inside his rib cage, its beam conducted along an optical fiber under the skin of his arm. It emerged from beneath the nail of his right forefinger. When he locked on target, all he had to do was point casually and activate. The invisible beam would do its work in perfect silence.

Nobody would notice what he had done. There were people pointing at her and shouting everywhere. He had several exit routes planned, each of them with a number of handy spots to don a new disguise in case some busybody should, by a fantastic chance, run a holo of the event and somehow spot him. It was almost beneath him to take such precautions against these innocent lummoxes, but a professional had to be thorough.

Kornfeld stood to make another address. She seemed to have most of the assembly on her side now. He hadn't been paying the slightest attention to her speeches or the debate. It wasn't his job. The dramatic moment was correct. He activated. The sighting device in his eye framed her face, the frame blinked when it was on target, an intense spot of blue light appeared between her eyes. He raised his hand and extended it.

Then his concentration was broken by something unbelievable. There was a tingling in his left hand. The chrono on his middle finger was vibrating in a simple, unmistakable pattern. There had to be something wrong, but the message was clear: *Abort Mission.*

He had seldom felt such rage in his life. He was keyed to the highest pitch to perform this assassination, not only as a duty, but as a work of art. Such a perfect moment might never come again. But Daniko Vladyka was a professional, and he lowered his hand. By no gesture had he betrayed his emotions to those standing near him.

There was nothing to keep him in the stifling chamber, so he turned to leave. That was when he noticed the security people closing in. What a bother, he thought. Making his way out through these amateurs would not be nearly the satisfaction that the assassination would have been.

As he entered the short tunnel that led out onto the main concourse, he touched off a smoke bomb that carried with it an overpowering scent of ozone. Amid the uproar this set off, he stepped unseen into a covered tunnel he had mapped out earlier. This led to a tool room that apparently hadn't been used in years. When he stepped out a few minutes later, the smoke was clearing and he had a new face and clothing.

The incident had caused excitement, but no panic. People accustomed to dealing with shipboard fires and breached walls didn't panic easily. The security force looked wildly about, but none spared a second glance for the elderly, professorial man with the silver hair.

THIRTEEN

Vladyka, in *Ivo the Black*, rendezvoused with the featureless ship three hours out from Avalon. His mole in the North Polar port had passed him through, a simple duty for which the man was well compensated on an annual basis.

He was still fuming. What might have been the high point of his career had been thwarted by bad timing. The ship he approached was larger than *Ivo*, a simple cylinder with no marking or lettering whatever. At one time, such craft had been favored by pirates and hijackers.

The ships matched velocity and docked. Vladyka pulled himself aboard the other vessel and drew himself hand over hand along a dimly lit tunnel to the control room. The man inside was as featureless as his ship. He was smallish and wore a dull gray coverall. Vladyka recognized him as Shevket's head of intelligence operations. He'd had no idea the man was even in space.

"What," Vladyka demanded, "is the meaning of this—this *coitus interruptus* of a mission?"

"Calm yourself, Daniko," said Roman Korda. "The general has made many contingency plans. He was monitoring that unspeakable woman's performance back on the motherworld. As soon as he realized the gist of

189

what she was saying, he signalled me to put into effect plan L, and I signalled you to abort. It is now desirable that she remain alive."

"If the general, or you, had signalled an instant later, she would be dead," Vladyka said. *Somebody* had to know how close he had come.

"I knew you could accomplish it, Daniko," Roman soothed, tired as always of having to stroke the egos of temperamental, high-strung field operatives. "But what is the death of one miserable woman? Wait until I explain the general's brilliant plan. You will be responsible for some killings that will be remembered for the rest of human history."

Vladyka was intrigued. "Of course," he said, mollified, "I would never question the general's judgment. Please explain my new duties."

Korda spoke for a long time, and as he did, Vladyka grew more and more excited. By the end of the recitation, he had entirely forgotten about the aborted assassination of Sieglinde Kornfeld-Taggart.

Carstairs stood on a terrace of the Great Palace of the United Nations. He looked down at Lake Geneva, the quiet waters reflecting the perfect blue of the sky. The palace was a marvel of architecture, the setting was perfect, the view was spectacular. It was as if all the efforts of man and nature had been bent to creating one flawless, peaceful place in a woefully imperfect world.

"God, I hate this fucking place," Carstairs said.

"It's a bit different from England," Mansfield agreed cautiously.

"Doesn't look like anybody's ever worked here. I'll bet nobody has since the construction crew left. Give me the docks any day."

"Was this such a good idea, sir?" Mansfield said. Instinctively, he spoke in a low voice. It was futile, since spying instruments could pick up any enunciated sound, and cameras could interpret lip and tongue motions, however subdued.

"Oh, for God's sake, Greg, speak out. If those two

slimy barstids hear us, so what? Do you think they'll decide to kill us all over again? We've been assured that this is the one place in the world where you can talk without being overheard, but who knows? It was designed by conspirators to facilitate conspiracies, so maybe it's true, but what of that?"

"It is the first time," Mansfield said, pointedly, "that you've accepted a summons like this. Always before, *they* came to *you*. No matter how powerful they were, no matter what absurd title you labored under, they came trooping to your office, hat in hand. That was how everyone that counted knew who held the real power. All the rest was mere stage dressing."

"Right. Well, things change, Greg. Time marches on. Our boy Shevket is top dog now, for a while, anyway. And here the bugger comes now, all puffed up like a frog full of swamp gas."

Shevket crossed the terrace, closely followed by Larsen. As if on a signal, the rest of his entourage stopped and the two continued until they were within two feet of Carstairs.

"Welcome to Geneva, Mr. Carstairs," said Larsen. "And you also, Mr. Mansfield. We do not see you here often enough."

"Too often for my taste," Carstairs said. "Once a year for the opening session's as much as my stomach can take."

"It's a mistake," Shevket said coolly, "for one who would wield power to avoid the places where power resides. It has been a miscalculation of many rulers who failed. Louis Sixteenth at Versailles, for instance, or Tiberius at Capri."

"It seems to me your reading of history's a bit shallow, General," Carstairs countered. "Those were men who inherited their power. The ones who grabbed it for themselves didn't waste their time in decadent old cities full of parasites." He gazed around him at the crowds scurrying about the palace.

"You didn't catch Alexander hanging around the gym in Athens, fondling the bare bums of all those ephebes, now, did you? No, he was always out conquering someplace or else up in Pella. Did your old hero, Genghis Khan, sit around stuffing himself with egg rolls in Peking or whatever was the Chinese capital in those days? Not a chance, mate. He stayed up there in Mongolia and pulled the strings. No flock of court eunuchs for him. I think old Napoleon might have made something of himself if he hadn't been so addicted to Paris. If the bugger'd gone back to Corsica and run things from there, the whole world would be speaking French right now."

Shevket reddened but Larsen cut in smoothly. "Why, Mr. Carstairs, your proletarian manner is just a pose! You've been a secret scholar all along."

"Even a poor boy can learn a few things by reading a bit," Carstairs said. "Of course, we draw different conclusions; can't help that. We don't all choose the same way to implement what we've learned, either. Some of us choose to organize working men as a way to power; others prefer to work with criminals."

"Carstairs," Shevket said, his face flaming, "you go too far!"

"Do I now?" Carstairs said. "Perhaps so. After so many years of having the likes of you and all the rest here queueing up to kiss my arse, I might have got too used to being the one who decided what's too far and what isn't."

Larsen and Mansfield went deathly pale, but abruptly Shevket relaxed and grinned. "That is an admission, coming from you. Come along, Mr. Carstairs. There are some things I would like for you to see before we must endure that tedious state luncheon."

"That's fair," Carstairs said. "If you can show me anything interesting about this place, you'll be the first one since I first came here forty years ago."

Shevket and Carstairs crossed the terrrace, Larsen and Mansfield three paces behind them, Shevket's entourage ten paces behind the second pair. They passed through a lavish portal, descended a ceremonial staircase and walked to a balcony overlooking a gigantic room full of humans and little, rolling robots, all rushing about and shouting like traders in a stock exchange. This, supposedly, was the room where much of the world's political work got done.

"Fine sight," Carstairs said. "Ambassadors, representatives, military attachés, speakers, the works. All of them pretending to be running the world's business. I probably get more work done in an hour over my old telephone than the lot of 'em all year. What am I supposed to see here?"

"Look more closely," Shevket urged. "What do you notice that is different?"

"Seems to be a younger crowd," Carstairs said.

"Very good. We in the Victory party have been clearing out a great deal of dead wood. Bringing a new spirit to the world."

"Also a great many more uniforms in evidence."

"There you have the most important change," Shevket said. "The one part of society that truly matters is at last going to achieve its deserved prominence, unpolluted by the influence of merchants and politicians."

Carstairs laughed uproariously. Shevket grew deadly grim. "Will you share this humor with us, Mr. Carstairs?"

"General, I can't believe you're serious! I've dealt with the military leadership all my professional life, and I've never encountered such a set of scheming politicians as them! You're an intelligent man, General Shevket. You can't seriously believe that a modern military establishment constitutes some sort of pristine warrior elite. They're a bunch of buggers with jobs and careers, and when there's a war, they control a pack of draftees that just want to go home. I've bought and sold your warriors, General, and believe me, they came cheap!"

The two men faced each other across a distance of less than a foot. Shevket kept his hands rigidly behind his back, but his uniformed following leaned forward like a pack of hounds straining at a leash. Larsen and Mansfield stood with their faces professionally bland, but nevertheless with the attitude of men expecting to be struck by lightning.

At last, Shevket spoke. "There will come a time, Carstairs. It is not yet, but it will be soon. Good day, sir!" He spun on an obsidian heel and stalked away, followed by his well-leashed entourage.

"My God, Anthony," Mansfield said, watching the uniformed backs as they disappeared, "you're insane to provoke him like that." He took out a handkerchief and mopped his sweating brow.

"Think so? I don't. I know he wants to kill me. I've known that for months, and so have you. The question is when. Well, Greg, we've learned that the time ain't now! That's worth a bit, right?"

"Anthony," Mansfield said, "I shall never understand your cold-bloodedness in the face of ruthless men like Shevket."

"Not a bit of it, mate," Carstairs said. "I haven't a drop of cold blood in my body. It's all piss and vinegar and adrenaline. I may not show it, but I'm always ready to go for their throats with my teeth."

Mansfield managed a faint smile. "I meant it in the French sense, of course, *sang-froid*. The ability to maintain a calm demeanor in the midst of a mutual desire to kill. But then, I suppose that's why you've run the world for so long, while I and others like me have been your followers."

Carstairs grinned and punched him in the chest. "Come on, we'll lick these bastards yet. Get killed ourselves doing it, of course, but we'll have some satisfaction out of it."

FOURTEEN

"How are we doing?" Derek asked.

"Not bad," Sieglinde said. "One hundred twenty definites and about fifty maybes."

"Can we turn out that many drive units in time?"

"It looks as if we'd have to." She was on one of her infrequent visits to Avalon. She spent almost all her time in her lab these days. The shielding problem was highest priority now that the drive units were fully designed. Individual labs had been established to design the mounting of the units since there was, naturally, no standard design for asteroids.

"I guess it was Fu's presentation that turned the trick for us," Derek said. Chih'-Chin Fu had put together a masterly holographic program for all levels of education that explained the drive and its possibilities. There was an immediate resurgence of enthusiasm for interstellar travel, encouraged greatly by the prospect of the coming war with Earth.

"I hope you're ready for some bad news," Derek said.

"I hope you never live long enough to hear all the bad news I've had in my life. What's yours?"

"Not only are some of the worlds opting for war, but there's been a revival of Shaw's private army. Apparently some of Shaw's old people are still around. They're calling themselves—get this—the Avengers."

She sighed. "I might have known. Those people have had nothing to do for years except get together and get drunk and lament for the good old days. At last they have a chance to relive their glory days. Well, there can't be enough of them to mount a credible threat."

"They're being joined by others," Derek said. "There are younger people, too. I guess, for some, the quick excitement of a war right now is more attractive than waiting for years to reach a new star system."

"Have you caught that man Vladyka yet?"

"No," Derek admitted. He brushed at the sleeve of his new uniform. He was now a captain in the security force. Ulric had recommended him for the commission because, in Ulric's words, "He's now renowned as the sneakiest little bastard in the whole Confederacy."

"No leads?"

"There was a sighting reported on Thera. Val's gone over to investigate but I don't expect much. The man's slippery, and appearance is too easy to alter. What really bothers me is the nature of his mission. I still don't understand how he failed to kill you. Val insists he had some kind of implanted laser and he was pointing it at you, but he didn't fire."

"I don't suppose it was a sudden attack of conscience. I suspect that, when we find out what he's up to, it'll be something supremely awful."

"That's a safe bet." Derek checked his chrono ring. "It's about time." The two left the port lounge and entered the departure terminal, which had been temporarily cleared of all commercial traffic. A small group of people stood surrounded by a much larger group and a whole flock of floating holo cameras.

The crowd parted for Sieglinde and Derek. The center group all wore brilliant silver coveralls. A tall young man saw Sieglinde coming and grinned at her. He was Dieter Taggart, her eldest son, called back from the Oort Cloud expedition to lead the first voyage under Kornfeld Drive. The target system was Sigma Pavonis.

She hugged him fiercely, then held her much taller son at arm's length. "I don't like it," she said, not caring what the cameras recorded. "The shielding isn't perfected yet. In six more months—"

"We don't have six months, Mother," Dieter said. "We're not on peacetime status anymore. It has to be tested now. More important, people have to see that the drive works."

She released him. "I know you'll make me proud. Go take care of your ship." Abruptly she turned and walked away, stone-faced. Hastily, Derek shook hands with his cousin and the others, then hurried after Sieglinde. While she was here, he was charged with her safety. His men were everywhere, with shoot-to-kill orders for anyone who even looked as if he was threatening her.

"He's a good skipper," she said as he caught up with her. "Gave me hell growing up. They all did. But I suppose it's force of personality that makes a good commander." Derek had never heard her talking in this disjointed fashion. The last few months had put new lines on her face. But then, he thought, in that time she had been under personal and professional stress such as few people had ever known.

"But," she said, "I would never have expected this from Martin!" Far worse than Dieter's voyage with untested shielding was Martin Shaw Taggart's decision to stay behind. Sálamis had voted to stay and protect those Island Worlds that decided to remain in the solar system. Personnel had been given free choice to go or to stay with Sálamis.

"Everybody has to interpret his own duty, Aunt Linde," he said, feeling inadequate. "I'm having a hell of a time convincing Val to go."

She stopped and looked at him. "Derek, I like Valentina, but I think you should seriously rethink your relationship with her. She's a spy and a saboteur and an assassin. She was raised to be that way and she's never been anything else until she came here."

He shrugged, an Earth gesture he had picked up from Valentina. "Nobody's perfect. Besides, as I understand it, that's exactly what old Sam Taggart was, and Fredrike Ciano, and probably about half the founders of our clans. There's even a rumor that old Goro Kuroda could get a little bloody-handed at times."

"Make up your own mind," she said impatiently.

"Let's go to HMK," he suggested. "Fu says the show'll be most spectacular there."

The place was mobbed. Nearly everybody who lived in Avalon was there, and visitors from nearby asteroids and ships had come in as well. No personal or institutional holo system could match the one Fu had set up in HMK, with similar sets installed in much of the Belt and on the planets and satellites, all connected by the new superluminal communication system. They found him beaming up at the incredibly realistic asteroid that floated in the vast open space.

"Isn't it fabulous?" he said. "Such fidelity! Absolutely no distortion! It's the crowning point of my career!" Derek half-expected to see the old man start dancing with excitement.

The asteroid chosen was a small one, previously known only by a number, but now called *Nova*. The interior had plenty of space for the small crew, but the leading end had been left solid rock, just in case of a shielding failure.

The image flashed to the interior, where Dieter and the bridge crew were strapping themselves into acceleration chairs. They went through a preliminary check, then he faced forward. No matter where anyone was sitting, standing or floating, he seemed to be looking the viewer straight in the eyes. "I taught him that trick myself!" Fu said, gleefully.

"I wish to speak to humanity everywhere," Dieter said. "We are now at one of the great turning points of the human race, possibly the greatest. With this voyage, humankind will become a truly starfaring species. What you are about to see is a ship made and inhabited by humans, drawing its power from the heart of a collapsed star. It is the overwhelming, unlimited power we have always dreamed of, and it will be used to spread our race throughout the galaxy—someday, throughout the universe. On behalf of myself and the crew of *Nova*, good fortune to you all."

The scene shifted back to the exterior of the asteroid, where lights began to flash around the Kornfeld Drive exhaust. A series of numbers began to blink, counting down from one hundred. People held their breath and Sieglinde brushed at her eyes repeatedly. Tears have a tendency to cling to the eyelashes in low gravity.

Gradually, a mass chant started. "Ten—Nine—Eight—" The lights began to flash rapidly. "Five—Four—Three—" The lights extinguished entirely. "One!" There was a moment when nothing happened. People began to think something had gone wrong, then—

"My God!" Derek shouted, unheard in the uproar of exclamations. The display was nothing like the blinding white light of the antimatter photon drive. The torrent that shot from the rear of *Nova* was so brilliant that it was painful to look at, but everybody looked anyway because it was unthinkably beautiful. Dampers cut in to reduce the dangerous glare, but the streaks and flashes remained searing. Gradually they faded, and there was no sign of the ship. People fell silent, moved but fearful at the same time.

Derek whispered what everyone was thinking. "Could any ship have survived that?" There was a deathly hush, then Dieter's voice came across with perfect clarity.

"Starship *Nova* on course, accelerating at one g. All systems functioning perfectly." A thunderous cheer broke out. There was much whooping and backslapping. Perfect strangers hugged one another as if they had been personally responsible for what they had just witnessed.

"Come on, Derek," Sieglinde said, jerking at his sleeve. "Let's go get stinking drunk and tear up a bar someplace." He hugged her and they pushed through the crowd, leaving the ecstatic Fu to his instruments.

"They're safe so far," Derek said.

"Of course they're safe now, idiot!" she shouted, furious and joyful in equal measure. "I never had any doubts about the drive! It'll be a month before they reach dangerous velocity. That's when faulty shielding can be a problem."

"Did I ever tell you you're a terrible liar, Aunt Sieglinde?"

Vladyka turned from the display in the ship's holo tank. The others in the cabin still stared in open-mouthed awe. It almost looked as if they had wished they had been going along. He had no intention of letting them nurture thoughts of that sort. "Very pretty. So that is how the cowards plan to leave us. Good riddance. Those too gutless to fight shouldn't contaminate us with their presence." Vladyka was now Colonel Sparta, founder and commander of the Avengers. His followers were mostly young and all bloodthirsty. He let them design their own uniforms and most had opted for rigs including high boots, swashbuckling cloaks, jackets consisting mainly of pseudo-leather straps with a great deal of chrome metalwork, wristbands and other eccentric touches.

Vladyka was amused by the make-believe warrior look and designed his own uniform after the same fashion. With his heavy musculature, it was far more impressive on him than on most of his followers, who had the spindly physiques common to low gravity. His hair had been shaved into three parallel, upstanding strips, with a tail of artificial hair hanging behind. His skin was darkened to deep gold, his cheekbones raised and tilted, his eyes given a Mongol slant. Contacts made his irises bright red. He looked the very picture of ferocity. The final touch was a set of steel teeth.

"It can't be long now," said a boy who called himself Geronimo. They had all chosen vainglorious noms de guerre.

"Very soon," Vladyka confirmed. "The Earthies will be moving against us now that they know the exodus is starting. The rock bombs are already moving into position."

A young woman called Valeria approached him. She favored skin-tight black pseudo-leather and was always trying to attract his attention. "Will you take me with you on the first attack?"

He draped an arm around her waist and cupped a rather bony hip in one palm. "Perhaps. There will be a lot of competition for slots on that voyage." She had a nicely rounded bottom but little else, and he preferred his women to be more full-fleshed.

"How many cities do we have targeted?" said a man called Leonidas.

"Fifty. But don't expect to see that many cities wiped out. The Earthies have powerful defenses in place. I revere the memory of Martin Shaw, but he was too restrained. The opportunity to destroy Earth was there, but the softliners of Eos—the Taggarts and Kurodas, the Cianos and Sousas—had no stomach for big-scale killing."

"Why wait?" Valeria asked. "Why not hit them now, before they expect us?" Her abundant hair was blond and she had a black band painted across her eyes.

"Bloodthirsty little bitch, aren't you?" he said affectionately. "Don't worry, you'll have all the blood you can stand before long. But if we're to have all the support we need, we have to let the Earthies strike first. After that, it'll be all our way. With half of the islands running, who's to protect the Confederacy but us?"

He knew that Earth would strike first because he had already seen to that little detail. He had planted nukes in two carefully selected asteroids, timed to go off just as he had his rock bombs perfectly positioned. He had no idea whether any of the rock bombs would really impact as Roman Korda had said, but he rather hoped so. Even wiping out a couple of asteroids with a few thousand deaths would be nothing like destroying even a small Earth city. He had no idea what Shevket's plan was, but his orders were clear. Shevket was willing to make a few sacrifices to consolidate his power, that was plain. He laughed uproariously.

"What's funny?" asked a follower.

"Life is," Vladyka said, fondling Valeria's sleek rear.

"Drinks all around, my comrades!" They all drew liquids and Vladyka raised his. "Death and destruction!"

"They're safe," Sieglinde said, breaking into the council meeting. As usual, nobody had had any inkling that she was in Avalon. She had breezed through their security checks without bothering to show her pass.

Mustapha Isherwood, Security Council chief, looked at her in annoyance. "Welcome as always, Linde. Who's safe?"

"*Nova*. I've put the shield through its final checks and it works flawlessly. The one aboard *Nova* is a good one."

Derek had never seen her looking so relieved. She looked ten years younger than when he had seen her last. "Speaking of *Nova*," he said, "she's already at one-tenth light speed and only a little more than a month out."

"Right about now," Sieglinde mused, "the ship that left thirty years ago under antimatter drive never yet attained one-hundredth the speed of light."

"They're going to be relieved when we show up with their new engine and shielding," Derek said. "Of course, we'll need to decelerate our ships to match velocity with our slow-moving cousins."

"Wouldn't you," Ulric commented, "facing a voyage of several centuries?"

Morton Bass grumbled. "I admit I'm an administrator, not a scientist, but this shielding business sounds like magic to me."

"It's simple enough," Sieglinde said. "Development and testing took up all the time. Once you understand the wave-nature of matter, the rest is easy."

"Wave-matter?" Bass said. They all prepared themselves with stoicism, knowing they were in for one of Sieglinde's explanations. Luckily, she usually kept it short.

"It was theorized as far back as the early twentieth century, by Schroedinger and de Broglie. We have a matter sensor and a protective field generator in each ship. The field itself is a by-product of Ugo Ciano's original research on his well-known GUFT, which I uncovered from his lab notes and developed further."

"GUFT?" Bass asked, resigned.

"Great Unified Field Theory," Ulric elucidated.

"Ugo had a unique approach to the unified field theory," Sieglinde said. "This particular force field is somewhat analogous to the nuclear force that binds protons within atomic nuclei and works only over a short range relative to the size of an atomic nucleus. My field works the same way, but it's repulsive rather than attractive and its effective range is immensely greater.

"The way it works is: The wave-front of matter approaching the ship or asteroid colony is detected by the matter sensor, which operates at virtual light speed. The approaching matter will encounter a repulsive force that is proportional to the square of the velocity of approach and inversely proportional to the fourth power of the distance from the protective field generator. Simple."

Bass cleared his throat. "Let's just pretend I understood that and go on about our business, shall we?"

"Hear, hear," somebody said.

"Luckily," Sieglinde went on, ignoring all comments, "the shield units don't require the precise placement that the drive units must have. They're already going into the star vessels and work will speed up now that I've confirmed that the technique and equipment have been perfected. How long do we have?"

"Shevket's new fleet is approaching battle readiness. All efforts at sabotage have failed. Cruise testing begins in three months. They'll be ready to come for us in four." Ulric looked across the table to the man in Sálamid uniform. "Is that correct, General?"

"Exactly, and we'll need every bit of that time to get ready. The instant hostilities open, we will attack, but we may not be able to buy much time."

"For that reason," Isherwood said, "it has been decided that everyone leaves at once, no matter what destination they've picked."

"What about the Avengers?" she asked. There were

several seconds of infuriating silence. Obviously, she had struck a sore spot.

"They're well-organized, they have ships, they're moving rock bombs into position, and we can't catch them at it," said the general.

"They're going to try something crazy," she said.

"What can they accomplish?" Ulric demanded. "Thirty years ago, such an attack would have been devastating. Today, it will provide the Earthies with a pretty fireworks display. Probably be the event of the season. Those idiots might as well be shooting cast iron cannonballs."

Sieglinde held her own counsel until the meeting broke up. "Derek, I want to talk to you."

"Naturally. I'm still in the old Ciano quarters. Antigone's never in these days; she's working on getting the Avalonian drive unit installed."

"Where is Valentina?"

"I don't know," he said, miserably. "She's become obsessed with catching Vladyka." They ducked into the tube-train tunnel and boarded a car headed toward the Kuroda complex. The trains were full of workers headed to or coming off their jobs. Nearly everybody was now involved in the star drive project. "She has some crazy idea about finding him and she won't tell me what it is."

"Maybe she knows more about this business than you do. Trust her instincts."

In the Ciano quarters they drifted into the smokelike furniture. "Derek," she began, "you still have a lot to learn about intelligence work. I didn't want to say anything in that council meeting because I'm not sure whom I can trust. This war won't be like the last one. They were clumsy then. You can bet they've spent the last three decades planting moles in our governments and operations."

"Who do you suspect?" he asked.

"Anybody I haven't known practically all their lives. That's not the point here. The point is, who are the Avengers?"

"Them? Mostly they're a bunch of dumb kids—"

"About your age, in other words."

"We can't all be smart. The ones we know about are mostly losers with no prospects—the kind you might expect to flock to an outfit made up of misfits. Plus, there are some of Shaw's old bunch. Hey, you don't think Shaw's behind this, do you? He disappeared after the war and nobody's ever proved he died."

She shook her head. "No, I'd feel much better about it if I thought he was running this lunacy. I was close to Martin in those last weeks of the war. He was Thor's friend, remember? No, Martin was physically destroyed by the Earthies' torture. Only his will kept him alive. In the end, he went off to die alone somewhere, like an old lion. He didn't want to expire ignobly in a hospital with people watching. Besides, he had a flair for the dramatic and he knew there'd be legends that he was out here alive someplace. Believe me, that very prospect has been haunting the Earthies ever since."

She seemed to shake off the odd mood. "That was then. This is now. So what we have is a handful of old vets, a bunch of thrill-hungry kids, and a leader rumored to be called Colonel Sparta. This pack of nobodies has ships, they're travelling among the Island Worlds undetected by the Sálamids, and they're shifting big rocks and icebergs all over, also undetected. Those are expensive operations, Derek. Hasn't it occurred to you to wonder who's financing all this?"

"Well, when Shaw started out—"

"Martin Shaw had a merchant fleet *before* the war started. He was joined by other merchant and smuggling skippers who brought their own vessels and pooled their resources. These raggedy fools have nothing like that."

"Some tycoon with a fleet, then?"

"Maybe, but I doubt it. Everybody with enough brains to get rich is heading out."

"Who, then?" Derek demanded.

"How about Shevket?"

After a stunned moment his mind began to whir and click. "You think maybe Sparta's an *agent provocateur?*"

"Either that, or a puppet for one. I don't know what Shevket would really plan, but one of the oldest war-mongering tricks is to provoke, or better, create an incident that gets everybody to believe that right is on their side."

"My God. I wonder if that's what Val—"

"Bet on it," Sieglinde said.

The mass meeting was held in the *Althing* chamber. Representatives of all the departing Island Worlds were there, although the great majority were there only in holographic projection. In the frantic effort to get the drive units and shields installed, few had the leisure to travel between worlds.

"Destinations," Sieglinde said. "That's what we're here to discuss. Of course, everybody gets to choose their own destination, but let's have a little coordination here."

"What business is it of yours where we go?" yelled someone belligerently.

"If you don't have a destination picked out," someone called back, "I can make a suggestion."

"Order! Order!" shouted Isherwood. "For all anybody cares you can change destinations in mid-course and you'll just disappear from human history, but for now let's have some sort of consensus. We have to leave at the same time and future generations will want to know where to look to find their relatives."

"Why all at the same time?" asked a representative from Delos.

Sieglinde answered. "Since we have plenty of energy to burn for boosting, there's no real need to use an optimal orbital location for the departure. By the time we leave, the Earth fleet will probably be after us. If we're already on our way, they can't catch us. While we sit, we're vulnerable. Some of the asteroid colonies will have to take a circuitous route around the sun before they can get aimed in the right direction to reach the stars they've chosen. If everybody goes at once there's far less chance of anybody being caught alone.

"The nearest solar systems have been pretty thoroughly studied by interferometric telescopes, so we have a fairly certain selection of stars with clement conditions, possibly including Earth-like worlds."

"Who needs 'em?" someone yelled.

"There are those among us," she said patiently, "who still want to settle other planets, as you well know, so pipe down. Any single system should be more than adequate for all the Island Worlds, but we all know that this bunch is too cantankerous to stand being in the same solar system with one another if there's a chance to get away.

"We recommend that a minimum of three asteroids make up each caravan. That guards against systems failures, insures an adequate gene pool in case you should be cut out of contact with other humans for several generations and, let's not forget, there is or has been at least one other starfaring species in this galaxy, and I suspect there are far, far more."

She cut into the subsequent murmur. "The odds-on favorite is Tau Ceti. Who's going there?" More than thirty hands went up.

"Sigma Pavonis? That's where Avalon is going. *Nova* will be there ahead of us, and that'll help when we get there." Another large contingent raised their hands.

"Alpha Centauri? You people get to catch up with the old antimatter starships and fit them with the new drives. Naturally, you'll have to decelerate first to match velocity with them. Maybe you'll meet some old friends you thought you'd never see again." More hands went up.

"Eighty-two Eridani?" More hands. She read out a long list of nearby stars that were almost certain to have promising planetary systems. Some had many takers, some had few. There were even a very few solitaries who chose against all advice to go it alone. These few were mostly religious communities that wanted to get away from the contamination of unbelievers.

After the holographic representatives blinked off, Sieglinde looked over her list. A small group of Avalonians crowded around her. "Thirty-three destination stars," she said. "Of course, some are probably lying and will end up going someplace else, but this is roughly accurate. If we can just get out of here before the Earthies nuke us all, we can pretty well ensure that the human race will last as long as the universe does, unless something comes along soon that can wipe out a whole arm of the galaxy."

"Hell," said Magnus Roalstad, "there's even one crazy bunch that hasn't settled on a star. They're just heading for the center of the galaxy. Think they'll find God there."

"It'll be their remote descendants if they ever make it," Sieglinde said. "My drive is fast, but that kind of distance will still require centuries. Oh, well, it's their choice."

"That's why I was urging that we refrain from scattering too much," Isherwood said. "If we stay relatively close, we'll all be able to benefit from new developments, be able to swap new discoveries. Those tiny expeditions won't have large enough scientific establishments, and some of them will be out of touch with the rest of humanity for a long, long time."

"At least that should encourage the greatest possible human diversity," Sieglinde said. "That might be the best idea after all. For better or worse, the die is cast now. We can't go back."

"Where are Katrina and Taeko being quartered?" Sieglinde asked.

"They wouldn't take anything in the Kuroda stronghold," Nadia said with a snort. "They're your daughters, you talk to them. Their husbands must be saints to put up with them."

At least the girls were going in Avalon. Like her son, her daughters were stubborn, independent and headstrong. Just like their parents, she thought ruefully. They would go whole years without contacting her, but for the duration of the voyage, they might grow closer. They would be reunited with Dieter when they arrived, but it still broke her heart to think about Martin. Well, she told herself, *he's said that if he lives through the war, or if the cause collapses completely, he'll follow after us*. It was all she had to console herself with.

Derek came in, looking gray and drawn. He looked much, much older than the puppyish boy who had brought her the little green egg that had changed history. "What is it?" she said, knowing it would be bad.

"It's started. Mauritius and Easter Island had been nuked. No survivors, at least eight thousand dead."

The emergency meeting was held in the Security Council chamber. The near-euphoria of recent days had been replaced by near-gloom. They had been jerked violently from their dreams of the stars to present reality.

"They were destroyed simultaneously," Ulric reported. "To the second." The holo over the table showed a scene familiar from the last war—shattered rocks still oozing lava, barren of life.

"How were the nukes delivered?" asked Isherwood.

General Davidson, the Sálamid liaison, answered. "We were able to detect nothing at all. Either the Earthies have a new delivery system we know nothing about—"

"Crap," Sieglinde said. "If they had something like that, they'd've hit all of us at once and timed it to happen simultaneously. Those nukes were planted, probably been in place for months."

"That," Davidson said stiffly, "was what I was about to say. We also consider that the likeliest possibility."

"Then there may be more of them," said Isherwood.

"Unlikely," Davidson said. "Everyone is looking for them now. Any more will be easy to find and dismantle. I suspect that this is a political incident."

"I agree," Sieglinde said. "Shevket's precipitating this war. He's doing it for both sides. He's just given us an excuse to start shooting. I suspect Earth's excuse is already in motion. He can always screw around with the chronology later to balance the history books. After all, if he wins, he'll be writing them."

"This is all a little Byzantine," Isherwood said.

"What else did you expect?" Sieglinde asked.

They all looked up as an apparition took the place of the smoldering rocks. It was Chih'-Chin Fu, dressed in his usual newscasting robes and looking like a Confucian scholar.

"This is Chih'-Chin Fu," he said gravely, "reporting from near-Lunar orbit. Today, within an hour of the destruction of Mauritius and Easter Island, Earth sustained a massive attack from rock bombs. Of fifty that came in, forty-eight were obliterated before they reached Earth's atmosphere. Two got through to their targets. New York and Hong Kong were obliterated, with at least forty million dead."

There was a stunned silence as scenes of the devastation rolled across the holographic viewing area. "Generalissimo Shevket," Fu's voice went on, "has assumed dictatorial powers, decrying the state to which he claims the Earth First Party had allowed Earth's defenses to fall. He has demanded an explanation from Mr. Anthony Carstairs and has called for that official to be stripped of all powers. The general vows to take personal command of the fleet within the week and crush the Confederacy once and for all."

"We're ready to go in thirty days," Sieglinde said. She turned to Davidson. "How long before the Earth fleet begins to reach us?"

"Elements are already on their way," the general reported. "Shevket will merely take command of the flagship *Conqueror*, still in Earth's orbit. Leading elements should reach us within twenty-four days. We will, of course, intercept all of them if we can."

"Do it," she said. "Damn! We're so close!" She didn't waste time fretting. "If you'll excuse me, I have a call to make. I'm about to call in an old IOU. I think I can buy us the time we need. But don't count on it. Tell everybody redoubled effort is needed." She walked out.

"That woman," Isherwood said, "is utterly insane."

Ulric Kuroda stared at him bleakly. "I've always said so, but I'm her kinsman. How would you like a broken nose?"

FIFTEEN

Carstairs sat behind his desk, collar open, feet propped
on the leather top, sleeves pulled up. He leaned back
in his ancient, squeaky roller chair, a bottle of Newcastle Brown Ale clutched in one of his powerful hands.
Across from him, in holographic projection, sat Sieglinde
Kornfeld-Taggart.

"Tony, it's never been my way to call in old favors,
but I'll be honest with you. I'm desperate. It was due to
my work that you were allowed to pretend that you
won the last war. I'm asking you—"

"Say no more," Carstairs cut her off. "We go too far
back for any of this nonsense. How much time do you
need?"

"I have to have six days, Tony. Six days. After that,
we'll be out of your hair and you Earthies can settle
affairs any way you see fit. How about it?"

He ran a palm over his scalp. "Not much hair left for
you to get out of," he said, "but I take your meaning.
All right, luv, you'll have your six days." He was grati-
fied to see how relieved she looked. At least somebody
still believes I can deliver, he thought.

"Just one thing, Linde. I need to know something
about your antimatter engine." She explained what he
needed to know and he filed it away in the part of his

brain that never forgot anything. "Fine. Listen, old girl, if we should live through this, what do you say we get hitched? Christ, between the two of us, we'll rule the galaxy in no time."

She smiled sadly. "Come out to Sigma Pavonis and I'll take you up on it." Then, seriously, "Tony, I'm going to miss you. You were the best enemy I ever had."

He raised his bottle. "You'll get your six days." He cut off the communication. He felt much better. He had long since decided what to do, but it helped to know that someone who counted would appreciate what he was up to. He drained the bottle and arranged for transportation to the flagship *Conqueror*.

He had himself driven to the port in his surface car, one with a human driver. "Let's go the long way," he told the uniformed man, "through London." The shuttle would wait for him, so there was no rush.

The city was densely packed, as always. The mood was different, though. Instead of the usual apathy, people were frightened or hysterical. The news about Hong Kong and New York had struck hard. They all knew that it might have been London instead. The younger crowd was rioting and demonstrating, calling for death to all offworlders. Offices of offworld businesses were being trashed, looted and burned, as were liquor stores and other establishments, more or less randomly.

He was interested to note that there were banners and placards calling for his own death. Many were professionally done, obviously made up well in advance for just such an occasion. That was Larsen's touch, he judged. He couldn't fault him for foresight and planning. He had always loved London. Now he found that he wasn't sorry to be leaving it behind. Maybe those bastards out there were right, he thought. Maybe this place just isn't worth saving. I hope they do a better job of it where they're going. I doubt it, though. It'll just be humanity buggering up all over again.

At the port, the military shuttle was ready to go. He got some strange looks as he boarded. Nobody was quite certain of his status. He seemed to be in disgrace, but nobody knew exactly what that meant. Carstairs' position had always been nebulous. "How long till we reach *Conqueror?*" he asked once they were spaceborne.

"Two hours until we dock," the commander said.

"Good. When we get there, I want you to be ready to take off all personnel."

"All personnel? But—"

"Can this shuttle hold them all?"

"Yes, easily, but—"

"Then see to it. I'm still head of the Defense Department, and I outrank all uniformed military personnel."

"Yes, sir."

When the man was gone, Carstairs reached into his briefcase and took out a bottle of Glenfiddich. "Put me in touch with Admiral Mboya," he ordered a communications computer.

Two hours later, the shuttle was dock-to-dock with the huge flagship. Carstairs pulled himself into the lock, queasy and reminded all over again why he hated going into space. Well, it won't be long this time, he thought. Mboya was at the lock to greet him.

"Sir, I must protest. We have all been at battle stations since the attack. We can't just—"

"You can," he said. "There won't be another attack. You can take my word for it. I still hold all my offices and they can't be taken from me without a convocation of the senior Party members and a U.N. Council meeting."

"But the generalissimo—"

"You let me handle the generalissimo. He's coming here to meet me soon. We're going to have our own private little conference right here aboard this vessel."

"I see. We shall stay nearby, ready to assume battle stations within an hour of notification."

"Fine, just don't stay too long. Now get along with you, Gus."

"Aye, aye, sir." The admiral turned to enter the shuttle, then he turned back. "And, sir, good luck."

The officers and crew of the ship pulled themselves

through the lock in orderly fashion. It did not take long. The huge ship was largely automated and functioned with a crew of fewer than one hundred. The locks closed, there was a hiss of escaping air, and the two vessels drifted apart.

Carstairs checked his watch. Shevket wouldn't show up for several hours. His challenge was being delivered about now. It was still possible that things might go awry, but he was certain he had read the man accurately. He had dealt with numerous Shevkets in his time. He headed for the ship's utility section, back near the engine room. It was time to get to work.

Three hours later, sweaty from the effort, Carstairs was taking his ease on the bridge, clipped into the admiral's chair. Pretty lights blinked everywhere and there were all sorts of holo sets in evidence. He had always considered military power to be rather childish, but sitting here in this chair, he could understand how a warlord could get addicted to it.

A holo flashed on above him and he saw Shevket's flushed countenance. "Carstairs!"

"That's *Mister* Carstairs to you, Turk! I'm still your superior."

"Oh, be serious. Earth First is a thing of the past. I am seizing control of the U.N. Your political position means nothing. Armed force is everything and I have it."

"Come on in and let's talk it over," Carstairs invited.

"There is nothing to talk about."

"Oh? But I can see here on this little screen that your ship's not far from here."

"Yes. The fact is, I am coming aboard, but it's because I owe myself one satisfaction and I intend to collect on it. I imagine you were terribly surprised to find that the admiral had secured all the ship's weaponry when he left. That's according to regulations, by the way."

Carstairs' eyebrows arched. "Why should that disappoint me?"

"Don't insult my intelligence. It is obvious that you

called for this meeting so that you could blast my ship out of space as I am calling."

"Oh. Well, best-laid plans of mice and men and all that. When shall I expect you?"

"Ten minutes." The image blinked out.

Carstairs finished the pint of Glenfiddich and let the bottle go drifting off wherever the interior breeze took it. When Shevket arrived in the lock, he wasn't alone. There were at least a dozen others with him, and Carstairs hoped one of them was Larsen.

When Shevket came onto the bridge, he was alone. He looked around him smugly. "I approve. You decided to stage our last meeting in a place of power. You wished for me to come to you, and I approve of that as well. You have a greater flair for the dramatic than I credited you with, Carstairs. Of course, it is still futile. This is *my* ship and therefore my power. And no one is ever going to see our last meeting. I ensured that you will broadcast no holos from this ship."

"Figure you're pretty safe, eh?"

"Oh, quite. Like everyone else who boards a military vessel, you were scanned in the lock. You came aboard unarmed, without explosives or poisons. All you have is your bare hands, and I assure you, should it come to that, I will best you. He tapped the hilt of the dagger he always wore.

"Actually, Mehmet, what I really wanted was a little talk. Satisfy my curiosity."

The Turk shrugged. "It can do no harm. What do you wish to know?"

"Well, I see how you've gained and consolidated power. Personally, I'm not sure why anybody wants to rule the world, but that's because I've done it for so long and know what a pain in the arse it is. But things like that look attractive when you've never experienced them. All very clever. But why did you destroy New York and Hong Kong? I know the defenses were perfect. It was your agents who brought those rocks here and you let some of them through. Why?" He hit a switch and a huge holo of the nearby planet appeared.

East Asia was showing, and a dark cloud of dust still hung over the area where Hong Kong had once been.

"Several reasons. There had to be a high body count in order to rouse some real war rage. And it had to be something inconsequential."

"Inconsequential? Forty million dead—you call that inconsequential?"

"Actually, it is closer to fifty million. No matter. One thing the planet has no shortage of is people. Just walking upright and babbling in some language doesn't make any creature valuable. Most useless of all are the urban destitute. New York? What importance has the place had for the last hundred years? There is no manufacture there. You yourself very wisely relocated all the world's banks to Zurich. What was there in New York but people? And what people! Nothing but useless blacks and the decadent remnants of the old United States, spawning Hispanics and the sweepings of the Caribbean. Nothing but useless mouths and empty bellies, most of them worthless even for purposes of war.

"Hong Kong was much the same, but its commercial enterprises were getting a little out of hand."

"So, this is as much your war on Earth as a war with the outerworlds?"

Shevket sneered and clasped his hands behind his back, booted feet widespread just as if he were standing solidly planted in a gravity environment. "The outerworld scum? What do I care for them? They are rivals for power, so they must be destroyed, and they must be *seen* to be destroyed. As for Earth, I shall build a better planet—one built on a healthy moral basis. Power, domination, masters, warriors, and slaves. No wonder an entire planet went mad, with the driveling nonsense of democracy and equality."

He snapped his whip against the leg of his boot. "Well, I shall change it all. In order to do it, I shall burn out these festering pockets of humanity. Believe me, Carstairs, in the future, there shall be far fewer, and far better, Earthmen."

Carstairs mused over the holograph of Earth. "It's

still a pretty place, from this high up. Still blue ocean and green land and white clouds. I love the place, for all its faults. I'm not going to let you have it, you know."

Shevket laughed. "You're an old man, Carstairs, dreaming an old man's dreams. Give up your fantasies. It's time to finish this." His black-gloved hand closed around the coral dagger hilt.

"Just a moment. I've one last thing to show you." He touched a control and a small holograph appeared before his seat. "You see, I knew you'd come here, Shevket. I knew it because you're a bloody sadist, and all sadists have childish minds. You could never just have me killed. You had to come here and do it yourself so you could gloat like the child you are. You could never be satisfied until you heard me acknowledge your superiority. Well, Shevket, look at that. Do you know what that big cylinder is, down in the engine room?"

Shevket was shocked and honestly puzzled. "It's the antimatter drive. What of it?"

"More precisely, it's the antimatter chamber of the Ciano-Kornfeld field generator. Designed by a friend of mine, by the way—lady the name of Kornfeld-Taggart. She's a very clever woman and she made sure nobody would ever tamper with her engines by making her own seal for them. There's one way to get into one, though. See that item leaning against it? That's a laser shortbeam cutter. It's used in mining and heavy industrial applications, such as repairing battle damage on a ship like this."

He saw the realization dawning in Shevket's eyes. "Shevket, did you ever wonder what it's like when matter and antimatter collide?"

To his credit, Shevket did not waste an instant in words or inaction. He snatched out his dagger and launched himself at Carstairs in a single motion. The distance was too great, though. All Carstairs had to do was press a single switch.

"Something's coming in from Fu's Lunar station,"

said Roalstad. The council was wrapping up work for the shift. They were all very tired.

"We might as well see it," Isherwood said. "We can always hope it's good news." He was rewarded with a few dry chuckles.

Fu appeared in their midst. "Something extraordinary has occurred in Earth orbit. This evening, at 1800 hours Greenwich time, Earth Fleet flagship *Conqueror* was destroyed by an explosion of unknown origin. There are rumors that the ship was unmanned at the time, but all reports are contradictory. I will deliver further reports as they come in, but the U.N. has clamped down a complete news blackout. This is Fu, signing off."

"Now what the hell is this all about?" Ulric said.

Sieglinde looked even wearier than before. "That was Tony Carstairs buying us the time we need. Let's not waste it." She returned her attention to her tables of figures.

Derek was tired as well, but not so tired that he couldn't focus on his main worry. There were just a few days to launch. Where the hell was Valentina?

Daniko Vladyka finished a drink and eyed his followers. They were mostly inert from the long victory celebration. They had delivered their missiles, had the satisfaction of seeing Hong Kong and New York transformed with all their inhabitants into columns of ascending hot ash. Then Vladyka had accomplished their "getaway" with great panache. They had been carousing ever since.

"Just two," said Geronimo. "I wish it could've been all fifty!" His words were slurred to near-unintelligibility.

"Cheer up," said Vladyka. "The war is just starting!"

He left his seat and headed for the bridge to send off his clandestine report. They were still under acceleration, so he had artificial gravity to work against. It always felt much better to him than free-fall. They were passing near Luna, which would give them a gravity-assisted slingshot boost to their next destination, where he would collect more rock and bombs or dispose of his crew, depending upon what orders were waiting for him.

As he went up the ladder, he heard a slight sound from the bridge. There wasn't supposed to be anybody in there. Just as a precaution, he activated his finger-laser. As he entered the bridge, he saw a black-clad back and a mane of blond hair. The woman was doing something with the controls.

"Valeria," he said, "what are you doing?"

She stood and faced him, eyes bright. "I just sent a holo of our mission to Fu's Lunar station, complete with your identity and your secret communications with Shevket's hatchetman."

For an instant he was stupefied. "You—what? Valeria!"

"It's Valentina!" She drew her pistol with incredible swiftness. The beam was already hot as she drew, slashing through the front of her holster, burning a track across the deck, slicing upward through his groin and deep into his viscera.

Vladyka's reaction was almost as swift, and far more precise. The microburst beam shot from beneath his fingernail and burned a hole just below and an inch to the right of her left breast. The blood in her heart flashed to steam and the organ exploded within her chest, flinging her backward, sending her crashing into the ship's controls, her pistol still firing, slicing into computers and backup systems.

Attitude rockets fired in crazy sequence. Before the deadman systems could shut them down, the ship was in an irretrievable end-for-end tumble. Centrifugal G-forces flung the befuddled Avengers toward the tail and front of the ship, helpless to make any move to rescue themselves.

Emergency lights flashing, the ship once called *Ivo the Black* tumbled out of control, arching downward for several minutes, finally impacting the lunar surface, creating yet one more crater in the Sea of Tranquility.

"I'm afraid there's no mistake, Derek," Ulric told

him. "The sign off she used was the one we assigned
her. We don't know for sure what happened after she
made her report, but something hit the moon within a
few minutes after her sign off. Fu is certain that it was
Vladyka's ship."

Derek couldn't say anything. He studied the backs of
his hands as if he had never seen them before. Finally,
he swallowed something in his throat and spoke. "Any
survivors?"

"Not even a distress signal from the ship. Whatever it
was, it happened fast." The older man studied his young
kinsman for a minute. "Take the rest of the shift off,
Derek. Come back—"

"The hell with that," Derek said, leaning over the
emergency procedure charts he had been assigned. If
anything went wrong on launch, everybody had to know
exactly where to go and what to do. "I have work to
do." He began reorganizing the maintenance section
manpower more efficiently. Ulric studied his work for a
moment, then quietly left the room.

"Three minutes," Sieglinde said. She was in her acceleration chair in Avalon's new flight control room. "So
far, no attacks from the Earth fleet." Her image was
broadcast into every holo set in the Sigma Pavonis fleet.

Derek was in his quarters in the Ciano section, which
was in even greater chaos than usual. Avalon was about
to lose the spin-induced gravity produced by rotation.
Under acceleration, they would be thrust away from
the direction of travel—a new kind of gravity entirely.

Derek wasn't thinking about the necessary reorienta-
tion, or about the voyage which he had been anticipat-
ing all his conscious life. He was thinking instead about
the recording that had arrived from Fu a few days
before. Mercifully, Valentina hadn't included her image.

"I suppose," she said, "that it would be terribly trite
to say that by the time this reaches you I'll be dead.
Actually, I have no idea. It's very likely, but as far as
you are concerned, I might as well be. I'm going to kill

Vladyka, and expose Shevket if I can, and in any case, I'm staying here.

"Derek, I'm one of the old Earth breed. You and your people are the star-rovers. You are going to have a long life traveling among the stars, and believe me, you'll find somebody who wants to share that kind of life with you. I have to make this brief, Vladyka's coming up to the bridge soon. Leave us dying old people to our dying old world. I—" That was where the transmission cut off. He wondered whether she would have ended with an "I love you," but he doubted it. Ruthless as she was, Valentina was not that cruel.

"Nine, eight, seven, six, five, four, three, two, one." Then he was pressed back against his seat as the island world of Avalon, along with nearly two hundred others, headed for the edge of the solar system on titanic columns of flame.

SIXTEEN

Derek strained against the weights in the gym. All around him, others were going through similar routines. It would be a long time before they reached their destination, but he fully intended to be in shape to explore planets at full gravity when he did. He finished a set and knocked off. After a shower, he dressed and left the gym.

He still had more than an hour before his next class. He was going to have plenty to do on his way to the new star system. There was a whole education to get in. He was studying planetary biology, theoretical xenobiology, first-contact theory and higher physics. The list would, eventually, be endless. He wanted to achieve a full professorship in time. Besides, there was his job in Avalonian administration. There was a lot to do between now and arrival. And he wasn't getting any younger. He was almost twenty-two.

Musing, he walked along the newly carpeted corridors, not truly paying attention to where he was going. Eventually, he stopped and looked up. Somehow, he had walked to the museum. He was about to turn and walk away, but an almost masochistic urge overcame him and he went in.

It looked a little different. There had been some rearrangements because of the new gravitic orientation. The long window was at a different angle, but it now faced in the direction they were travelling. The exhibits were in the same relationship, and he felt a stab of pain, remembering the last time he had been in this place. It was not very long ago, but he felt so much older now.

He made himself walk all the way to the end. There was no one else in the museum. The stars in the window looked subtly different as the ship's velocity increased. He stopped abruptly at the last exhibits. A few paces past the last of them stood a small female figure. For a moment he froze, then she turned and looked at him.

"Hello, Derek," Sieglinde said.

"Aunt Linde. What brings you here?"

"Same as you, I suppose. Just wandering aimlessly. We'll have something to put here pretty soon. They're going to install holos of *Nova*'s launch, and some of our own. Someday soon, we'll have exhibits of our first planetfall. No stopping us now. For good or ill, everybody can build my drive units." A few seconds before the mass exodus, she had transmitted data to the Island Worlds, both those that were leaving and those remaining behind, explaining how to construct both her antimatter and collapsar drives.

"Then why do you look so sad?" he asked.

She stared out the long window. "Just remembering the past. It seems like I've lost everyone. Thor is gone, and Martin Shaw. Fu stayed behind, and my son Martin. Even Tony Carstairs is gone. I feel like there's nothing left of my life."

"Hell, Aunt Linde, you're barely sixty years old! Statistically, you haven't even reached one-third of your life span. Think of all there is out there, still to see!" It exasperated him that she should be more depressed than he was.

"I know. I've worked for this all my life, but now that I have it, it hardly seems worthwhile." She stared out the window for a long while, then said, "Except for one thing."

"What's that?"

"It's these damned engines. We've been going for a couple of months and we're barely at twenty percent the speed of light. If everything works as I think it will, we'll get up to ninety-nine percent light speed. With a year's turnaround and deceleration time, that still leaves sixteen years to get to a destination just a hundred light-years away. It's too slow, Derek!"

"Well, considering it couldn't have been done at all before— "

"Not good enough. If I'm going to spend my time travelling, I don't want to see just five or six star systems in my lifetime. I want to see a hundred!"

"Everybody says superluminal travel is supposed to be impossible," he pointed out.

"So what? I've been told that before. If anybody can do it, I can!"

"That's the kind of talk I like to hear. Think you can do it before we reach Sigma Pavonis?"

"Hell, yes!" She whirled on her heel and stalked back through the exhibits. "I have to go to my lab. I'll see you later, Derek." She was lost to view among the exhibits, but he could still hear her voice, fading away toward the entrance. "I'll lick this yet. Lifetime, hell! Before I'm finished, we'll hit a hundred new star systems every goddamn *year!*"

He grinned and turned back to the window. The stars were all out there, waiting. The depression was gone as if it had never been. He felt a tingling and he learned forward, as if urging the great ark to higher speed. He stood there for a long time, savoring the feeling of being a human being standing between the stars.

Here is an excerpt from the brand-new "Hammer's Slammers" novel by David Drake, coming in November 1987 from Baen Books:

COUNTING THE COST
David Drake

The C.O. of the Executive Guard strode into the Consistory Room with a mixture of arrogance and fear. He moved like a rabbit loaded with amphetamines. "Gentlemen!" he called in a clear voice. "Rioters are in the courtyard with guns and torches!"

Tyl was waiting for a recommendation—*Do I have your permission to open fire?* was how a Slammers officer would have proceeded—but this fellow had nothing in mind save the theatrical announcement.

What Tyl didn't expect—nobody expected—was for Eunice Delcorio to sweep like a torch flame to the door and step out onto the porch.

The blast of noise when the clear doors opened was a shocking reminder of how well they blocked sound. There was an animal undertone, but the organized chant of *"Freedom!"* boomed over and through the snarl until the mob recognized the black-haired, glass-smooth woman facing them from the high porch.

Tyl moved fast. He was at Eunice's side before the shouts of surprise had given way to the hush of a thousand people drawing breath simultaneously. He thought there might be shots. At the first bang or spurt of light he was going to hurl Eunice back into the Consistory Room, trusting his luck and his clamshell armor.

Not because she was a woman; but because if

the President's wife got blown away, there was as little chance of compromise as there seemed to be of winning.

And maybe a little because she was a woman.

"What will you have, citizens?" Eunice called.

The porch was designed for speeches. Even without amplification, the modeling walls threw her powerful contralto out over the crowd. "Will you abandon God's Crusade for a whim?"

Tyl watched the mob.

Weapons glinted there. He couldn't tell if any of them were being aimed. The night-vision sensors in his faceshield would have helped; but if he locked the shield down he'd be a mirror-faced threat to the crowd, and that might be all it took to draw the first shots. . . .

The crowd's silence had dissolved in a dozen varied answers to Eunice's question, all underlain by blurred attempts to continue the chant of "Freedom!"

As Tyl waited, poised, a hand-held floodlight glared over the porch from near the flagpole.

He stepped in front of the President's wife, bumping her out of the way with his hip, while his left hand locked the faceshield down against the blinding radiance. The muzzle of his sub-machinegun quested like an adder's tongue while his finger took up slack on the trigger.

"Wait!" boomed a voice from the mob in amplified startlement. The floodlight dimmed from a threat to comfortable illumination.

"I'll take over now, Eunice," said John Delcorio as his firm hand touched Tyl's upper arm, just beneath the shoulder flare of the clamshell armor.

The Slammers officer stepped aside, knowing it was out of his hands for better or for worse, now.

President Delcorio's voice thundered to the crowd from roof speakers, "My people, why do you come here to disturb God's purpose?"

"We want the murderer Berne!" called the bull horn. The words were indistinct from the out-of-synchronous echoes which they waked from the Palace walls. "Berne sells justice and sells lives!"

"Berne!" shouted the mob, and their echoes thundered BERNE*berne*berne.

"Will you go back to your homes in peace if I replace the City Prefect?" Delcorio said, pitching his words to make his offered capitulation sound like a demand. His features were regally arrogant as Tyl watched him sidelong behind the mirror of his faceshield.

The priest with the bullhorn leaned sideways to confer with another man. While the mob waited for their leaders' response, the President used the pause to add, "One man's venality can't be permitted to jeopardize God's work!"

"Give us Berne!" demanded the courtyard.

"I'll replace—" Delcorio attempted.

GIVE*give*give roared the mob. GIVE*give*give ...

A woman waved a doll in green robes above her head. She held it tethered by its neck.

Delcorio and his wife stepped back into the Consistory Room. Tyl Koopman wasn't going to be the only target on the balcony while the mob waited for a response it might not care for. He kept his featureless face to the front—with the gun muzzle beneath it for emphasis—as he retreated after the rest.

*　　*　　*

"Firing me won't—" Berne began even before Tyl slid the door shut on the thunder of the mob.

"Be silent!" Eunice Delcorio ordered in a glass-sharp voice.

The walls shuddered with the low notes of the shouting in the courtyard.

Everyone in the Consistory Room had gathered

in a semicircle. There were only a dozen or so of Delcorio's advisors present. They glared at the City Prefect with the expression of gorgeously-attired fish viewing an injured one of their number ... a peer moments before, a certain victim now. Their eyes were hungry as they slid over Berne.

The door behind the President rattled sharply when a missile struck it. The vitril held as it was supposed to do.

"John, they aren't after *me*," Berne cried with more than personal concern in his voice.

"If you hadn't failed, none of this would be happening," Eunice said, her scorn honed by years of personal hatred that found its outlet now in the midst of general catastrophe.

She turned to her husband, the ends of her black hair emphasizing the motion. "Why are you delaying? They want this criminal, and that will give us the time we need to deal with the filth properly with the additional troops."

Vividness made Eunice Delcorio a beautiful woman, but the way her lips rolled over the word "properly" sent a chill down the spine of everyone who watched her.

Berne made a break for the door to the hall.

A middle-aged civilian tripped the City Prefect. One of Dowells' aides leaped on Berne and wrestled him to the polished floor as he tried to rise, while the other aide shouted into his communicator for support without bothering to lock his privacy screen in place.

Tyl looked away in disgust.

"All right," said the President, bobbing his head in decision. "I'll tell them."

He took one stride, reached for the sliding door, and paused. "You," he said to Tyl. "Come with me."

Tyl nodded without expression. Another stone

or possibly a light bullet whacked against the vitril. He set his faceshield and stepped onto the porch ahead of the Regiment's employer.

Something pinged on the railing. Tyl's gun quivered, pointed—

"Wait!" thundered the bullhorn.

"My people!" boomed the President's voice from the roofline. "I have dismissed the miscreant Berne as you demanded. I will turn him over to the custody of the Church for safekeeping until the entire State can determine the punishment for his many crimes."

"Give us Berne!" snarled the bullhorn with echoing violence.

The President raised a hand for silence from the crowd. The chant continued unabated, but Delcorio and the Slammers officer were able to back inside without a rain of missiles to mark their retreat.

Four soldiers were gripping the City Perfect.

Delcorio made a dismissing gesture. "Send him out to them," he said. "I've done all I can. Quickly, so I don't have to go out there—"

"Pick him up," said Eunice Delcorio in a voice as clear as a sapphire laser. "You four—*pick* him up and follow. We'll *give* them their scrap of bone."

She strode toward the door, the motion of her legs a devouring flame across the intaglio.

Berne screamed as the soldiers lifted him.

Tyl stepped out beside Eunice, because he'd made it his job ... or Hammer had made it his job ... and who in blazes cared, he was there and the animal snarl of the mob brought answering rage to the Slammer's mind and washed some of the sour taste from his mouth.

Eunice gestured. The guards threw their prisoner toward the courtyard.

Berne grabbed the railing with both hands as

he went over. His legs flailed without the organization needed to boost him back onto the porch, but his hands clung like claws of cast bronze.

A bottle shattered on Tyl's breastplate. He didn't hear the shot that was fired a moment later, but the howl of a light slug ricocheting from the wall cut through even the roar of the crowd.

"*Get* inside!" Tyl bellowed to Eunice Delcorio as he stepped sideways to the railing where Berne thrashed. Tyl hammered the man's knuckles with the butt of his submachinegun. One stroke, two—bone cracked—

Three and the prefect's screaming changed note. His broken left hand slipped and his right hand opened. Berne's throat made a sound like a siren as he fell ten meters to the mob waiting to recieve him. . . .

November 1987 * 65355-5 * 288 pp. * $3.50

To order any Baen Book by mail, send the cover price plus 75 cents for first class postage and handling to: Baen Books, Dept. B, 260 Fifth Avenue, New York, N.Y. 10001.

DRAKE, DAVID
Birds of Prey

The time: 262 A.D. The place: Imperial Rome. There had never been a greater empire, but now it is dying. Everywhere its armies are in retreat, and what had been civilization seethes with riots and bizarre cults. Against the imminent fall of the Long Night stands Aulus Perennius, an Imperial secret agent as tough and ruthless as the age in which he lives. But he stands alone—until a traveller from Earth's far future recruits him for a mission so strange it cannot be disclosed.

55912-5 (trade paper) $7.95
55909-5 (hardcover) $14.95

DRAKE, DAVID
Ranks of Bronze

Disguised alien traders bought captured Roman soldiers on the slave market because they needed troops who could win battles without high-tech weaponry. The leigionaires provided victories, smashing barbarian armies with the swords, javelins, and discipline that had won a world. But the worlds on which they now fought were strange ones, and the spoils of victory did not include freedom. If the legionaires went home, it would be through the use of the beam weapons and force screens of their ruthless alien owners. It's been 2000 years—and now they want to go home. 65568-X $3.50

DRAKE, DAVID, & WAGNER, KARL EDWARD
Killer

Vonones and Lycon capture wild animals to sell for bloodsport in ancient Rome. A vicious animal sold to them by a trader turns out to be more than they bargained for—it is the sole survivor of the crash of an alien spacecraft. Possessed of intelligence nearly human, it has two goals in life: to breed and to kill.

55931-1 $2.95

Have You Missed?

DRAKE, DAVID
At Any Price
Hammer's Slammers are back—and Baen Books has them!
Now the 23rd-century armored division faces its deadliest
enemies ever: aliens who *teleport* into combat.
55978-8 $3.50

DRAKE, DAVID
Hammer's Slammers
A special *expanded* edition of the book that began the
legend of Colonel Alois Hammer. Now the toughest, mean-
est mercs who ever killed for a dollar or wrecked a world
for pay have come home—to Baen Books—and they've
brought a secret weapon: "The Tank Lords," a brand-new
short novel, included in this special Baen edition of *Hammer's Slammers*.
65632-5 $3.50

DRAKE, DAVID
Lacey and His Friends
In Jed Lacey's time the United States computers scan
every citizen, every hour of the day. When crime is detected, it's Lacey's turn. There are a few things worse than
having him come after you, but they're not survivable
either. But things aren't really that bad—not for Lacey and
his friends. By the author of *Hammer's Slammers* and *At
Any Price*.
65593-0 $3.50

**CARD, ORSON SCOTT; DRAKE, DAVID;
& BUJOLD, LOIS MCMASTER**
(edited by Elizabeth Mitchell)
Free Lancers (Alien Stars, Vol. IV)
Three short novels about mercenary soldiers—never be-
fore in print! Card's hero leads a ragtag group of scientific
refugees to sanctuary in Utah; Drake contributes a new
"Hammer's Slammers" story; Bujold tells a new tale of
Miles Vorkosigan, hero of *The Warrior's Apprentice*.
65352-0 $2.95

DAVID DRAKE

"Drake has distinguished himself as the master of the mercenary sf novel."—Rave Reviews

To receive books by one of BAEN BOOKS most popular authors send in the order form below.

AT ANY PRICE, 55978-8, $3.50 . . . . ☐

HAMMER'S SLAMMERS, 65632-5, $3.50 . . . . . . ☐

LACEY AND HIS FRIENDS, 65593-0, $3.50 . . . ☐

FREE LANCERS, (ALIEN STARS #4),
    65352-0, $2.95 . . . . ☐

BIRDS OF PREY, hardcover, 55912-5, $7.95 . . . ☐

BIRDS OF PREY, trade paper, 55909-5, $14.95 . . ☐

RANKS OF BRONZE, 65568-X, $3.50 . . . . ☐

KILLER, 55931-1, $2.95 . . . . ☐

Please send me the books checked above. I have enclosed a check or money order for the combined cover price made out to: BAEN BOOKS, 260 Fifth Avenue, New York N.Y. 10001.